FATAL ROOTS

A COUNTY CORK MYSTERY

FATAL ROOTS

SHEILA CONNOLLY

WHEELER PUBLISHING
A part of Gale, a Cengage Company

GALE
A Cengage Company

Copyright © 2020 by Sheila Connolly.
Wheeler Publishing, a part of Gale, a Cengage Company.

Wheeler Publishing Large Print Cozy Mystery.
The text of this Large Print edition is unabridged.
Other aspects of the book may vary from the original edition.
Set in 16 pt. Plantin.

LIBRARY OF CONGRESS CIP DATA ON FILE.
CATALOGUING IN PUBLICATION FOR THIS BOOK
IS AVAILABLE FROM THE LIBRARY OF CONGRESS

ISBN-13: 978-1-4328-8001-9 (softcover alk. paper)

Published in 2020 by arrangement with The Quick Brown Fox & Company LLC

Printed in the United States of America
2 3 4 5 6   24 23 22 21 20

Na dean nos is na bris nos

CHAPTER ONE

The pounding at the front door woke Maura from a sound sleep. Did she have to answer it? She'd put in a late shift at the pub the night before, and she hadn't planned to show up this morning until opening time. The pounding came again, and she could hear a female voice call out, "Hello? Anyone at home?" Irish accent, so she was probably local, or at least Irish.

Maura managed to pry her eyes open. The sun was shining, always a wonderful thing in this part of the world. She had few visitors, and unfamiliar women of her own age were rarely among them. The visitor didn't sound scared or panicked, so she wasn't looking for help. Maura sighed and sat up slowly, then came to her feet and walked barefoot to the front window on the second story, the one over the door below. She pushed it open and leaned out.

"Can I help you with something?" she said.

The young woman below shaded her eyes. "Are you Maura Donovan?"

"Yes."

"Any relation to Michael Sullivan?"

Who did she mean? Maura wondered. The man who had owned the house that was now hers because he'd left it to her in his will, or a living one she knew nothing about? What she did know was there were a *lot* of Sullivans in the area, and probably quite a few named Michael.

"Not if you're looking for the man who used to own this place. I never met the man, but this used to be his property. Why do you want to know?"

"If you're the owner, I'd like to talk with you. Before you ask, I don't want to buy it or sell you anything, but I'm studying archaeology, and I'd like to explore your land, if that's all right with you."

Maura sighed. The only archaeology she knew about in the region was the Drombeg stone circle, which the Mick who worked for her at Sullivan's Pub had shown her when she first arrived. She hadn't gone looking for any more, because she didn't have the time, and she wouldn't even know what she was looking for. But it couldn't hurt to talk to someone who had managed to track her down to a small townland in the out-country. "Let me put on some clothes and I'll be down."

"That'd be grand. Thank you!"

Maura dug out a mostly clean pair of jeans and a shirt from the pile waiting to be washed. Laundry was something she seldom got around to doing. She also pulled on socks and shoes, because the house was shaded by old trees and the floor downstairs was made of concrete, so it was always cold, even in summer. She made it down the rickety wooden stairway against the back wall and opened the door to the stranger. "Come on in. I'm Maura. Who are you?"

"My name's Ciara McCarthy. I'm working on a postgraduate degree in the Department of Archaeology at University College Cork, and my thesis will be on early Irish ring forts in Cork."

"Uh, slow down for a second. Please," Maura interrupted. "In case you can't tell, I'm American, although my grandmother and her son — my father — were born near here. I've been in Ireland just over a year, and I haven't seen much of it. I've never been to Cork city, except for the bus station. I don't have a college degree, and I haven't got a clue what a ring fort is. So you'll have to start at the beginning and explain all this to me. Why is it you want to talk to me? Oh, and would you like some breakfast? Coffee?"

"Yes, please. And forgive me for barging in on you like this, so early, but I really want to get started, and the weather's been so nice lately I hate to let it go to waste. I'll give you the short version. Ring forts are the most common archaeological monuments in rural Ireland, and most of them date to the early Middle Ages, up to about the year one thousand AD. There's still a lot of controversy about who made them and why, but there are lots in Cork. One thing that makes them even more intriguing is that there's a lot of folklore attached to them, and the people on whose property they lie treat them with respect. You might say they're scared of them, and even nowadays they leave them alone. That is, they don't just plow them under to give their cows more room."

Maura poured boiling water from her kettle over the coffee grounds in her coffeepot and found two mugs. "Bread okay? Because that's about all I've got to eat at the moment."

"That's fine. You want me to keep explaining?"

"Yes," Maura said firmly, as she sliced the bread and added a chunk of local butter to the plate before setting it in front of Ciara.

"First of all, they're circles, but they're not usually made of stone. So you might not notice the ring forts if you drive past them, because they're big and not very high and they're often overgrown with brambles and the like, but once you recognize them you'll find them everywhere. Others are long gone, or have been raided for building materials, mainly in the past. But there are maps that were made in the middle of the nineteenth century, when more of them were still intact, that show them all over, and I've been tracking these down. Once I think I've found them all, I plan to analyze their locations, how they relate to each other, how close or far apart they are — things like that. What do you know about your property?"

Maura placed a second plate with sliced brown bread and a chunk of butter on the table, then sat down. "Not a lot. I told you, I don't know much about Ireland. My grandmother moved to Boston before I was born, with my father, and then he died, and she raised me. I guess she was worried about how I'd get by once she was gone. She knew Old Mick Sullivan, who owned

11

this place. He was some kind of distant relative, and he had no family to leave it to, so he and my grandmother fixed it that I'd inherit it, but she never told me. I didn't find out until I got here. Old Mick also owned a pub in Leap, which is now mine, and it's where I work. But I haven't had time to do much exploring. As for this property, I signed a bunch of papers, and I know there are a lot of bits and pieces of land that belonged to Mick scattered around, but I couldn't tell you where they are, or if there's anything on them that would interest you."

"Not a problem! I've got copies of the old maps, and I can tell you that nothing much changes around here, except maybe somebody puts in a new road. Like the one at the bottom of the hill on the north side — that's relatively new. Your cottage here is just over a hundred years old, I think, and it's probably not the first house on this site."

"And there were people living here and building these ring fort things like a thousand years ago?"

"Roughly," Ciara said. "So I came here to ask if you'd mind if I did some surveying of where there are any old structures. It may be that there are none on your land, but I'd bet money there are some nearby, and it's kind of hard to guess who owned which pieces or how much, back before anybody was writing history down. I won't be in your way, but I thought it would be polite to ask your permission."

"No problem. I'm not here much anyway. I'm at the pub from opening to closing. I'm still learning the business, and sometimes we're shorthanded."

"You live here alone?"

"Yeah, mostly. Look, I don't mind if you want to poke around. I don't have anything worth stealing, and I'm sorry I can't tell you more about what's in this neighborhood. You might want to talk to one of the guys who's at the pub a lot — we call him Old Billy, and he was a friend of the former owner Mick. He's over eighty, but his memory's sharp. Or Bridget down the lane — she's as old as Billy, and she's lived right around here most of her life, and she seems to know everybody and everything. Maybe they won't know where to find these fort things, but they can tell you where to look."

"Thank you for the suggestions. This is my first real field survey, and I want to learn as much as I can and record all the details. It's a challenge, you know?"

"I'm sure it is. You said you already have maps?"

"I do. Luckily the property boundaries haven't changed much. Do you know how much total acreage you have here?"

"Not at all. I just signed whatever papers the lawyer handed me. Old Mick had lived here all his life, I gather, and his ancestors before him. I don't think he sold off anything. Or farmed it, for that matter — I've been told he made his money at the pub. He didn't seem to need much, and he wasn't keeping cows or sheep. Some of the other owners here do. How long do you think this will take you?"

"Longer than I have," Ciara said ruefully.

"Are you staying around here somewhere?" Maura asked.

"It's only an hour to the university, so that's not a problem. Though I've enlisted some university friends to help, with photos and the like. And this county is a large one."

"Well, let me know if you need someplace to crash now and then. And I guess I'd like to know more about a place that's mine. Owning something like this is still pretty new to me."

"I could show you the basics, on your computer."

"Uh, Ciara, I don't own a computer. I barely know how to use one."

"Oh. Well, I can bring my laptop along,

14

though the images wouldn't be very large. But it might be useful to you to know where your land is. From what I can tell, sometimes local farmers are looking for a little extra grazing land, and they might pay you to use it."

That was something Maura had never considered, but she'd never learned anything about farming when she was growing up in Boston. She could tell a cow from a sheep, but that was about as far as it went. "It's mostly cows, I think. There's a creamery up at Drinagh that's pretty big. Sometimes I see their milk tankers go by on the main road."

"There are several major ring forts scattered around Drinagh. And other places too. There's still so much we don't know about them! But one thing seems clear: people still believe there's something supernatural around them. Sometimes they're called fairy forts."

"What does that mean?"

"That you shouldn't mess with them. I've read that up until several years ago farmers were destroying a lot of them, but bad things started happening to them, like tractor accidents or sick cattle. So in the past decade or two they've stopped tearing them apart. Which is good for me. Same thing's happened with new construction, close to the towns. A company wants to build a new factory where there's a fairy fort, but they can't find any local workers to build it because the workers are scared of what might happen to them."

"Sorry, but that sounds weird to me."

"Weird but true," Ciara said, smiling. "I treat the ring forts with respect, but I'd like to know who built them and why. I make sure I don't do any damage. So, do you have to get to your pub?"

"I should leave soon, and I need to shower. Feel free to go wherever you want, although I can't tell you how my neighbors will react, since I haven't met a lot of them, but like I said, Bridget — she lives in the yellow cottage just downhill — loves company, and I'm sure she can tell you a lot about the history of this townland, which is Knockskagh. But I would like to know more about what you're looking for, and what you find."

"I'll print out the maps for Knockskagh, so you can see where the circles might be or once were. I'm really glad you don't mind my wandering about. I'll get out of your hair now. If you'd like to see where I'm guessing your land is, maybe we could take a walk in the morning? If you're in the pub most of the time?"

"It'd have to be early, but you may have noticed the sun comes up pretty early in June. Come by and maybe we could spend an hour or two checking things out."

"Thank you!" Ciara swallowed the last of her bread, drained her coffee mug, and all but bounced out of her chair. "And thank you for the breakfast. I hope I'll be seeing more of you."

"I'd like that," Maura said, mainly because it seemed polite, although she wasn't sure she'd have to time to chase down old circles in the fields. But she should know something about the property she'd inherited, and about the history that came with it. "I'll be up early. And I'll keep my fingers crossed that it doesn't rain."

"Tomorrow, then," Ciara said, and made her exit.

Maura sighed. What had she let herself in for? She knew vaguely that she had more land than the small piece the cottage sat on, but she had had no intention of looking for it, much less doing something with it, and nobody until now had come to ask her about it. But after more than a year in West Cork, maybe she should know more about where she was living, and its history. Did they teach that in schools around here? In

Boston, her history teacher had devoted about two class hours to the American Revolution, and Lexington and Concord and Paul Revere. But, she realized, she didn't have any knowledge of the history of West Cork, apart from the bit about the O'Donovan who supposedly jumped his horse over the ravine next to the pub — a story she took with a grain of salt, because she had doubts about whether any horse could have made that jump. But it made a nice dramatic story and people still remembered it.

Were fairy forts in the same category? She might as well go with Ciara at least once and find out what all the fuss was about.

CHAPTER TWO

Despite Ciara's interruption, Maura arrived at Sullivan's before anyone else. Admittedly, business would be pretty slow early in the day, but she welcomed the time to clean up the place. A couple of months earlier Rose Sweeney had persuaded her to expand the kitchen and make it usable, and the improvements were moving along slowly but steadily, although Maura still had no idea when they would be finished. Maura had inherited Rose along with the pub, and though she was still a teenager, she had proved to be a hard worker, and she knew more about running the place than Maura did. In addition to her shifts at the pub, she was now taking cooking classes in Skibbereen. Whether they would ever progress to serving more than sandwiches was still an open question, but Maura was giving Rose free rein to get the old kitchen up and running. Fancy dreams were one thing, but reality was something else.

Sophie and Niall, a sister and brother she'd met and kind of rescued earlier in the spring, were working at two different restaurants in Skibbereen, with the promise to return to Sullivan's if business ever picked up. Maura wasn't holding her breath, but she was keeping her fingers crossed. Rose had met Sophie while they were taking the same cooking class in Skibbereen, and Maura knew Sophie had real talent as a cook. Niall had turned out to be a great bartender, and he was beginning to attract a younger crowd, not to mention more women.

There were rooms upstairs, but under Old Mick they had been neglected for a long time. Maura hadn't quite made up her mind whether to offer them as a plus for employees, which weren't easy to find, or whether to actually rent them out. She gave Ann Sheahan at the Leap Inn across the road first rights to any paying guests, not that she and Ann had discussed it, though she had volunteered to take Ann's overflow, if any. But Maura's main hope was that her current staffing would be adequate to cover the summer tourist season until the kitchen remodel was finished.

Mick Nolan, her sort-of boyfriend was the

next to arrive. "Yeh're in early, Maura," he commented. "It was wild last night."

"And profitable, I hope," Maura said. "I was planning to sleep in, but I had an early visitor."

"Someone yeh know?"

Maura shook her head. "Nope. Although most people who find me up in Knockskagh usually do know me, because my cottage isn't exactly easy to find if you don't know where to look. This was a grad student at the university in Cork. She wants to do some archaeology work on my land. Of course, apart from the cottage, I have no idea where my land actually is. I got the impression when I first found out about it that there are small pieces scattered all over the place up there, but I've never looked for them."

"Could be," Mick said. "The English often set it up that way, a while back. They weren't happy about giving away any land at all to the Irish, so they made it hard for the farmers to use it without wastin' a lot of time. Imagine herding your cattle from field to field every other day."

"Mick, I don't know squat about managing cattle. I grew up in Boston, remember? No cattle there. But I can see your point. It wasn't an efficient way to do things, if you were a farmer. Are things better now?"

"Some," Mick said. "Or there may be fewer dairy farmers, with larger land holdings — there's a lot of milk comes from this part of the country. So what's this Cork woman lookin' for?"

"Ring forts, she said. About which I know exactly nothing."

Mick smiled. "How long is it yeh've been in Cork?"

"Over a year now, more or less, but I never have the time to wander around the countryside looking for things I don't even recognize. You know about ring forts?"

"I do, but I grew up in this county. Pay attention when yeh're drivin' around and you'll most likely see a few of the bigger ones. There's one just over the hill from yeh, on yer way to Ballinlough, but the road's crumbling away now, so yeh'd have to walk it."

"Right past that lovely piggery, right? I'll keep that in mind. Anyway, the woman's name is Ciara McCarthy, and she says she wants to do some serious surveying — find as many of these things as she can and figure out how they relate to each other. If they do. She also said something odd."

"And what would that be?"

"That there's something weird about ring

forts, like they're sort of haunted. People leave them alone, mostly."

"The fairies don't like to be disturbed," Mick said.

Maura looked at his face to see if he was joking. He wasn't smiling. "You too? Seriously? Should I be watching for fairies? And what would they look like?"

"Depends on what yeh believe. There's a long history of fairy folk in Ireland, and there's plenty of people who believe in 'em. Or half believe, in case it's true. There's those as have wireless connections and satellite dishes, but they still won't mess with a fairy tree."

"And what the heck is that?"

"Usually a hawthorn tree, or an ash. Yeh find them at the edge of a field, standing alone, or in the middle. It's said to be bad luck to harm them. Do yeh not know the name of yer townland?"

"I can spell it, but that's about all."

"It's *cnoc sceach,* though the Irish spelling won't be the same as you've been writin' it, and not what yeh'll find on a map. It means 'hawthorn hill.' If yeh come upon a single tree, don't hurry to cut it down."

"Great," Maura muttered. "So now I've learned about at least two things that bring bad luck if you harm them. Isn't there anything positive around here? No good luck?"

"That's a whole different kettle of fish. Find yerself a book about Irish fairies, why don't yeh? And promise yeh won't be cuttin' down any trees or messin' with any circle yeh may find."

"Fine, I promise. I wasn't planning to cut down any trees anyway. Should this Ciara person worry? Or do you think she knows about the old traditions?"

"If she's done her research, she should know. Wonder what the university has to say about them?"

"We didn't talk about it, but she asked me if I wanted to go along with her tomorrow morning — she said she'd show me where those scattered pieces of my land are. And she's got some old maps, which show the circles, some of which are probably gone now."

"Take yer time. We've enough people workin' here now to cover the crowds here."

Maura wondered how she would handle trekking through fields. And bogs — she'd already discovered the hard way that there were upland bogs you couldn't see until you sank a foot into one. She'd been raised in a city — one with sidewalks — and she still had a lot to learn. She hoped Ciara knew more than she did, because she didn't relish the idea of trying to haul her out of the mud. And how did Ciara feel about cows? Because it was all too likely that these big circles she was looking for would be smack in the middle of a field full of cows — and their by-products.

"Is there anyone she should stay away from? I don't think she'll wander through any herds of cows, but she might spook them by accident and tick off the farmer who owns them. She seems to be a city girl, like me."

"She was smart enough to let yeh know she'd be lookin' around your place. Maybe the uni gives instructions to its students, so they don't get themselves shot."

"People around here really do that?"

"Not often, but it happens."

"I'll be careful, I promise. Do you think your gran Bridget would know about the fairy circles?"

"She would have done, when she was young. Like yeh say, it may be that a lot of 'em are gone now, and she's not up fer walkin' far. But I'm sure she'd love to talk about 'em."

"I'll tell Ciara. So, do we have a few quiet days to look forward to?"

"We might. Fer a lot of our foreign visitors, their kids are still in school, so June's not the best time fer 'em. Come July we'll be busier. Might be a good time to start servin' food."

"Rose told me she was going to look for some used cookware at the farmers market. Might save some money."

"She's a smart girl. She's likely to find some pieces at a good price, and there's not much need for a lot of things, nor do we have the room to spare. She should keep her eyes open fer plates and such, unless yeh want to spend all your time washin' dishes a few at a time."

"Not my favorite thing," Maura told him firmly. "It's almost opening time. I'm going to open the door and let the place air out."

She went over to the front door and pulled it open. The building was old, she knew, and so were all the doors, and the windows were old too. The interior was kind of shabby, but it felt comfortable. And the tourists seemed to like it. The local customers didn't pay it much attention, but they seemed to feel at home, and often they came in for a pint. And it looked authentic, not because it had been decorated that way, but because the pub had been in business for a long time.

She stepped outside the door and looked

up and down the road. It always surprised her that this was a national highway, since she seldom saw more than a couple of passing cars at once. The weather was unexpectedly lovely — exactly what visitors wanted to believe Irish weather was like, with blue skies and green hills and a lot of cows in the meadows. The air smelled of hay, not auto exhaust, with a dash of cooking food from the closest restaurants and cafés.

Mick joined her, wrapping an arm around her shoulders. "It's a fine day," he said, staring out across the harbor.

"That it is. I hope we get more of them."

"I think we've got company," he said, nodding at a car that had pulled into the parking lot of the Inn across the road.

A woman climbed out the driver's side, and a girl who looked like a teenager came out the other side, loudly slamming the door behind her. Maura looked at the older woman, then looked again. "That's Helen, isn't it?"

"Yer mother? I'm guessin' it is," Mick replied.

"And the other person?" Maura didn't really expect Mick to answer, but she had a pretty good idea, although she was having trouble believing it. "I think that's my sister.

Or half sister. What on earth are they doing here?"

"Looks like yer goin' to find out."

Maura debated between retreating into the darkness of the pub behind her or pasting a smile on her face and welcoming her mother. There was no reason not to choose the second option; Helen had spent some time with her earlier in the year — for the first time in Maura's life — and they had parted on good terms, she thought. But the question of bringing her half sister along hadn't come up. If she remembered correctly, the girl's name was Susan, and she was about ten years younger than Maura. Maura was pretty sure they had little in common apart from Helen. But there had to be a story behind her being here, because Maura didn't really think Helen had brought Susan along just for fun. Susan didn't look particularly happy to be here at the moment.

By the time Maura had run all those thoughts through her head, Helen was only a few feet away. "Helen!" she called out. "I didn't expect to see you here again anytime soon. And this must be Susan?" The girl stared blankly at Maura but didn't answer. Maura was ready to declare that for Susan, this was not a fun vacation trip.

"Maura, it's good to see you," Helen said, and gave her a cautious hug. "I would have given you some warning, but this all came up so quickly I didn't get a chance. It's about the hotel."

That might explain a few things, Maura thought. "Listen, come on in and have some coffee or something, and we can sit down and talk about it. It's not very busy at the moment."

"Thanks, I'd like that. Susan and I took a red-eye flight overnight, so we haven't slept, and I'm pretty sure I'm not very coherent at the moment."

Maura stepped back and held the door open as Helen and Susan entered. "Mick, you remember Helen. And this is her daughter — her *other* daughter — Susan. Can you start some coffee?"

"Happy to. Helen, it's good to see yeh again. Find yerselves a seat and I'll bring yez the coffee when it's ready."

Helen aimed for a table in the front corner. Susan followed, without looking at Maura. Maura waited until they were settled, then took a chair. "So, change in plans for the hotel?" Maura began. "Did your group vote to keep the hotel or dump it as fast as they can?"

"They voted to keep it, for now," Helen

said, "but they're going to revisit the question after a year. Since John is . . . no longer involved, they gave me control for now, but I already know it won't be easy."

"And you brought Susan along this time?" Maura asked, trying to think of any reason that would have been a good choice.

"Yes. Tommy's going to some wilderness camp, but Susan didn't want to go to a camp. Her father and I thought sitting around the house stewing all summer was a bad idea, so I told her she'd come with me. She's never been outside the country before."

And she'd never met me, Maura thought. "Did you tell her about me, and how we met?"

"Hey, I'm right here," the girl protested. "No, Mom never talked about her life before she married Dad and had me and my brother. Then she dumped the whole story on us, all at once, right after she got back from her last trip here. I didn't want to come, but she didn't give me a choice."

Maura swallowed a smile. "Hey, kid, she never got in touch with me at all. When she left Boston, I was too young to remember her. So you could say she dumped her history on me too, only a few months ago. We'll have to compare notes."

Susan's eyes widened — apparently she hadn't expected Maura to see her side of things. "Good idea. Mom says we'll be around for a while."

Mick slid coffees across the table and retreated silently.

"So, Helen, what's your plan?" Maura asked. "You staying at the hotel? You thinking of making changes now that you're in control?"

"Yes to the first question. I want to take the second part slowly, but I realize this is peak tourist season, so I may not have that luxury. I'm sure I'll keep busy, but I'm not sure what Susan will find to keep herself busy."

"Rose should be in soon — remember her? She's pretty close to Susan's age. And I've hired a couple of kids — brother and sister — which really helps. And we're working on the kitchen. So, I warn you, Susan — if you don't find something else to do, I'll put you to work here."

Susan just looked glum. "Great. I can go home and tell my friends I've been working in an Irish pub all summer."

"And what will they think about that?"

"I don't really know."

"We can play it by ear. Helen, are you heading over to the hotel now?"

31

"As soon as the caffeine kicks in. I don't think I can stay awake much longer."

"Thanks for stopping here first. It's good to see you. And to meet Susan."

Helen downed the last of her coffee and shepherded Susan back to their rental car. She pulled out carefully, and then they were gone.

"Well, that was interesting," Maura said to Mick.

"She gave yeh no warning?" he asked.

"Not a word. We parted on fairly good terms, I think, but she never discussed bringing Susan with her. Poor kid — what the heck is she going to do with herself while her mother is working? She seems a bit young for a job."

"That I can't say. But Rose was no more than Susan's age when she started workin' here," Mick pointed out.

"Mick, I think Rose was *born* older than Susan. We'll see."

The morning passed quickly, with a small but steady flow of customers. It was close to noon when Maura noticed a girl standing on the other side of the road, staring at her. Susan? Then the girl looked quickly in both directions — where there were no cars at all — and crossed.

"Hello again, Susan. Are you looking for

something?" Maura asked when the girl was close enough to hear her.

"And you're Maura, the big sister, that nobody told me about." Susan's tone was edgy. "Can I come in?" she asked.

"Half sister. Sure. Come on in. You want something to drink? There's coffee or tea or soda."

"I just want to talk," the girl said, brushing past Maura. Mick looked up when she walked to the bar, then looked at Maura, who shrugged. "Hello, Susan. Did Maura ever introduce me? I'm Mick. I think I'll go clean up in the back room," he said, and went through the doors in back. *Tactful of him,* Maura thought.

"Bar or table?" Maura asked the girl, who was looking increasingly unsettled.

"Bar, I guess. And coffee."

"Pick a stool, then. I'll get the coffee. Oh, wait — some rule somewhere says I'm supposed to ask you if your mother knows where you are."

Susan snorted. "We flew in yesterday, stopped here, went to the hotel. Mom took a nap, then told me she had an afternoon meeting to go to. I left."

"So of course you decided to come back to my ratty pub?" Maura asked, as she filled a coffee mug. She set it on the bar and pushed a sugar bowl toward the girl. "How'd you get here?"

"Taxi. I asked at the desk. Look, this isn't easy. My mother didn't tell me I had a sister living in Ireland until she announced she was taking me to Ireland, like, the next day."

"Well, don't feel sorry for yourself. I didn't meet her officially until earlier this year. She just kind of showed up. At the time she didn't happen to mention she would be back here now, much less with you. Your father and brother didn't happen to come along too, did they?"

"Nope, girls only. My brother had other plans anyway."

"How much did she tell you about me, when she got back?"

Susan sipped her coffee, made a face, and added more sugar. "Not much right away. I know she felt bad about dumping you, but she'd made a whole new life and she didn't seem to know what to do. Then her job sent her back here, and she decided to bring me. Don't ask me why."

"I'd guess some mother–daughter bonding thing. Either that or she thought you'd get yourself into trouble if she left you alone. We don't have to be friends or anything, and you don't have to like me. I'm glad to meet you, and I'll answer whatever questions you ask, but it can end there. So, call your mother and tell her where you are, before she calls the gardaí. That's the police. You have a mobile, right?"

"Well, yeah, of course."

"Then call, and maybe we can go find something to eat."

Silently Susan fished her phone out of a pocket and headed for a corner, where she made a call. From what little Maura could hear, it didn't go well. But why would it? Susan had sneaked away in a country she'd never seen before, to find Maura, whom she'd barely met and had heard of only weeks earlier, and hadn't bothered to tell her mother where she was going. Not a smart thing to do, anytime or anywhere. Even Maura knew that much.

Susan returned after about three minutes. "Meeting's over. She's going to come here as soon as she can get ready. She's pissed."

"She has every right to be. You didn't tell her I had any part in this, did you?"

"Why would I do that? This was my idea, and I got here, didn't I?"

"You did. But she may lock you in your room for the rest of the trip."

"I haven't got anything else to do," Susan muttered, her voice sulky.

"Well, let's take care of the food — we

35

have time to get some before she gets here. But you'll have to settle for Costcutter bread and butter, or something like that. We can walk — it's just up the street."

"Whatever."

"Mick?" Maura called out. He appeared quickly.

"What's going on?"

"Susan and I are going to go find something to eat. Susan sneaked out of the hotel to come here, but I told her she had to call her mother and let her know where she was. Would you mind staying here in case Helen shows up and tries to chew on the woodwork?"

"No worries. I'll try to keep Helen calm."

"Good luck with that," Maura said under her breath.

Maura led Susan out the door and turned up the street. "Who's he? Do you work for him?"

"Not hardly. I own the pub. He works there, and has for a while, since before I got here."

"Huh. You two a couple?"

Maura shrugged. "We haven't decided. Maybe. I don't know. Anyway, this is Leap, County Cork, in the Republic of Ireland, population two hundred and fifty people. Three or four pubs, depending on who feels like opening at any time. Two churches, one school. One gas station, which is one place where you can get food — it's not bad, but if you want a real choice, you have to go to Skibbereen. They have good restaurants there too, not just at the hotels. And in case you don't notice, there's a lot of open land around here and a lot of cows. It's a dairy region."

"You grew up in Boston, right?"

"I did. This is very different, and I think I like it, but it takes getting used to. The fact that I inherited the pub and a cottage certainly makes a difference. And I have no reason to go back to the States. I hope you get to see more of this area."

"Yeah, like Mom is going to let me out of her sight."

"You're the one who gave her a scare. Please remember to apologize." They crossed the road in front of the church, and Maura said, "Okay, here we are. What do you want to eat?"

Fifteen minutes later they came back to Sullivan's to find Mick waiting in the doorway. "She's here. And she's spittin' nails, although mebbe that's the jet lag."

"Might as well get this over with," Maura told him. "Hello again, Helen. I've got your wandering child here with me."

"Could I have a private word with Susan before we chat? The back room, maybe?"

Maura nodded. "Go right ahead."

Helen headed for the door to the back room, and Susan followed, without looking at Maura. The door shut behind them.

Maura turned back to Mick. "Well, this should be interesting," she told him.

"And she didn't ask her mother's permission to drop in this morning?" Mick asked, smiling.

"Exactly. And I knew nothing about it until Susan showed up at the door."

They busied themselves with what little cleanup remained. Rose was still at one of her cooking classes, and Maura wasn't holding her breath waiting for customers. It was at least twenty minutes before Helen and Susan reappeared.

"Let me apologize for any inconvenience Susan has caused," Helen began quickly.

"Helen, she's a kid, and you just dragged her across an ocean. Then you left her in your room. She wanted to see me. I don't quite know why, or what you've told her about me or the pub or the village or Ireland, but it's not a problem. Maybe you could explain? Do you want some coffee or anything else? Please, sit, and slow down."

Much to Maura's surprise, Helen did,

dropping into a chair at a corner table. "I'm sorry. Oh, I already said that, but I mean it. The whole hotel package changed almost overnight, once we lost John, and I was sent over on short notice to see if I could fix it. If I can't, I'll get the blame and probably be out of a job. I'd like this to work, because I think it's a great place, but getting the hotel back on its feet won't be easy. And I had no time to plan anything."

"Which is why you brought Susan along?"

"More or less. Susan didn't want to go to a camp like her brother, so I suggested to my husband that she could come with me. He liked the idea, but I'm not sure she did. She's never been outside the country before."

Maura glanced at Susan, who was staring out the front window and pretending she wasn't there.

"Not like you gave me a choice," Susan muttered to no one in particular.

Maura swallowed a smile. "What did she think you were going to do here?"

"I was going to figure that out when we got here," Helen said. "I guess I didn't think this through very well."

"I can find something to do," Susan protested.

"Helen, Rose should be in soon — remember her? She's pretty close to Susan's age. We're working on building out the kitchen. So, I warn you, Susan — if you don't find something else to do, I'll put you to work here. That should impress your friends."

Susan snorted.

"Try it. You might like it. Helen, are you going back to the hotel now?"

"Yes. And Susan's coming with me for now. I'm sorry if I overreacted, but when your child disappears in a foreign country, you get scared. Give me a little time and we can start over."

"That's fine. Susan, I'll ask Rose if she needs some help. There's still a lot of physical stuff to be done in the kitchen space, and we haven't even begun to think about appliances and plates and pans and all that stuff."

"Oh, good heavens," Helen said suddenly. "I promised to look into whatever appliances the hotel wants to replace. Susan, remind me to check with the contractors and see what's available — maybe Maura can use the recycled pieces here."

"That would be great," Maura told her, although she wasn't even sure what she needed yet. "Susan, you can call me tomorrow, and maybe you can come meet Rose and the others."

"Cool." Susan at least looked less angry than she had.

"Then let's go, Susan," Helen said. I think I need another nap. Thank you, Maura." And they were gone.

Maura turned to Mick, who was behind the bar pretending not to listen. "Looks like it may be an interesting summer."

CHAPTER THREE

When Helen and Susan had left, Maura found she was happy. She'd been carrying a lot of resentment around with her all her life because her mother had vanished from Boston and never bothered to contact her, so getting to know Helen when she had first visited Ireland had been kind of challenging. Then Maura had had to clear up the murder of Helen's boss, whose company owned the hotel outside of Skibbereen, which had made things even more complicated. But they'd managed to work their way to something like a relationship.

Now Susan had been added to the equation, and from what little Maura had seen, Susan wasn't too happy about any of this — meeting her secret sister, seeing the pub, being stuck with her busy mother in an unfamiliar place for who knew how long. Susan needed something to do with her time, and there weren't a whole lot of options in this part of West Cork. Would Helen find some sort of job for her at the hotel? Or should Maura try to work her in at the pub? Maura needed to talk with Rose.

"She favors yeh — the girl, I mean," Mick said, as he collected the empty cups.

"You mean you think she looks like me?" Maura asked. That was something she hadn't considered.

"And like yer mother. I've no clue what your father looked like, as a grown man."

"I've only seen a few pictures, but I always thought he looked Irish. Not that I knew what that meant. Anyway, Susan doesn't seem to be thrilled to be here. Maybe it's just her age, or maybe she had secret plans for back home, but somebody's going to have to find something to keep her busy, if she'll be staying long." Which Helen hadn't bothered to mention.

"Give her some time to settle in. And she can meet the rest of the crew here — they're nearer her age."

"That they are. I feel kind of old when I'm with them, especially since they know more than I do about running this place. So, what do we need to do today?"

"Only the usual. Don't worry yerself — business will pick up soon enough."

"I hope so."

Maura couldn't hear any sound from upstairs: apparently Sophie and Niall had left for their current jobs very early. She still hadn't gotten used to having — what should she call them? Boarders? Guests? Employees? She couldn't complain, because they worked hard and kept the place cleaned up. It was good to have Niall working behind the bar, especially on those occasional nights when things got busy. She'd inherited Rose's father, Jimmy, when she first arrived, but he hadn't really pulled his weight, and she'd been relieved when he got married again and moved in with his new wife. The few times he'd been back to the pub, he'd seemed less than happy to be a dairy farmer, but Maura wasn't inclined to offer him his old job back. Having Niall on staff gave her an additional excuse to turn Jimmy away. Not that Sullivan's required a bouncer, or whatever they were called in Ireland, but every now and then things got a bit rowdy, and having another male presence was helpful.

Rose came bustling in after her class in Skibbereen. "Mornin', Maura, Mick. Another slow day? Mebbe I can get some work done on the kitchen. We need to get it workin'."

"Helen's back in town," Maura told her.

44

"Yer mother? Will she be workin' to fix up the hotel?"

"Looks like it, maybe. They still have to figure out what they want to do with the place. And this time she brought her daughter Susan with her."

"Daughter . . ." Rose said thoughtfully, then brightened. "That'd be your sister?"

"She is, or at least, half sister. She's about sixteen and she doesn't want to be in Ireland with her mother, who won't have much time for her anyway. I was hoping maybe we could find something for her to do — as long as it's not serving drinks, which I know is illegal."

"I'll think about it. Didn't yer mother offer to give us any kitchen appliances she replaces at the hotel?" Rose asked.

"She remembered, and she's going to see what she's got. Whatever she's getting rid of is probably a lot newer than what we've got."

"Didja know she was comin'?"

"Nope. And you missed all the fun: Susan escaped from the hotel and was waiting outside when I got here this morning."

"Yeh're joking!" Rose said, until she looked at Maura's expression. "Yeh're not? Yer mother musta been boilin' mad. What's Susan like?"

"Not too happy at the moment. I don't

think she wanted to be here — it was her mother's idea. Plus apparently Helen didn't tell her about me until she had to. She sneaked away while her mother was at a meeting this morning to come here. I don't know what she might have done if she hated me on sight — headed back to the airport, maybe? Anyway, I thought maybe you'd have some ideas about what she can do around here."

"She sounds a bit young to be workin' here at the pub."

"I agree," Maura told her. "And I'm not sure she's ever had a job at all. Well, think about it. Oh, and I met someone else this morning, back at my cottage."

"And who would that be?"

"An archaeologist from Cork, getting a degree at the university. She's looking for fairy forts. Do you know what they are?"

"Of course — I was raised around here. What's she want with 'em?"

"She says she's doing research — you know, how old they are, who built them, that kind of thing. Do you know where there are any?"

"I do, although sometimes they're hard to see. Will she be stayin' around long?"

"As long as the weather's good, I guess. She said she'd show me the rest of my bits of land, which I haven't had time to explore. Do I want to find a fairy fort on my property?"

"Why would yeh not?" Rose asked.

"Well, so far all I've learned about them is that a lot of people think they're bad luck and won't go near them."

"There's plenty of room to share with the cows. Have yeh asked anyone else?"

"No, not yet. She only showed up this morning, but we're going to walk around tomorrow morning. If you think you and Mick can handle the business."

Rose looked around the room and grinned. "I think we can manage. Yeh might want to talk to Old Billy. Where will yer archaeologist be stayin'?"

"I don't know if she knows yet — she's only just arrived. I told her she could crash at my place if she needed to, but I don't really want a roommate for long."

"Yeh mean, other than Mick?"

"Well, yes. But I like my privacy, and I rarely clean house or keep much food in the cottage. If you meet her, ask her how long she'll be here and what kind of a place she'd like to stay at."

"There's still the third room upstairs."

"So there is. She must have a car to get around, or she'd never have found my place.

47

At least she was polite enough to ask if she could go tramping around my land. She probably knows where to find the parts of it better than I do. And she's got maps."

After the excitement of the morning, things calmed down at Sullivan's. Old Billy came in midafternoon and settled himself in his usual seat by the fireplace, which wasn't in use at the moment. But even the summer weather was unpredictable, so the fireplace was always ready. Maura went over to say hello.

"Hey, Billy. You ready for a pint?"

"I won't say no. Business slow?"

"Kind of. Should I be worried?"

"It'll work itself out — it's still early in the season, and there's plenty goin' on come next month."

Maura settled herself in the shabby armchair across from Billy's. "Can I ask you something?"

"Of course yeh may."

"I had a visit this morning from a woman about my age, who's in graduate school at Cork University and who's spending some time looking for fairy forts around here. I realized I didn't know a darn thing about them, but I figured you would. What can you tell me? She said she'd take me along to look for some on my land, and she told me it was Mick Sullivan's land, and you knew him well, so I figured maybe you'd know if there are any ring forts up around Knockskagh."

"Ah. When I was young, I remember there were several, but I couldn't say they're still there. Time was farmers thought they just got in the way and tore them down — and often regretted it. More recently people leave them alone, for they believe disturbing them can bring bad luck."

"You aren't the first person who's told me that. Why would that be, do you think?"

"Hard to say, but the forts go way back, long before anybody bothered to write anythin' down. Have you not noticed any?"

"No, but I didn't know there was such a thing, so I certainly wasn't looking. And I spend a lot of time here, and usually end up driving back after dark, so I wouldn't be likely to see them. Could you talk to this woman, if she comes in here and you remember anything? I gather we're going looking for some tomorrow morning. Unless you tell me that would be bad luck?"

Billy smiled at her. "Not if yeh respect 'em. And you may be surprised at how many yeh find, once yeh start lookin'."

"I'll tell her. I don't know how much she knows about the country, since I think she

49

comes from somewhere around Cork city. I hope she doesn't end up in a bog."

By late evening the crowd had thinned. Billy had left to get his supper, and Rose and Sophie were deep in conversation about how to fit out the kitchen. "You mind staying till closing?" Maura asked them. "It's not exactly busy."

"We'll be fine," Sophie told her. "You can go on your way. When will you be in, come morning?"

"On time, I hope, but I met an archaeologist who invited me to go exploring with her. I'll try to make it in by opening time. If I'm not in by afternoon, send out the dogs, because we'll probably be stuck in the mud somewhere."

"Take yer mobile with yeh," Rose cautioned.

When Maura stepped outside, the sky was still light, although the sun had sunk below the horizon. She was surprised to see Mick leaning against the building, looking out over the harbor. "Waiting for me?" Maura asked.

"I wondered if you'd care for some company," he said.

"I'd like that. Ciara said she'd come by in the morning, but I think she can handle seeing you. Unless you want to come exploring with us? You can pull us out of the muck when we fall in."

"I'd be glad to be of service."

"Then let's go."

"Your car or mine?"

"Both, I guess. You may want to get to Leap on time in the morning, but I may be wandering the countryside with a student, and who knows how long that will take?"

"I'd be happy to meet the woman. Is she likely to be doing this the old-fashioned way, just poking around, or will she show up with ground-penetrating radar or drones or what have you?"

"How on earth am I supposed to know? Would a drone help?"

"Likely it would. The raths are much easier to see from above. At ground level they look like hedges, and you can seldom see the shape of them."

"I guess that makes sense. Hey, how come these things have so many names? Ring fort, fairy fort, rath? Are they different?"

"Tradition, I'd guess. There's no real difference among them."

"Big help. How do you know all this?"

"I like the history. People lived here a long time ago, and they left little behind them. Maybe this Ciara will learn something about how they lived."

"Sometimes I wish I'd spent more time in school, but Gran and I just couldn't afford it after high school, except for a class now and then. Besides, Boston doesn't really have anything so early, or if it did, the city swallowed it all up."

"That's not a problem here. Things move more slowly in Ireland."

"I'm learning that. Ready to go?"

"I am."

CHAPTER FOUR

Mick was finishing his second cup of coffee, and Maura was trying to figure out where she'd left her only pair of waterproof boots, when Ciara knocked at the door in the morning. "Come on in," Maura called out, rummaging in a pile of odds and ends under the stairs.

"Good morning, Maura," Ciara said, then stopped at the sight of Mick. "Oh, I'm sorry. I didn't mean to interrupt anything."

"Don't worry. This is Mick Nolan. He works with me at the pub. In fact, he's been there a lot longer than I have," Maura told her. "His gran lives down the lane, in that yellow house. Mick won't be coming with us, because somebody has to open the pub. Although I'm sure he knows more about these fairy rings than I do. Do you have a plan, or are we just going to wander around until we fall over one?"

"I've brought a copy of one of Griffith's

maps — have you seen them?"

"Uh, no, and I don't know what they are. Go ahead and tell me," Maura said, piling the few breakfast dishes in the sink.

"Richard Griffith was an Irish mining engineer who became boundary commissioner for Ireland in 1824," Ciara began enthusiastically. "He defined townland boundaries, laying out in exact lines the edges of areas that had long been fluid or traditional, although he also left out a lot of the older place names, or rewrote them to sound more English than Irish. The country needed the boundaries so that the Ordnance Survey could be accurate for valuation — that is, how much the land was worth. Griffith was appointed as the first commissioner for the General Survey and Valuation of Rateable Property in Ireland in 1827, following the Valuation Act of 1826, an act he was involved in drafting, and he held the position until 1868. I could explain to you why there are so many small pieces of land, all of which are recorded based on who owned them and who lived on them, but you won't need it today. I'll get you a copy of the Knockskagh pages, but today all I want to do is get a feel for the land and its topography, since I've never been here before. And I think you should see all the bits you own, and how they connect — or don't. Let me add that starting in the later nineteenth century, the government decided to consolidate properties, so farmers ended up with the same amount of land but all in one piece, which made life easier for them. This went on for quite a while. I don't know if any of this affected your Mick Sullivan's land, and it shouldn't have anything to do with where the raths were located, because they're far earlier, well before anybody had established boundaries — as far as we know, at least. Is that enough for today's lesson?" Ciara smiled.

"That should do for now." History had never been Maura's strong suit in school, and certainly not Irish history.

"Then let me show you an example — it might make more sense to you then. Excuse me, Mick — I need to spread this out."

Maura cleared the few crumbs off the table so Ciara could unroll a map, which was clearly a modern photocopy. "Is this where we are?" she asked, pointing to a blurry square on the map.

"It is. Here's where your house is." Ciara pointed to one small lane in the middle of the map. "Or maybe I should say *was,* because the one we're standing in was built well after Griffith was in charge and this map was made. But there was a building here, at least. You'll notice that the map shows mainly the roads and things like lakes. The houses are kind of sketched in, if they're there at all. Anyway, your lane ends right here, at the next farm. And you know that road at the bottom of the hill, to the east?" When Maura nodded, Ciara said, "It wasn't there when this map was laid out. Some people still call it the 'New Road' or the "Bog Road,' although it's been there for more than a century. Or so I've read."

"And how were the circles laid out?" Maura asked, finding herself getting interested.

"Ah, that the question, isn't it? There are plenty around, and there were probably more once upon a time, but it's hard to say how their locations came about. That's one of the things I'm interested in exploring. Are you familiar with the stone circles?"

"Just Drombeg," Maura said. "Mick took me to see it not long after I arrived here."

"Then you'll know they're usually aligned with celestial events, like the solstices. The raths or fairy forts or ring forts are true circles, carefully laid out, but they often don't have an entry, so they don't align with much of anything. They're sometimes but not always on a hill, but they aren't exactly lookout points. It's really interesting to study them because there's so little evidence to work with. But it's a great way to spend the summer. Oh, and take another look at the map."

"What am I looking for?" Maura asked.

"Griffith included whatever circles were around in the mid-nineteenth century. On a map of this scale, they're tiny, but just look for circles and you'll find quite a few."

Maura peered at the map laid out on the table, and soon found there were a lot of small circles scattered around with no particular pattern. "Will you show me which pieces of land are mine? And if there are any circles on them?"

"I will, but right now I'd rather get out and start looking, while the weather's fine. One thing you don't really see on Griffith's maps is the elevation, so I want to find out if you can see from one ring to another. Don't worry — I plan to be around for a while, so we don't have to see them all today. You can get familiar with your land, and then we can go looking for them. That is, if you want to?" Ciara looked suddenly uncertain. "I know I get excited by hunting for them, but a lot of people don't care. As long as you don't mind my wandering around, you can go your own way. But if you'd like to come with me, I'd be happy for the company."

"Let's see how it goes," Maura said. "My schedule at the pub can be a little unpredictable. Do you need help?"

"I'm good — I just thought you might enjoy it. I've invited a few of my friends to come down, with some equipment, like drones, and maybe some ground-penetrating radar — property of the university, since we can't afford to buy them ourselves. Not that this is a treasure hunt or anything like that — most of these are not burial sites — but it wouldn't hurt to check, and I want some accurate measurements. Mick, would you like to come along?"

Maura realized Mick had remained silent for Ciara's lecture, but she was so enthusiastic that it was hard to interrupt her.

"Some other day, mebbe. I've seen a few around here, but I never paid them much mind. I'll ask me gran if she remembers anything. She knew Mick Sullivan well, and it could be that he mentioned something. But thanks fer offerin'."

"You ready to go, Maura?" Ciara asked.

"I guess. Mick, are you going to see your gran now?"

"I thought I would. Then I'll meet you at the pub?"

"Sounds good. I promise I won't take too long."

"No rush. With our new staff, we can manage, at least during the early part of the day. If any of our friends stop in, I can ask them if they know of any rings."

"Sounds good to me," Maura told him. "Oh, if Helen stops by, tell her I'll be in later, or I can meet her at the hotel. But I'm guessing she and Susan will need a little time to settle in."

"I'll do that. Good to meet you, Ciara. Stop by Sullivan's when you can, although I doubt it's up to Cork city standards."

"Thanks, Mick. Maybe I'll bring my friends around, when they show up."

"I'll see you out, Mick," Maura told him, and followed him out the door. She said quietly, "I don't know what to make of her, or what she's doing. Do I need to know something about these rings or forts or whatever?"

"There's no money involved, nor any buried treasure. It's interestin' that they've been where they are for a thousand years but nobody seems to know anything about them."

"Except that they're scared of them. How can people with modern machines and the Internet be scared of piles of dirt?"

"It's a long tradition, passed down through families. And families rarely strayed far in the past, or if they did, they ended up in another country. Like New Zealand. That's not to say yeh can't look fer the things, as long as yeh don't damage them."

"Does anyone do that? Travellers, say?"

"Not that I've heard. But there are stories about farmers whose tractor falls on 'em when they try to clear their land."

"Great," Maura said, a bit glumly. "I'm glad I wasn't planning to plow anything. Or build anything. I've got all I need right now."

"Yeh can help this Ciara find people to talk to — people who know more about the local traditions. Or myths, you might call 'em."

"Does that count as scientific research? Just talking to old people, I mean. Still, she may be around for a while this summer, so it's worth looking into. Does having her hanging around make you uncomfortable? I mean, we don't get a lot of private time."

"We'll manage." He gave her a quick kiss. "I'll call on Bridget, and then go to Leap."

"And I'll follow you in a couple of hours, if I don't meet some angry fairies."

Back inside, Ciara appeared to be studying the map she'd shown Maura earlier. She had her cell phone in her hand and was comparing it to the map. "Reception's kind of unpredictable on this hill, you know. I'm not trying to call anyone, but I wanted to use the compass app. Do you have a compass?"

"No, I've never needed one. It's not like there are many roads around here to choose between."

"Good point. Well, this is just an exploration, and I can come back. Ready to go?"

"I guess. We're lucky again with the weather today."

"That we are. But these rings somehow have survived for a long time, so who are we to complain if we happen to get wet?"

"Which way do you want to look?"

"Actually, I'd like to find a high hill and get a sense of how the land is laid out. I know we're on a hill here, and there are small lakes or ponds over the top on the other side, so there shouldn't be anything to see in that direction. Which means I guess we should go west. The land seems to climb toward the north. How about a camera? Do you have one?"

"Only what's on my phone. I don't take a lot of pictures, or send any."

Ciara sighed. "I should have done my homework and brought more tools, but I can always find some, or ask my friends to bring some extras. Let's go!"

Maura dutifully followed Ciara out, shutting the door behind her. She knew her cottage was on a hill, but that didn't mean it would be easy to go up, since fields were irregularly shaped, with fences or hedgerows between them, and they were full of grazing cattle or sheep who were not necessarily friendly. Had Ciara spent any time in the country, or was she making assumptions based on what she'd read? And then there was the fact that some local residents, no doubt, would not want strangers tramping through their land.

Ciara stopped halfway down the hill, past Bridget's cottage, and surveyed the landscape. "I'm guessing it's boggy at the bottom of the hill."

"I'm pretty sure it is," Maura told her.

"That patch straight ahead belongs to you," Ciara said.

"What?"

"That's what the map says, although the road is more recent. And it was Michael Sullivan who owned all this before you?"

"That's what the documents I signed say. He was in his eighties when he died a couple of years ago. No wife or children. That's why he left it to me." With a little persuasion from Gran, Maura thought. No matter how it had come about, she was grateful.

"Hey, about this Mick Nolan. Where does he fit?" Ciara asked cautiously.

Nobody around here asked anything like that, Maura reflected. Where *did* he fit? Or was it just a passing thing? She was afraid to guess. She liked being with Mick, but she still wasn't sure it was something that would last. "I guess we're sort of together. It hasn't been very long. And he works for me, not the other way around."

"No worries — I wasn't about to make a play for him. He's from around here, isn't he?"

"Yes, mostly. Bridget is his gran. He looks out for her." Time to change the subject. Maura wasn't comfortable talking about her maybe love life with someone she barely knew. "Which way are we going?"

Ciara pointed across the shallow valley to the north. "See that kind of lump up the hill there?" Maura nodded dubiously. "I'm betting that's a fairy fort. You see any cows in the field?"

"Uh, no. But they could be at one end or the other, out of sight."

"Well, let's go find out."

"Lead the way, Ciara."

Chapter Five

Maura hadn't done a lot of hiking, even close to her home. Some parts of the fields were littered with bushes and weeds, with the occasional patch of what she understood was called upland bog. Sometimes there were areas with cattle prints, which made the land lumpy and muddy. Why would anyone put a round enclosure up here? Whatever the reason, it wasn't obvious.

As they approached, with Ciara in the lead, the structure became less and less obvious. Up close it looked like a pile of brambles, but Ciara had said the bramble pile had to be maybe a thousand years old or more. Maura had never been much of a gardener, but it amazed her that the assorted plants had survived this long.

Ciara stopped a hundred or so feet from their target and turned slowly around, gauging angles and distances. "Do you see another circle anywhere?" she asked Maura.

"Un, no? But I've never noticed any at all. What were these good for?"

Ciara smiled ruefully. "There are several schools of thought on that. Some people believe they were no more than cattle pens, to protect the cattle from predators. Others think they served as a sort of enclosure against human invaders. Others think they were ceremonial sites."

"In other words, nobody knows," Maura commented.

"Let's just say that nobody agrees. That's one reason I want to check their individual locations and how they relate to one another. Maybe that will show us a pattern. Or we can connect them to houses, if there is any evidence left of those. Odd, isn't it, that a cattle pen could outlast a human dwelling?"

"Seems unlikely to me — didn't humans use stones to build? Or did people back then steal the stones when they were building something new? Or did they just keep moving when their house fell down? Anyway, have you ever talked with people who raise cattle now? I mean, how many cows could you put in one of these rings, with enough food?"

"I haven't talked to many farmers," Ciara admitted.

"And why haven't they burned down?" Maura pressed on. "They're just plant materials, aren't they? No stones holding them together?"

"That's where it gets interesting. You're right — if they're just branches and vines, they could easily have burned at some point. Since they didn't, one could infer that people had an unusual respect for them, and protected them, or at least kept them in good repair."

"And after a thousand years or so, nobody's figured it out?" Maura asked.

"So it would appear. That's why I'm doing this research. I'll admit there's no particular value in knowing what these were, how they were used, but people still feel there's something eerie about them. The cautious ones leave them alone. Others tear them down, and turn up dead in a farm accident shortly after that."

"Ciara, there's a lot I don't understand about Ireland. I never thought I'd have to worry about old plants, but I don't have any reason to mow them down."

"I'm glad to hear it. You want to get closer?"

"Will I be safe?" Maura wasn't sure whether she was kidding.

"If you're careful," Ciara said, and took

off toward the ring.

The circle turned out to be bigger than it looked from a distance, Maura discovered. And it was surprisingly precisely round, even after so much time. How had anybody planned that? "Is there anything inside the circle?"

Ciara was busy taking pictures. "That's hard to guess. Because of what I said, about people fearing them, nobody likes to dig them up, so it's hard to say if there's anything buried — human, cattle, or treasure. That's why I wanted to try out ground-penetrating radar, which is noninvasive. But I'm not pinning too much hope on that, since even the stone circles don't usually include any sort of burial, or if they do, the burials are often much later than the circles themselves."

"So why are you so interested, and what do you hope to prove?"

Ciara smiled. "I think proving a negative is still useful. If we can say that ninety percent of the surviving raths show no evidence of human sacrifice or burial, then the academic community will have learned something. And maybe help to protect those that have survived, because people won't start poking around looking for gold or something valuable. What're the oldest cemeteries around here, do you know?"

"That's not really my kind of thing, so I've never looked. I suppose I should, since my grandmother was born around here, and her parents or the rest of the family should be buried somewhere. But if they couldn't afford tombstones, I'm told it's hard to find where they might be. And I don't even know their names. My gran didn't talk much about her life here." Maura knew where her father was buried, near Boston, but wasn't even sure Gran had been able to afford a tombstone when he died. She couldn't recall ever visiting it, if it existed.

Maura checked her watch and was surprised to see it was already past ten. "I should head for Leap. The pub should be opening soon, and I've still got to go back and get my car. Do you have plans?"

"I'm fine — I'll hike around a bit longer, but all I'm doing now is checking out what I should look at more carefully. It's nice to have plenty of time."

"If you have the time, stop in the pub in Leap and I can introduce you to some other people. You really should talk to Old Billy. He was a longtime friend of Mick who owned the place, and he might know more about the land here than I do. Do you know when your friends are coming?"

"I need to talk to them again, now that I have a better idea of what's where. But sooner rather than later, I'd guess — they're just doing me a favor, but this isn't their main field of interest. You go ahead. I want to stay here for a bit and see if I can commune with any long-dead farmers."

"Good luck. See you later," Maura said, then turned to figure out her way home.

It was close to eleven by the time she arrived at Sullivan's, but things seemed to be going smoothly, mainly because there weren't a lot of customers. The clanging from the kitchen space in the back made it clear that the construction process was well under way. Mick came out of the back room. "Didja find what yeh were looking for?"

"Well, we found one ring, but I'd never noticed it before. I can't say I'm excited by any of it. Ciara seems to be, but even she admits there's a lot she doesn't know about them, and nobody else does either. I'm still boggled by the fact that they're still there after so long. I mean, we've seen houses around here that are less than a hundred years old, and they're falling apart. What's the difference?"

"It's the fairies guardin' the places," Mick said.

Maura took a harder look at his expression to see if he was joking. It looked like he was. "Have you seen Billy yet today?"

"It's still early fer him. Why do yeh ask?"

"I thought he might know more about Old Mick's land than I do, which wouldn't be hard. Or does nobody ever talk about fairy forts? Is that supposed to be bad luck too, just mentioning them?"

"Yeh'll have to ask Billy. I'm not even sure I can say there're any on the Nolan land, but I've never been a farmer. Now you've got one ring."

"At least one," she corrected Mick. "Ciara said there might be more, if I can figure out what other pieces of land I may have. But finding them is not tops on my list."

"Yeh didn't know yeh had the land?" Mick asked.

"No, I did not. Or why. When I showed up here, I didn't know Mick Sullivan existed. And then this lawyer shows up and tells me to sign a lot of papers, but I can't say I read them carefully. So it seems I've got land I can't even find. What am I supposed to do with it?"

"Has no one asked yeh about grazing on it?"

"Uh, no. But I'm almost never there by daylight. How much land does it take to graze one cow or one sheep?"

"I couldn't tell yeh. And acre apiece, mebbe? But if you've no plan to use it, yeh might think of selling it to someone who would."

"I suppose. But I have no idea how much it's worth. And it's not like I need the money."

"You could use it to pay for the kitchen," Mick pointed out.

"I wouldn't know how to find out how to sell it," Maura said dubiously.

"Maura Donovan, yeh work in a pub, do yeh not? All you need to do is tell a few people, and the word will get round."

"Can I find out where it is first, please? If it turns out it's right behind my cottage, then the blasted sheep or cows will keep me awake all night."

"Up to you, Maura," Mick said. Then he looked beyond Maura toward the front door. "Look's like yeh've got company again."

Maura turned to see Susan standing in the doorway, looking uncertain. Maura strode over to her quickly. "You coming or going?"

"Does it matter?" the girl said defiantly.

"Just wondering. You're welcome to come in. Or if you're looking for lunch, you can go back to the Costcutter, or to Ger's next door."

Now it was Susan's turn to look past Maura, at the number of empty tables, and the cobwebs in the corners, all too obvious on a sunny day. "Can I get something to drink, like a Coke, maybe?"

"Sure." Maura stepped back and let Susan come in. Susan, her sister. *Half sister.* This was going to take getting used to. Maura had to admit she was curious about a lot of things. Among them, why was Susan in the pub right now? Not that she minded. "Sit wherever you like. Listen, don't take this wrong, but does your mother know where you are this time?"

Susan snorted. "She's in a meeting — again — and she didn't know when it would end. I don't know why she wanted me to be here in Ireland if she's never going to have time to see me. But this time I told her I was coming here. Really."

"How'd you get to Leap?"

"The woman at the hotel called a cab for me, and said the hotel would pay. I think she wanted to suck up to Mom, who's probably her boss."

"Have you ever left the country before?"

Susan shook her head. "My school took a field trip to Montreal in Canada, but that's about it. I was really surprised when Mom said she was coming back to Ireland. She never talked much about it, but when she did, it sounded like she didn't like it."

Maura wasn't sure what she was supposed to say or do right now, but she might as well get everything out in the open. If Helen was pissed off, too bad. "Well, there were some peculiar things that happened on that trip, so I can't say I'm surprised. Susan, when did she tell you about me?"

Susan shook her head. "She never talked much about her life before she met Dad. Finally last year she said she thought Tommy and I were old enough to know she'd had another child before us, and walked away from her and never even contacted her. Is that true?"

Even though Maura knew it, it hurt her to hear it. It was like Helen had tried to erase her, until she'd finally figured out that wouldn't work. "It is. When her husband — my father — died suddenly, I think she panicked and just left. Like she couldn't imagine living in a crummy apartment with her Irish mother-in-law and a baby. At least I had my grandmother to take care of me, but it wasn't easy for us. And as far as I know, your — our — mother never looked back, never got in touch with Gran or me.

And then she just showed up here. What did she say when she came home after that trip?"

Susan's mouth twitched. "You mean after she almost got arrested for murdering her boss? She did say that you were the person who got her out of it. I guess that was her way of jumping into the story."

"It's true, sort of. I sure didn't expect any of that — the whole murder thing. Not the best way to get to know someone, like a long-lost mother. Or maybe it was, because she had to tell the truth. Did she want to come back now because of her job or because she wanted you to meet me?"

"She didn't explain. She knew she had to come back here, and I guess she didn't want to dump this whole load of stuff on me and disappear. She told me I was coming with her, no argument. Of course, I'll admit I was kind of curious about this unknown sister in another country. But her job was to save the hotel, not entertain me, so I was kind of at loose ends."

"Does she think the hotel was in trouble?"

"Not exactly. She said she'd have to work hard to save it, but I think she wants to. Anyway, here I am. What is there to do around here?"

"Depends on what you like. I warn you,

I'd take movies and concerts and shopping off the list. This isn't that kind of place. But there are a lot of things going on in the summer, like festivals and events — not that I have time to check them out. You can probably find something to keep you busy."

"Why don't you have any time?"

"Because I've never owned anyplace and I've never run anything in my life, much less a pub in a small town in Ireland, and I've still got a lot to learn. But I think I like it."

Maura heard the sound of a ringing phone, and Susan fished a mobile out of her pocket. "Yeah, Mom. No, I'm in Leap. I wanted to talk to Maura." She fell silent, and Maura could hear Helen's loud voice. "Why don't you come here? You said you wanted me to get to know her. Well, she's sitting in front of me." Another round of silence from Susan. "Yeah, yeah. I'll stay here and wait for you. Bye."

"She didn't sound happy," Maura commented.

Susan ignored Maura's comment. "So, what's it like, running your own pub?"

"Sometimes it's busy, other times not. Lots of people in the area come in regularly, more for the talking than for the drinking, and now there's live music a few nights a week. How old are you?"

"Sixteen this past April. Why?"

"Just trying to find out if you're old enough to work here for a bit. You have to have a relative working here too, but I think you and I have that covered. And you should meet Rose — she's not that much older than you. She's working in the back, rebuilding the kitchen, because she wants to cook and serve food."

"Cool. Mom would pitch a fit, but at least she'd know where I was. Can I go meet this Rose?"

"Go right ahead. I'm sure she'll be happy to see you."

CHAPTER SIX

Maura watched as Susan sauntered into the back room, where the pounding promptly stopped. She sighed. How had her life suddenly become so complicated? Again? Susan was certainly an unexpected addition, although Maura thought she kind of liked her. If she got along with Rose, things would be easier.

"What's the story?" Mick asked from behind the bar. He'd been suspiciously quiet.

"Like I'm supposed to know?" Maura said. "Apparently Helen insisted that Susan come along with her, but it doesn't seem that she had any plan for keeping Susan busy. Helen was in a business meeting this morning, so Susan found herself a cab at the hotel and just showed up. At least she's curious, not just sitting in her room and sulking. She's also barely sixteen, so I can't exactly turn her loose. I told her to go talk to Rose — at least they're more or less the same age. Wonder if Susan knows anything about carpentry?"

"Seems unlikely," Mick said. "How long's she stayin'?"

"Nobody's said. Have you heard any rumors about what's going on with the hotel?"

"Not exactly. There's folks that are curious, but I don't think they're worried. The place has been through plenty of changes before. Helen surely must know that."

"If she knows how to do her job, I'd think so. Or maybe she's here just to close things up at the hotel. I don't see her trying to make a life for herself here — she's not Irish. I wish I could say how my father felt about staying in Boston. At least there were jobs there, ones that didn't involve cows. But then, maybe he liked cows. He was still pretty young when Gran took him to the U.S. But I never knew him, and Gran didn't talk about him."

"Have yeh looked to see where he was born?" Mick asked softly.

Maura shook her head. "I didn't know where to start. The first real map I've seen was the one Ciara brought. I can't even pronounce most of the townlands. Bridget would know, but we've never talked about it. Is your grandmother hiding something, or does she think I'm not interested? I mean, it's kind of late to start putting together my family history, and it's too late to ask Gran for the details. But I can't exactly feel sorry for myself, can I? I've got a home and a business, and I owe that to Gran. It's just that she never mentioned how her husband died, and I never asked because I didn't want to upset her, especially after my father died. I guess we just looked ahead, not backwards, and ignored the past. So I don't know much, and I can't help Susan out about my past, or her mother's."

"Yeh've only to ask, if you want to know more. I can talk with Bridget with yeh, if yeh want."

"I'll let you know. But thanks for offering."

Their conversation was interrupted when Susan and Rose came out from the soon-to-be kitchen. Susan was laughing, and she looked pleased with herself. "That was fun, Rose. Look, if my mom doesn't mind, I'd be happy to help, if you'll just tell me what you need done."

"Hang on," Maura interrupted. "You know enough about construction to manage on your own, Susan?"

79

"Pretty much. My dad and me, we've worked together on some house improvements, and I think I've got the basics down, like how to use a hammer. And I can help with clean-up."

"Let's see what your mother has to say about it. Was there something she wanted to do together with you while you were here?"

Susan shrugged. "She didn't mention much. Maybe she didn't know how busy she would be, but I'm pretty sure she never planned to run around playing tourist. I think it would be cool if I could help pull this place together."

"That's fine with me, if she's willing." Maura looked up to see two guys outside who looked about her own age, and who seemed lost. When they came in, the taller asked her, "This is Sullivan's, right?"

"That it is. Why do you want to know?"

"Ciara McCarthy's a friend. She wanted us to come out and help her with something she's working on, and we have a few free days. Do you know her?"

"Since yesterday, yes. So you're archaeology students?"

"Kind of, but not the same way she is. But she wanted us to check out some scientific ideas. Do you know where she is?"

"I saw her this morning, but she didn't say where she was staying. I live a couple of miles from here, and she says I own at least one fairy fort, which was news to me. She was still looking for more when I came to work here. Oh, sorry — I'm Maura Donovan. I run this place."

The taller young man said, "I'm Darragh, and this is Ronan." The second guy had yet to say a word, but he nodded at Maura.

"You two want something to drink?"

"That'd be grand. And I'll call Ciara's mobile and find out where we should meet."

"Good idea. Have you ever been to this part of Cork? Mick, you want to fill a couple of pints?"

"Happy to," he said, and turned to the taps.

Darragh was still talking. "Can't say that we have. Ronan's from the west, and I'm from the south of Dublin. We all met in Cork city. I'm told things are pretty wild around here, but you can tell us where to go looking for Ciara, right?"

"Of course." Maura turned away from the bar and realized Susan was sitting silently at a table and staring at the guys. Maura took a critical look at them. They seemed to be uniformly good-looking, but they were a few years older than Susan. Maura hadn't even spent enough time talking with her to know if she had a boyfriend back in the States, or wanted one. Maybe she should ask Helen if there were any rules about her daughter dating.

It looked like the guys had reached Ciara by phone. "You're Maura, right?" Darragh asked.

"I am. You found Ciara?"

"Yes. She said we should meet her in Skibbereen and figure out where to stay. Where is Skibbereen?"

"It's the next town over," Maura said. "Just take the road out front to the west and you'll find it — it's less than ten miles."

"You know where she's looking for raths?" he asked, as Maura slid the pints across the bar toward the young men.

"As of this morning, on my land, but she had to show me where. I'm so busy working here that I don't have time to go exploring. What are you guys looking for?"

"I don't know if Ciara's told you, but we want to try some scans to see if there's anything below the surface in or around the rings. Not like a treasure hunt, but just to see if there's anythin' buried there. Might help us understand what they were used for."

"Have people found things like that in

other places?"

"A few, but it's hard to tell if they're the same age as the raths or if what's buried hasn't been there very long. That's why we brought some machinery along."

"Sounds interesting," Maura said. "Not that I know anything about the things."

"What did Ciara say about what you found?"

"So far it's only the one, and it's nothing that I understood," Maura admitted. "I mean, I may own the land it's on, but I didn't know it was there. Or what that meant. I inherited the property, but I never knew the former owner. I grew up in Boston, so all this is new to me. Why are you interested?"

"Because it's a bit of history. Because we don't know much about the people who built these things, or why they're still there, but it means something to a lot of people."

"Ciara told me people still think the rings have some sort of special powers, and they leave them alone. How is that possible?"

"It's fairy business. I can show you some books, if you want to know more. You haven't seen anything — or anyone — unexpected, have you?"

"Only living, breathing ones," Maura told him, smiling. She spied Helen outside the pub, heading for the door, and she leaned closer to the man. "There's an example, maybe. She's my mother, but she abandoned me when I was very young and I'd never met her. Then suddenly she shows up around here, without any warning. This is actually her second trip, and she brought her daughter. My sister." Maura nodded toward Susan. "I didn't know until this year that I had one. Is there something supernatural going on with us?"

"Never say never." He looked past Helen, then said, "Ah, Ciara, there you are. I thought we'd be lookin' for yeh in Skibbereen. I've been talking to Maura here for a while. Any luck?"

"A few clues, possibly, but I've only just begun. Do you guys want to sit down and talk about it? Or go straight to the hostel? I've booked space for us. It's the other side of Skibbereen."

"It's early yet. Let's have a pint and enjoy this place — it looks like it's a century old or more. Then we can work out our plans for tomorrow."

"Fine," Ciara said. "Maura, could you draw me a pint? I see these two have had a head start. And we can fill you in on our plans after I've talked with this lot."

"No problem." Maura nodded at Mick

behind the bar, then pointed to Ciara while her friends found a corner table. Then she headed toward Helen, who'd walked in and stopped, and was apparently scanning the room for Susan.

"Is Susan here? She was when I called earlier."

"She's in the back," Maura told her, "looking at the kitchen remodeling and probably talking to Rose, who's as close to her own age as anybody she's met around here. How was your meeting at the hotel?"

"Long. And I wish I'd had more sleep. I don't think most of the staff has heard about what's going on and where they might fit."

"You want to sit down? Have some coffee?"

"Please."

Maura went back to the bar again. "She wants coffee, if you don't mind," she told Mick quietly. "She looks tired. Should I go get Susan?"

"Yeh might want to have a chat with Helen. Has she said how long she's stayin'? A week, or all summer?"

"Mick, you've seen her exactly as long as I have. But now that she knows where Susan is, she's not so worried. I'll take her coffee over."

Maura delivered the coffee and joined Helen at the table. "You look beat. Was there a reason you had to be in Skibbereen now, instead of waiting a bit?"

Helen shrugged. "I wanted to get the process rolling. Oh, heck — I'm not even sure what the staff on this end wants to happen. I figured I'd better find out sooner rather than later. The place has gone through a lot of changes, all before your time here. John had good ideas about what to do next, but he didn't get the chance, as you know. I need to take a hard look at the place now. How're things going here at the pub?"

"Unpredictable. I told you we decided to make the kitchen usable — or at least, Rose did. She's only a couple of years older than Susan, and she's already finished school. She's working on the kitchen." Maura paused before going on. "You know, Susan seems to know her own mind. It might be better if she kept busy. She can help Rose with the kitchen if she wants — she told me she and her father have done some repair-type work together. How long are you going to be around?"

"A few weeks, at least. I'm sorry I didn't make any plans to keep Susan busy. That was my fault. I didn't have time to plan much."

"What does she like to do?"

"A lot of things. You have some ideas?"

"Well, there's the kitchen, for one thing. I think I told Susan that she was old enough to work in the pub — this one or another one — as long as she doesn't sell liquor. If she has a relative here, it's okay, and I guess I count, so the law says it's okay. I wish I had more time to show her around West Cork, but this place keeps me pretty busy, especially in summer. What did you tell her about my father?"

"Not much, for a long time. He was ancient history by the time I married again, and it was too complicated. But you have every right to ask for yourself — I know I didn't treat you fairly, and it sounds like your grandmother didn't say much either. I'm sorry. But remember that when your father died, I was younger than you are now, and I didn't have any idea what to do. So I left. I've tried to make up for that for years, and I guess confessing to you is my last step. But I hadn't counted on explaining it all to Susan."

"I think you should have — explained it, I mean, and to all of us — but that's water under the bridge. My life is definitely interesting now, more than I expected, and I'm not complaining. But there's not much I can tell Susan. Does she have friends back home? A boyfriend? Hobbies?"

"Not that she tells me about. You can let her try working here, if she wants to, and you can keep an eye on her. If not, I'll figure out something."

"That works for me," Maura told her. "And if you want to see where my father was born, we can probably find that. But you don't have to."

"I did love him, you know. If he hadn't died unexpectedly, we might have had a good life, or at least a very different one. I'm sorry you never got to know him."

"So am I, Helen."

CHAPTER SEVEN

Susan came barreling out of the back room, liberally splattered with plaster and sawdust. "Hey, Mom, I wondered if you'd be here yet. Maura, it's going to be a cool kitchen when it's finished."

Helen interrupted. "Shoot, I promised you that you could have some of the discarded appliances from the hotel, and they're all still there somewhere, or will be, if we make any more changes. Let me know what you need and I'll see what I can do. And I'll try not to forget again."

Rose also emerged from the kitchen, looking as grubby as Susan. "Oh, hello, Mrs. Jenkins. Maura said you'd be back. I think Susan could be a big help, and the kitchen's far from finished. Maura, with another pair of hands, I think we could have it done in a few weeks."

"Sounds good to me, Rose," Maura told her. "But we still aren't ready to cook anything hot, right? You can go with sand-wiches and stuff if you want, at least for now."

"How old is this building?" Susan asked, all but bouncing with enthusiasm.

"Oh, two or three hundred years," Maura said.

"Seriously?" Susan exclaimed. "Has it been a pub that long?"

Maura smiled. "That I can't tell you. But it's known for being the boundary of West Cork, otherwise known as the Wild West of Ireland. There's a creek next to the building that separates Cork and West Cork, and it got famous because a guy named O'Donovan jumped across it on his horse to escape the English. Which is why this village is called Leap."

Susan did not look convinced. "Is all that true?"

"So I'm told, but I'd like to see the horse that could do it. And west of here, it's pretty much country. With a lot of cows, and some sheep thrown in."

"Wait — you said you grew up in Boston. So you grew up in a city, right? And now you're living in the middle of cow pastures?"

"That's true. Not that I see a lot of cows, because I'm usually not home until late, after the pub closes and it's too dark, and in winter the cows are in their barns. But it's quiet, and I've gotten used to the smell of manure."

Susan snorted at her comment. "You going back to Boston any time soon?"

"I haven't decided, but I doubt it. Here I own a house and a business. I don't think that's ever going to happen back in the States, unless I win a lottery. Besides, I like it here. I've got friends, and I'm learning a lot."

"I'm glad to hear that," Helen said. "Susan, we should be going now."

"Back to your hotel? It's really not my kind of place, from what I've seen."

"I know, but it's mine. We can talk about what else you want to do."

"Can I help out at the pub here? You said I could."

Helen looked resigned. "As long as you don't handle drinks."

"Yeah, I know, but Rose is putting together the kitchen and I could cook. You know, make sandwiches, that kind of thing, if enough is finished. It's not fancy or anything."

Helen looked anxiously around the room until she spotted Rose. "Rose, you sure you're okay with it if Susan spends some time here helping you out?"

"I'd be glad of the company — as long as she does the work. And I'll make sure she doesn't do anythin' she shouldn't. And doesn't do any drinkin'."

Helen smiled. "I guess I can't ask for more. Thank you, Rose. Susan, let's get moving. I still need more sleep."

"Fine, as long as I can come back in the morning," Susan said.

"Fair enough. Bye, Maura — I'll drop her off tomorrow, or try to find a ride for her."

Maura watched until Helen and Susan reached Helen's car before asking Rose, "Does she know what she's doing?"

"Susan? Sure, and she'll be fine. The kitchen will be ready in no time, and I'll start advertisin' meals."

"Rose, you are amazing."

The Cork students finished their drinks, and Ciara took charge. "Darragh! Ronan! Is the equipment in your car? Did you come in one car or two?"

"Two cars. The machines are in mine," Darragh said. "As much as I could borrow, anyways. You know where you want to use it?"

"I've found a few more rings, out past Maura's place. How long can you stay? We should figure out how many forts we can collect data for."

"It's pretty quiet in Cork city. We thought we'd stay around for a few days, maybe longer, depending on what we find."

"Hi, Ciara," Maura said as she ambled over. "You ready to leave?"

"Yes, and I'm thinking you want us to settle up. This place looks really old. Maybe you can give me a tour sometime?"

"It is — about three hundred years old, I was told. Since we've torn apart a few of the walls in the back, I'm sure you as an archaeologist would enjoy it. Did you find anything interesting?"

"I think so, but we need more accurate details. I think the fine weather will last, so we can get an early start in the morning. And the days are as long as they'll get now, which should give us plenty of time. At least the sites seem undisturbed, save for the cows."

"Sounds good," Maura said. "Let me know if there's anything else you think I should see. Oh, and here comes our most valuable resource: Old Billy, who's known this area for eighty-some years. I'm sure he'd love to talk to you about what he remembers, although I don't know if he's been out in the country much for a while. But I'd guess the fairy forts won't have changed, and he'd know about them. I'll ask if he's willing to talk now."

"That would be grand, Maura. Interesting how oral history survives."

Maura stood up and made her way over to Billy.

"Ah, Maura, yeh're lookin' well. Who are the nice young people you were talkin' with?"

"They're archaeology students from Cork city, and they're doing research on fairy rings. You know, I don't know anything about those, but I thought you might. Ciara thinks she's found at least one on what was Old Mick's property, which is now mine. It was news to me, but I've never gone looking and I don't even know what I'm looking for. Would you be willing to talk to them? Do you remember anything out that way?"

"Ah, sure, there's plenty between here and Drinagh, or time was there were plenty. I'll be happy to answer their questions, as long as they'll buy me a pint or two."

"Great! Thank you."

"Ah, Maura, I'm happy to share what I know. Was that yer mother I saw, when I was comin' in?"

"It was, and now I bet you're going to ask who the young girl was."

"And you'd be right. Though from the look of her, I'd guess she's yer sister. How're yeh getting' along?"

"Better than I might have expected, if I'd had a clue she was coming. But Susan seems smart, and interested, which is good. I may put her to work here with Rose while she's around. I don't know how long she and my mother are staying, but I think Helen's got a lot of work cut out if she wants to keep the hotel going."

"Same old problem, and it's survived before. But at least she's seen the place already, and she's had time to think about what needs doin'.."

"It's been a slow summer so far — not a lot of tourists. Will that make it easier for Helen?"

"Might do. It's hard to guess whether it'll be busy or not, but I'd tell her not to give up just yet."

"Good to know, Billy. Should I send the students over to you now?"

"Happy to see them. Mebbe they'll let yeh go with 'em — you need to see what's on your land."

"I know I should, but there never seems to be enough time, and I don't even know where to look. How much land did Old Mick have?"

"It's hard to say now. There's the bit around the cottage, but more than that. He kept buyin' and sellin' smaller bits, when he had cattle. But he gave that up quite a few years ago, or maybe just let his neighbors graze their animals. Yeh don't have any plans like that of yer own, do yeh?"

"What, I'm supposed to be raising cattle now? I don't think so. If you hear of anyone else who wants to use it, I'm more than willing, as long as I don't end up with cows in my kitchen."

Billy smiled broadly. "Used to be that was how farmers heated their houses — keep the cows inside in the winter, and let the children sleep up top where it'd be warm."

Maura had to smile at Billy's image. "I don't think I'm going to try that. Look, I'll send the students over, and if you don't want to talk now, tell them when they can come back. And thanks."

"Happy to help yeh, Maura."

Maura made her way back to the bar, stopping to tell the gathering of students that Billy was looking forward to talking with them, if they had the time. The trio conferred briefly, then stood and went over to Billy's corner and sat. Maura set about making herself a cup of coffee. "Odd day today, isn't it?" she said to Mick. "So far I've talked to my long-lost family, more or less found someone to help Rose build the kitchen, and discussed fairy forts with a couple of different people, which is ridiculous, since I don't know a darn thing about them. Has anybody paid for drinks, or are we simply drumming up business?"

"A bit of both. If Seamus and his gang come in later, he might help — he and his mates have been raisin' dairy cows fer a long time, and they'd know where to find the rings."

"I'll try to remember that, if I see them. You know, I've got kind of mixed feelings about this. I should know where I'm living, and how much land I've got. But nobody's ever mentioned fairy forts to me. I guess they've sort of become part of the landscape and nobody thinks about it, unless it comes time to mow the field. But if I'd found them on my own, I probably wouldn't have given them much thought. I mean, they just look like a tangle of old plants, not someplace that a bunch of thousand-plus-year-old fairies call home. It all seems crazy."

"You'd best not say that. People here have grown up with it, and their families before them. And most fairies mind their own business, unless you cross them. It's a way of keeping the local population polite, I'm guessin'."

"Then tell me, Mick — have you met any

fairies?"

He grinned. "I'd rather not say. But yeh might ask Bridget."

"I'll do that. You know, I'd bet she's on good terms with the local fairies, wherever they are."

Mick was still smiling. "I wouldn't doubt that."

The rest of the day passed quietly. It wasn't unpleasant: the sun shone on the harbor, highlighting the gliding swans, and a few new customers wandered in, oohing and aahing at the quaint nature of the pub, and how very Irish it seemed. Maura kept her mouth shut, after providing them with drinks; she didn't want to tell them it was in fact Irish (except for her), and that the old place had been collecting dirt and cobwebs for well over a century, which made it authentic. If she told them it was authentic dirt, would they walk out?

After a while she wandered into the soon-to-be-kitchen to see what Rose had accomplished. The high windows remained in place, although they could use some new panes to replace a few cracked ones, but Rose had recently added a fresh coat of paint, which brightened the room. She still wasn't sure if they needed new wiring and plumbing, able to maintain a serious stove and the small water heater that provided the sink with hot water. Rose was still tidying up, so Maura asked, "If you could have whatever you want, what appliances would you get?"

"A four- or six-burner stove with a griddle on top, and two working ovens. A standard refrigerator — leave the one behind the bar for ice. Mebbe an electric dishwasher, although that might be a luxury, as long as someone keeps washing."

"Microwave?" Maura asked.

"I'm not sure of that, but it would be easy to add. And plenty of cabinets, for food and dishes and pans. And we'd need to allow enough room for two people to work side by side at the same time."

"Sounds about right, although I've never worked in a kitchen. When I worked in a Boston pub, I stayed behind the bar, so I don't know everything that went on in the back. But it sounds to me like you've been paying attention at your cookery school."

"That I have. And I also know the competition. We've got to set ourselves apart here, since we've got Sheahan's across the road, and the Harbour Bar a couple of doors down, and Ger's for quick food. I've tried them all and I can't complain."

"Remind me again why we're doing this?"

"To keep people here longer, orderin' more drinks. Or askin' fer food on the nights we have the music."

"It all sounds good to me. Can Susan help?"

"With the buildin' or the food?"

"Both. Either. I haven't spent enough time with her to know how good she is, or how long she might last. And she's not here to stay — she'll have to go back to school in the fall, or maybe sooner."

"We can let her try things out, before our official openin'. Can we have a big party fer that?"

"I don't see why not. Thanks for taking this on, Rose. I wouldn't have known where to start. And you know I can't cook."

Rose grinned. "Why do yeh think I volunteered?"

CHAPTER EIGHT

When Maura came out of the kitchen again, she stopped for a moment to watch Old Billy holding court with the young students. She almost snorted at her own choice of word: they seemed young to her, but they were the same age she was, more or less. Had she missed some critical part of her life? Most of what she could remember was work and classes. She'd taken a couple of accounting classes in the evening, figuring that knowing how to work with numbers would always be useful somewhere. Not that she'd enjoyed it much, but at least she'd finished the course and could calculate profits and losses, which came in handy now.

Ciara and the two guys — Darragh and Ronan, she thought they were, but she'd never known anybody with those names before — were still seated at Billy's feet, hanging on his every word. That was fine with her. Billy was always truthful, and his knowledge of this corner of West Cork was broad and deep. And he liked an audience, maybe because everyone else who came into Sullivan's had already heard his stories. But nobody in the small group seemed to be in a hurry to go anywhere, and they even bought a second round of pints. She wondered how long they'd be around.

It was past nine when Billy told them all — somewhat reluctantly — that he needed his sleep, and could they continue their conversation at another time? The rest of them nodded in agreement and started to drain their glasses. Ciara stood up and came over to where Maura was keeping an eye on things. "Thanks so much for putting us together with your friend, Maura — he has an amazing memory. I hope we'll have a chance to talk with him again."

"He's led an interesting life. And then he settled at the end of this building when his old friend Mick took over the pub. Billy told me once that Mick didn't really care whether he made any money here. He saw this place as a good business and a place to just hang out with his pals, and that went on for years. But he's been gone almost three years now. Billy still lives in a small apartment at the other end of this building, and he's here at the pub every day. I'm sure he'd be happy to talk to you again. Do you all have a place to stay while you're here?"

"Yes, we're set — I found a hostel just past Skibbereen. We're going to try to head out to the ring forts early in the morning. I've spotted a few more sites up in the hills, and I'd like to start recording them, getting some measurements, things like that. Darragh's brought the radar machine, and Ronan can take pictures with a drone he borrowed. It's great for aerial views. We're looking forward to it. You can come along if you want."

Maura knew no more about drones and radar than about fairy forts. "Let me think about it. You've got me interested now, but I still have a business to run here. I'll let you know, though. And good hunting!"

"Thanks, Maura. If we find anything interesting tomorrow, we'll stop by here and celebrate."

It was still light when Ciara and her friends headed out. Maura still didn't quite know exactly where they were staying, but as long as she didn't have to put them up for the night, she wasn't going to worry. In some ways it was hard to get lost in this corner of West Cork — there simply weren't enough roads to make a mistake, or if you did, you knew soon enough when you found yourself staring at a field full of cows. Or a small lake.

Mick came up behind her. "No guests at yer place tonight?"

"Ciara said they had a place to stay, and there are only the three of them. You know, they seem younger and older than me at the same time. They're so excited about this archaeology project, but what are they going to do with it?"

"If all goes well, they'll learn something about Irish history," Mick said, and Maura was reminded that he had more education than she did. "Otherwise they'll be looking for work at universities, and there aren't all that many of those — mebbe ten, so few jobs. But I wouldn't want to spoil their fun just yet."

"I know what you mean, but they make me feel old. I don't think I was ever that young, and I've been working for a long time." She hesitated for a moment before saying, "Are you coming home with me tonight?"

"Would you like me to?"

"Oh, so now you're going to make me beg?" Maura softened her comment with a smile. Spare time and privacy were luxuries not to be wasted.

"We're still working out what we want, aren't we?" Mick said, his tone gentle.

Maura's smile faded. "I guess we are. I never got much practice with dating back in Boston. And Gran was always on her own, and my father was dead, and my mother was gone. I guess I have a lot to learn. But don't let me push you away."

"I won't, I promise."

Rose came out of the kitchen, scrubbing paint off her hands. "I lost track of time. Is everyone gone?"

"If everyone means Billy, my mother, my half sister, and three students, then yes. I hope things pick up soon. What've you got happening tomorrow?"

"A couple of classes in Skib in the morning, then back here, I guess. It might be that Susan will be here too, but I'm not sure yer mother's happy with the idea."

"I have no idea what either one of 'em's thinking, except I think Susan won't be in the way and I think she wants to help. Ciara and her pals asked me if I wanted to go with them looking at forts in the morning — they're still exploring, and they've got fancy machines to play with."

"Do yeh want to go?"

"I don't know. It's not like I'm needed here all the time, but I feel guilty if I'm not here, because it's my place and I'm supposed to be running it. When will you be in?"

"Before noon, most likely. If Mick comes in early, we can manage."

"Is Sophie taking the same classes as you?"

"She is. I think she already knows more than I do. Niall said he'd be by later in the day. He's better behind the bar than in front of the cookstove."

"Very true."

So, Maura decided, she had a choice about whether to tag along with Ciara and her friends to try to figure out some local history based on very few facts, with nothing of her own to add. At least she didn't have to decide before morning. Maybe if she didn't go with Ciara in the morning, she should stop by and visit with Bridget. Bridget probably knew more about which land belonged to whom than she did, and would know where the fairy rings were. Plus Maura had a feeling that Bridget would be interested in what Helen and Susan were doing here. She'd met Helen, but Susan would be a pleasant surprise to her. She hoped.

As she cleaned up the few tables in the pub, Maura wondered about the stories Ciara had told her regarding the ring forts.

Did anyone around here still believe in fairies? What an odd question in the world today, even if this was rural Ireland. But from what little she had been told, there were local people who still took fairies seriously. She herself hadn't met one yet — that she knew of — but she had seen enough things that couldn't be easily explained to ignore the idea. If nothing else, she was going to be polite to fairies, even if she never met one. Just in case.

No one came in after ten, so Maura told Mick she was leaving and that they should take two cars to her cottage so she wouldn't have to decide whether to go with Ciara in the morning. She could wait to see what the weather was like. Mick didn't comment, but then he seldom did. She wasn't exactly in a hurry to move this relationship any faster — in fact, neither of them seemed to be — but she'd like to have a vague idea.

They arrived in Knockskagh at the same time. There were no lights on in the nearest homes, including Bridget's. A waning moon provided some light, and Mick said, "Can we walk a bit? I've been inside the pub all day."

"Sure, as long as we don't walk through any cow pats," she told him. "Uphill or down?"

She couldn't see his smile, but she could hear it in his voice. "Up's toward the piggery, and it smells as bad at night as in the day," he told her. "What about we follow Bridget's field? It's level, at least, and she has no cows."

"Sounds good to me. I'm not particularly tired. Should we be worried that business is slow?"

"And why would yeh be wanting to do that? You own the place, and this one here, and all you need is enough to pay your staff."

"True. I guess I'm used to worrying. Gran had trouble finding a job that paid enough to cover the rent in the city, and we'd nowhere else to go."

"Until she sent you here," Mick said quietly. "She knew you'd be taken care of."

"I guess she did. I wish she'd had an easier life. I wish we'd had more time together. I miss her."

"I'm lucky to have Bridget. And you."

His last statement hung in the air. It was as close to a declaration as he'd come, but she understood that. He'd had problems in his life that were more painful than hers, and it had been a big step forward when he'd shared his story with her not long ago. And now here they were on a moonlit hillside in Ireland, and she had no idea what to say. *I'm glad to have you in my life?*

They were silent for a few minutes as they made their way along the barely paved lane. Maura finally said, "It is lovely, isn't it? It's nothing like Boston, which was all noise and lights and crowds."

"Do yeh like it?"

"I think I do. It gives me more time to think, and there's no hurry to it. Like these fairy forts that Ciara's looking at. They've been around for, what, a thousand years? And they're still here, and people tidy them up and then leave them alone. There's no rush to make changes. Were the people who built them the same as people today?"

"I'd tell yeh, yes and no. Remember how many of the Irish left the country for one reason or another, like in the Famine, and then never came back? There used to be far more, even in rural areas. And you've seen how long memories are. Leavin' the rings alone is kind of like honoring the ones who built them, who've been gone a long time."

"You think Ciara is wrong to want to know more about them?"

Mick thought for a moment. "She's young yet. The story she wants wouldn't be like the story that Bridget or Old Billy tells. We'll

109

see what she finds and what she does with it."

"I'm about the same age she is, you know."

"I think yeh have an older spirit, though yeh may not know it. Or maybe the fairies were waitin' for yeh to come home."

"So this is home?"

"Yeh don't think so?"

Maura stopped walking for a moment, to listen to the night. A distant cow lowing. Some kind of bird? She'd seen a lot of pheasants nearby, but did they sleep at night? In Boston she'd always felt on edge, worried about having enough money or finding a new job or staying safe on the streets at night. Here? She felt a sense of peace, which was new to her.

"I think I do. Thank you for letting me see it. Ready to go back now?"

"Happy to."

When they reached the cottage again, Mick said, "I'll be glad to open Sullivan's, if yeh want to go with Ciara."

"Remember that Rose will be in class in the morning. Think you can manage?"

"I'll talk to Niall, if it looks like we'll be busy."

"We need to use him a bit more — people do like him. I'll try not to take all day. I'm more interested in finding how much land belongs to me than looking for circles. Or if three busloads of tourists show up all at once, give me a call on my mobile and I'll be there."

"Fair enough. But there's music come the end of the week. I'll check with Rose fer the details."

"Traditional or modern?"

"Traditional, I'm thinkin'," Mick said. "It's what the tourists want. It's the younger ones who want current groups, but there aren't many of those around at the moment. But before yeh start worryin', it's going well, old or new, and we're makin' a bit of money. Just enjoy it."

"I'll do my best. And I think it's time for bed."

CHAPTER NINE

The coffee was made and on the table the next morning, and Maura had found a loaf of bread she'd forgotten she had, and there was always butter. Mick was in the shower when there was a knocking at the door. Ciara, so early? She really was enthusiastic about her project. Maura opened the door to Ciara and her two friends.

"Good morning! You're out early," Maura greeted them. "Come on in — there's coffee."

"Good morning, Maura," Ciara said. "We've heard it may rain later in the day, so we wanted to look at as much as we can before it starts. Then if it rains, we can map out our plans, and maybe do a bit of research online. You said don't have a computer?"

"Nope. Never did. I used a few at the library when I was in school, but I've never owned one. So far I haven't needed anything

I can't get on my mobile. Where do you think you'll be looking this morning?"

"The one you saw the other day — it's the closest. There's a big one this side of Drinagh a few miles away, another one up the hill beyond at Drinagh West, and others scattered around. We wanted to try a two-prong approach. Darragh will use the ground-penetrating radar to see if anything shows up below the surface, and Ronan will handle the drone, which will record some pictures. It's nothing fancy, but if Darragh finds something, Ronan can look at it in a different way — his drone is good at capturing geographic details. And we'll measure and take some notes. I only hope there are no cows around any of our targets."

"I did tell you about the ring fort up the hill, didn't I?"

"Past the piggery? I think you did. It's hard to recognize from the road, or what used to be the road, but I checked on an aerial view on my computer and it does look large, and it's an interesting site."

Maura smiled. "There have been known to be cows there. And the road is lousy."

Mick emerged from the bathroom with a towel around his waist. "Good mornin'," he said. "You'll be havin' a busy day?"

"At least half a day," Ciara said. "We don't

fancy mucking around in the fields in the rain."

"Maybe you can talk to Old Billy again," Mick suggested. "In case yeh're wondering, he's always at Sullivan's, and you'll have seen that he loves to talk."

"He does that!" Ciara smiled cheerfully. "We want to get to know the lay of the land a little better, so we can follow what he's telling us. Give us a couple of days."

Mick nodded once, then turned to Maura. "I'll be getting' dressed now so I can head for Leap. If yeh see Bridget, tell her I'll try to come by later."

Maura watched him climb the rickety stairs quickly, and admired the view. She wondered briefly what Ciara made of him, but she wasn't about to worry. "So, coffee? Yes or no?"

Ciara glanced at her friends. "I think we'd rather get started now. Will you be joining us?"

"If you're going to the circle we saw earlier, I'd like to know more about that one, since I guess it's mine. Can somebody actually own a circle, or does the government have other ideas? Like it's a public monument? But in any case, I should get to work by midday. We all have cars, right?"

"We do, since we have equipment to shift.

Three, actually, since I came early on my own, and Darragh and Ronan followed me a day later, and yours. But you know where we're going. And maybe we've time for that cup of coffee."

Maura filled cups, then joined the others at the table. "You didn't answer my question. Are fairy forts legally protected by anyone, local or national?"

"Not really. It's usually the land that matters to people, not what's on it. There've been times when people didn't hesitate to level the rings to give themselves more grazing land, back in the seventies, I think, but then there were a lot of accidents, so people thought twice about doing it anymore. Nowadays people take good care of them, even if they're using the field."

"And are there still fairies around?" Maura asked, trying to keep a straight face.

"There could be. That's another historic tradition. Time was people in the country took them seriously and were careful how they spoke of them."

"Were any of those stories due to a bit too much to drink? I thought I should ask, since I do run a pub."

"Not necessarily. Women often saw or heard things they couldn't explain, and not everyone had the money for liquor. And there were more outside the villages and towns than within them. It's an interesting history, but say what you will — the rings are still there. Some say they're portals to the fairy world."

"Do I want to know more about my own ring, or should I just stay away from it?" Maura asked.

"Just be polite to whomever you see on the road, and I'm sure they'll tell you whatever you want to know. Like you said, Irish country people love to talk."

"True, and I should get to know my neighbors better," Maura told her. "You ready to go?"

Ciara looked at her friends. "I think we are. I'll lead the way."

They reached the field that surrounded the ring in minutes. Maura was surprised again that she hadn't noticed an odd mound in the middle of the field, but then, there were no fields in Boston, except the Public Garden, so she'd had nothing to compare it to. Plus, seeing it only from ground level made it impossible to tell that it was a circle. Mostly it looked like a large lump.

The guys got out of their car, where they'd been waiting, and started unloading equipment. The pieces themselves weren't large, so it didn't take long. Maura didn't recognize either of the two main items, and they seemed out of place in a rolling pasture with a leafy lump in the middle of it. She wondered briefly what the heck she was doing here; she'd gotten along just fine not knowing anything about fairy forts or fairies in the time she'd spent in Ireland.

She and Ciara had walked around the perimeter earlier, and they hadn't found anything that looked like an entrance into the interior. Had there ever been one? Or had some later farmer filled it in to keep the cattle from disturbing the fairies? Maura had to stop herself from snorting. There was no way she could come up with a logical explanation of any of this. But Ciara and the guys looked like they were playing a giant game. Ciara couldn't stop smiling, and Darragh and Ronan followed her around, lugging their borrowed equipment.

"Can I walk along the top of the wall?" Maura called out, although she wasn't sure she needed anyone's permission.

"Sure," Ciara called back. "It's pretty sturdy — the base is earth, and it's been there a long time. But watch the brambles — they can trip you up."

"Thanks," Maura replied, and scrabbled up the bank on one side. It wasn't hard, and the top was fairly level, maybe five feet above the surrounding land. As far as she could tell, there was nothing to see inside the ring except more dirt and grass and weeds. She wasn't sure what she had been expecting — something made of stone, maybe? A small house, or the ruins of one? Tombstones? But if ever there had been a structure, there wasn't now. She tried to work out the orientation. Her best guess was that she was standing on the eastern side. The ring was a near-perfect circle, even after a millennium or so, and she wondered how anybody had laid it out. She also wondered again how it had survived, since she did know how often it rained in this part of Ireland. Why hadn't the earth simply dissolved away over time? One more question she couldn't answer.

She took a moment to pivot around and look at the rest of the site, and decided there really wasn't anything much to see. Sure, there might have been houses or cottages or whatever around it in the past, but clearly they hadn't lasted well. There were a few modern houses visible, but they bore no relation to the ring. She couldn't see her own cottage from where she stood, and she wondered if it would be visible if all the trees were taken down, but she wasn't about to do that.

She watched the students walk slowly around the interior, studying small details she couldn't even see from where she stood. She'd seen the Drombeg stone circle when she'd first arrived in West Cork, but that was made of large stones, the largest being taller than she was. The fairy fort was far wider, but there wasn't a stone of any size in sight.

Maura realized she was getting bored. In a way she envied Ciara, who was clearly excited to be where she was, doing what she was doing. But Maura was finding that she really wasn't interested in a dirt circle in a grassy field. No doubt there were others around, but they'd all look more or less the same, although they might vary by size. She wondered briefly if there was anything special about the leafy plants that covered the ring, but she didn't know anything about plants in general, and Irish field plants in particular. It was good to have seen this monument, on her own land, but she didn't feel the need to see any more of them. "Ciara?" she called out.

Ciara looked up at her. "What?" she called out.

"I think I'll head for Leap now. If you find anything interesting, you can stop by the pub and tell me about it, or stop by the cottage tomorrow morning. Good hunting!" Maura turned and stumbled her way down the side of the ring and headed for her car.

As she drove toward the village, she had to acknowledge that she would never have been much of an archaeologist. Maybe there was a good reason she had never had a chance to go beyond high school. More education might have been entirely wasted on her.

She arrived at Sullivan's before noon, but there were few patrons inside. She did hear giggles coming from the kitchen, so she assumed Susan had come back, and that she and Rose were having a good time, which pleased her. She could only hope they were accomplishing something, but there really wasn't that much that needed to be done, and they'd have to wait for the appliances, whatever the source, before finishing things up.

Mick was behind the bar. "Any great finds?"

Maura sat on a stool. "Not that I could tell. I got as far as standing on the edge of the fairy ring, but I really didn't see much but dirt and grass and stuff. Okay, it's a nice big circle, but there's not much to see."

"And were you expecting a fairy wedding or some such?" Mick asked, smiling.

"I don't think so. But I guess I was hoping it would look more special. The others seemed happy, though. I didn't stick around long enough to see how their research toys worked, but I told them to stop by here if they found anything interesting. And that's all I've got. Anything happening here?"

"Susan's back, as if you can't tell," Mick told her.

"Sounds like she and Rose are enjoying themselves. And I'm not going to complain if things aren't getting done fast. It's nice to hear Rose laugh — I don't think she has a lot of friends her own age. Did Helen say she was going to pick Susan up later, or does she have her own way to get back to the hotel?"

"She didn't say, and I didn't ask."

The day passed slowly and peacefully. Mick had been right, she decided. She owned the pub free and clear, and she had to pay only for as much as she sold. Tourist season hadn't peaked yet, and things would pick up. There was no point in worrying.

The sun was sliding toward the horizon when Maura heard her mobile phone ring, and she answered it quickly, expecting to hear Helen's voice. Instead it was Ciara, who sounded breathless and slightly hysterical.

"Maura? Something's wrong. Ronan and I made a quick trip to Skibbereen to get some lunch, but Darragh wanted to stay behind and run as many scans as he could before the rain started, which it hasn't. But when we got back, he was gone. Disappeared. With the radar unit. You're the only person I could think of to call. What should I do?"

"You sure he didn't just drop by a local farmer's house to ask some questions? Or maybe he thought he'd take a walk and got lost?"

"I tried his mobile and he doesn't answer. I don't know where to look for him or who to ask. I mean, I know he's a grown man, but he could have sent me a text message or something. Should I call the gardaí?"

"Ciara, I don't think they're likely to do anything until he's been gone a bit longer, and they don't have many men on duty. But I've got a friend there, and I can ask him, off the record, kind of. Let me talk to him first. Maybe he'll have some ideas. Are you still at the ring fort?"

"Yes. I didn't want to leave in case Darragh came back. He took his car, and I've got mine. At least it's not dark yet. But I can't think where he might have gone, or why. He was really looking forward to this trip, and trying out the equipment."

"Ciara, just stay where you are. I'll call my friend, and then I'll come join you, and maybe he'll want to come. But call me if you hear from Darragh, or if he comes back."

"All right. Thank you." Ciara hung up abruptly.

"What's wrong?" Mick asked as he came up behind her.

Maura turned to face him. "That was Ciara. Darragh seems to have disappeared and she's worried. He took his car and he's not answering his mobile, and Ciara doesn't know what to think. As you must've heard, I told her I'd call Sean Murphy and see what he thinks we should do. Can you cover here?"

"Of course. Maura, there's not much of anywhere out that way that he could go. Let's hope that Darragh only took a walk and got lost."

"Or the fairies took him," Maura muttered, and went into the back room to call Sean.

CHAPTER TEN

Once in the back room, Maura tried to figure out what she wanted to say. Sean was a friend, but he was also a garda. Luckily she hadn't seen or heard of any crimes recently, so she hadn't bothered him much, but he did drop by the pub occasionally, probably more to chat with Rose than to see Maura. But now Maura didn't know whether to believe Darragh's disappearance was something to be worried about, or if he'd just thought a walk in the country would be nice and he'd show up any minute now. Ciara certainly seemed upset. Was she usually a hysterical type? How well did she know Darragh?

Stop waffling, Maura, she told herself firmly. *Let Sean figure this out.* She pulled out her mobile and hit the speed-dial button for Sean, hoping he was at the station.

He answered quickly. "Good afternoon, Maura. I hope all's going well with yeh."

"Hi, Sean. I'm fine, the pub is fine, and we might get a kitchen soon. But I seem to have a secondhand problem. I'll give you the quick version." She quickly outlined the arrival of Ciara from the university, followed a day later by her friends, and their finding a fairy ring on land she didn't even know she owned. Then she reached the part about Darragh's disappearance. "So they went out to that ring earlier today, and I went along for a while, then came back to Leap. Ciara and Ronan went to get lunch after that, but she called to say that when they got back to the ring fort, Darragh had disappeared and she doesn't know where to look for him. She was going to call your crew, but I thought you might not take her seriously, so I said I'd call you. I told her to let me know if her friend reappeared — heck, for all she knows, he's taking a nap under a tree somewhere — but I haven't heard from her. So, what should she do? Or shouldn't she do anything just yet? After all, they're not children."

"Does he know the area?"

"I don't think so. Darragh said he came from south of Dublin somewhere, maybe Carlow, and he's taking graduate classes in Cork. He's only been here a day, so I don't think he's explored much."

"Is he an honest man?" Sean asked.

"How should I know? Oh, he brought along a ground-penetrating radar thing that he borrowed from the university. Ciara said that's missing too."

"Costly item, that. What is it you want me to do?"

"I don't know. He took his car, so who knows how far he went. And he seems to know a lot about fairy forts. Maybe the fairies took him?" Maura realized how silly that sounded. "I'm sorry — bad joke. Ciara's kind of in charge of this project, and she seems seriously worried. Can you come out and talk to her before it gets too dark?"

"Things are slow here. Where's the circle?"

"Oh, that's the other twist. Ciara came equipped with maps, and it turns out it's on a piece of land that belongs to me, that used to be Mick Sullivan's. It seems there are a lot of little bits and pieces of land that're mine that I didn't know about. But I have been to the circle from my cottage, so I know how to find it."

"Has this Darragh been to the cottage as well?"

"Yes, briefly. Why?"

"Could be he fell ill and wanted a place to rest. He could find his way, couldn't he?"

"Maybe. Ciara said she'd found them a

hostel the other side of Skibbereen. You want to meet me at my cottage and check, and then I can take you to the fairy ring?"

"That'll do. I can leave now."

"Good. And thank you. See you soon!"

Maura shut down the phone, feeling kind of relieved. Yes, this seemed to be happening on her land, but she didn't really know where all the parts were, and she wouldn't have found the fairy ring if Ciara hadn't shown her how to get there. She had no idea where to look for Darragh, though, or whether he was lost or just roaming around. Better that Sean did the looking.

She went back out to the bar to tell Mick she was going to meet Sean. "He's not heard of any trouble?" he asked.

"He didn't mention anything. He probably thinks Darragh is from the city or somewhere that isn't West Cork and he just got lost. But I'd rather he checked. Me, I'd just get lost too, especially when the light's fading. If we don't find him, I'll come back here, okay? Oh, and tell Susan why she hasn't seen me."

"I'll take care of it. And watch yer step out there. If it happens to rain tonight, that would erase any trace of the man."

"This seems silly — he could have remembered an errand or decided to go to the library or something and didn't bother to leave a note. I'll let you know what Sean and I find. With any luck, Darragh's back at the ring fort."

Maura waved at Old Billy seated in his usual spot by the fireplace, but decided to wait to tell him what was going on until she knew more. Or she could ask him where someone might get lost — he had to have more ideas that she did.

It took maybe ten minutes to get to her cottage, where Sean was already waiting. "Anything?" she asked as she climbed out of her car.

He shook his head. "The door's locked, and no one seems to be about. Do you want to check inside? He knows how to find yer place here, right?"

"Yes, I told you he's been here. I won't be long." Maura fished out the key that had been Old Mick's and opened the door, but nothing had changed since she'd left in the morning. The dirty dishes were still on the table, and she knew she hadn't much food in her small near-antique refrigerator. "Nobody home, Sean. Listen, is Ciara overreacting? She and her friends seem like serious, smart people, and I don't think they'd do something stupid, like wander off and fall into a bog. They're very focused, and they don't have a whole lot of time for their project."

"Then let's go talk to this Ciara person and she what she can tell us. Will you drive?"

Maura had to smile. "You're asking me? Sure. This is one of the few places I know how to find that's off any main road. Won't take long."

True to her word, a few minutes later she pulled into the start of an unpaved lane, blocked by a makeshift wire gate, and stopped. She could see the fairy ring a couple hundred feet away in the field, and Ciara and Ronan were sitting on the side nearest the road, waiting for her. There was no sign of Darragh, but maybe he was inside the ring? Ciara scrambled to her feet and waved to her.

"Okay, that's Ciara who's waving." Maura leaned toward Sean. "And the other person is Ronan — he's the guy who runs the drone, though I haven't seen it in action." Sean didn't answer but walked over to the gate and opened it easily, letting Maura pass through.

"No cattle to be seen, but we should shut the gate behind us. You own this field?"

"So I'm told. There's no farmer here to ask about where a stranger might have ended up, if that's what you're wondering.

Just me."

"Thought I'd ask," Sean said, then set off across the field. Maura followed quickly. When they were near enough, Maura called out to Ciara and Ronan. "This is Garda Sean Murphy — we've worked together on a couple of things. When I told him what you'd said, he thought he would check things out. You haven't heard anything from Darragh, or anyone who's seen him?"

Ciara shook her head vigorously. "Not a word. It's not like Darragh. He should be back by now. It's not like we're a couple or anything, but we've known each other for a while, and he's usually very responsible. He shouldn't have just disappeared like this." She looked near tears.

Sean took a step forward. "Why don't we sit down and you can tell me what you told Maura? I know it must be hard when you're in an unfamiliar place and all. Would that be all right?"

"Fine." Ciara sniffed. "How about the other side of the ring?" she suggested.

"That would be grand," Sean said, and extended his hand to help her off the top of the ring. Maura was impressed. He really was quite the gentleman.

When they had disappeared, Maura turned to Ronan, who'd spoken about a dozen words to her since he arrived in Cork. "Do you know anything, Ronan? I mean, have you worked with Darragh before? Has he ever done anything like this?"

Ronan shook his head. "He's, like, very focused, and he was looking forward to using the radar device. He didn't want to go with us into Skibbereen but told us to pick up some food for him. We weren't gone long."

For Ronan, that was a surprisingly long conversation, and Maura wanted to keep him talking. "Did you see anybody else, coming or going? Or watching from a distance?"

He shook his head silently.

"Did he mention anything else he wanted to check out today?"

Another silent shake of his head.

Maura was running out of questions. "Ciara said he took the radar thing with him instead of leaving it here. Was there something he wanted to do with it? Was he looking for something in particular?"

"I don't know!" Ronan all but wailed. "It can see a couple feet down into the earth, but mostly it tells you if there is or isn't something under the dirt, not what it is. And if it looks important, you can dig a bit. But we don't like to do that, because we don't want to risk damaging something important or messing with the original site, and it's hard to decipher what it is from the machine."

Sean and Ciara were certainly taking their time, given that nobody seemed to have a clue where Darragh had gone and where they should look. She decided she might as well keep talking. "What's the most interesting thing you've found?"

"Hard to say. Usually it's metal objects, which show up well. If it's a bowl or a vase or something, you can identify it easily by its general shape, but you can't see a lot of details. And it takes some practice."

"Ciara told me Darragh was going to go over the ground first, and then you were going to use your drone camera thing, and then you all would compare them. Have I got that right?"

"Close enough. But we'd only just started."

"How big are these things? I never saw either one."

"The radar machine is about the size of a small lawn mower, more or less. But it's far from perfect — it's not very big."

"Why did you think you were going to find something at all in a fairy ring? Some people have told me they weren't used for burials.

Although maybe there were portals to the fairy world in the rings."

Ronan managed a weak smile. "We're thinkin' that's a myth. I haven't met any fairies. Yet."

"Has Darragh?"

"Maybe. He doesn't talk about it. Look, this is your pasture, right?" When Maura nodded, Ronan asked, "Have you see any?"

"Fairies? Not that I know of. Everything I've seen since I started living around here has been either a real human or an animal. But I haven't been here long, and I haven't been looking. And nobody told me about fairies."

Finally Sean and Ciara came back around the fairy ring, but neither looked happy. "Any ideas, Sean?" Maura hurried to ask.

"I thought we should look carefully around the ring to see if there are any marks," Sean said.

"Like footprints, you mean?" Maura asked.

Sean nodded. "I don't hold out much hope, since the grass is so thick here, but if it rains tonight, we'll lose the chance."

"And if we don't find anything?" Ciara said anxiously.

"I'll talk to my detective. It may be he has some ideas. It's not often we misplace people hereabouts."

And when you do, you don't always find them alive, Maura thought to herself, but she managed not to say it out loud.

"Ciara, Ronan, where have you looked?" Maura asked.

"You mean, right around here?" Ciara said, looking bewildered. "I guess we walked around the ring a time or two, calling out, but we were looking mainly for the radar machine. It belongs to the university and we don't want to lose it."

"And you found nothing?" Sean asked carefully. Ciara shook her head. "Then let's take another pass at it before we lose the light. Look for anything yer man might've dropped, or where the grass is crushed. Maura says there's no cows grazing in this field, although one or two might have broken away from their herd and wandered over. Split up, so we can cover more ground. And we should stay close enough that we can hear each other if we call out."

In pairs, they moved a distance away from the edge of the ring, keeping their eyes on the ground. *Nice grass,* Maura thought, and no person or machine or animal had used it anytime recently. How was it that she hadn't even know about this field, or any others that might be hers? Probably because she didn't know squat about cows, and didn't plan to start a herd of her own. What would her gran have thought about that idea?

Funny how almost every visitor commented that Ireland was so green, Maura thought. Well, it was, but that was probably due to all the rain. She looked a few yards ahead of her, where some of the grass looked trampled just a bit. As she moved closer, she saw a splash of red mixed in with the green, and stopped walking. Then she took a few tentative steps closer, careful not to walk on any part that had already been messed up. The red was more obvious then, in stark contrast to the bright green of the grass.

Maura didn't want to get any closer, and didn't think she needed to. It looked like blood to her. Why would there be blood in an unused field in the country? Maybe Sean should take a look — he must know more than she did about blood. Maura swallowed, then called out, "Sean? I think I've found something."

She could hear him call out from the far side of the fairy ring, easy to hear in the warm dusk. "On my way," he said.

Maura waited until he appeared, then pointed silently to the patch of red on the grass.

CHAPTER ELEVEN

Sean saw the expression on Maura's face and said only, "Where?"

"There." Maura pointed again. "Is it . . . ?"

"Blood? I think it's likely. Are yeh all right?"

"I'm not going to throw up, if that's what you're worried about," Maura said sharply. Then she added more softly, "I'm sorry. I barely know the man. He's a student, or that's what I was told. I can't imagine how he could run into any trouble out here — I don't think he knows anyone in this part of Cork. I certainly don't expect him to wind up dead. Unless someone saw him with that radar thing and decided it was worth stealing, but I haven't seen many people around here, and I don't see any cows that someone would have to look after. This is a lot of blood, isn't it?"

Sean looked at her with a half smile on his face. "Not really. It only looks that way.

How'd yeh find it?"

"I saw a patch of red in the grass and walked toward it, and then I stopped so I wouldn't mess anything up. I didn't go around the patch either. I figured I should let you handle it. You think maybe Darragh had some kind of accident and went to find help? Or someone whacked him, stole the radar scanner, and then hid the body?"

Sean shook his head. "It's clear yer not a country girl." He knelt by the patch of blood and picked up something. "More like he startled a fox, made it drop its dinner." Sean picked up what seemed to be the remains of a rabbit, holding it by its long ears.

"Oh," Maura said, feeling foolish. "I guess I jumped to a conclusion after seeing the blood. So there are foxes around here?"

"There are."

"And they eat rabbits?"

"They do, as well as other small animals, when they can catch them. They won't go after cows or humans, and we've no rabies in Ireland."

"So this blood has nothing to do with Darragh."

"I'd say no. Save that the fox didn't get to finish its supper."

"I feel stupid," Maura said. "And Darragh is still missing."

"And he left no tracks, but then he has a car. Yer friend Ciara said his car's gone?"

"Yes, she did. You think he got bored and went for a drive?"

"I'd say yes, unless it was a batch of fairies lured him away."

"Ha ha," Maura said, her tone acidic. "Any sign of the radar machine? Ciara said he had it with him when she and Ronan left for lunch."

"I've seen no machine, nor any tracks of one, but there are plenty of places around here where it could be hid. Maybe he didn't want to haul it around with him or leave it in his car. We'd have to look more carefully."

"I'm sorry I wasted your time, Sean. What are you going to tell Ciara and Ronan?"

"I'd call off the search fer now. If I asked my mates at the station fer help, they'd only laugh. The man seems to have left of his own free will and driven away."

"You're probably right, Sean." Maura thought for a moment. Something was troubling her. "Can I ask you something else?" When Sean nodded, Maura went on, "You think these people — all three of them — are what they say they are? Students working on a project? Or is there something else going on?"

"They seem innocent enough, but I can't

say I know many who are takin' high-level courses like they claim, with fancy equipment. I may check with the university to see if they're registered, but don't say anythin' to them."

"I will say that they seem worried that Darragh's missing. Are you going to talk to them now, or call them over, or what?"

"I'll give them my opinion. There's really nothin' else they can do right now."

"Should I go back to Sullivan's? And if I do, should I say anything about this? Or maybe ask if they've seen Darragh somewhere around?"

"If anybody asked about visitin' archaeologists, yeh can talk about what you know. Do yeh know where they'll be tonight?"

"Probably at that hostel in Skib. But that doesn't mean she's going to want to sit around there and worry. If she wants to come to Sullivan's, I can handle that. And maybe calm her down."

"Then I'll go tell 'em it's too late in the day to look any farther, and I'll talk to them in the mornin'."

"Thanks, Sean. Let me know if you do find anything more."

"I'll do that. Take care, Maura."

She turned and marched back to where she'd left her car, and Sean waded through the grass toward where Ciara and Ronan were waiting anxiously. She'd let Sean handle things for the moment. She felt like an idiot, having overreacted about a dead rabbit, and the feeling in her gut told her she'd be seeing Darragh again. But why would he disappear, even for a short time? Would a radar machine, probably labeled as university property, be important to anyone around here? Most local people were farmers who raised cows and a few sheep, and nobody would need radar for that. Maybe a drone, in case the animals wandered too far. But Ronan had the drone. Still, maybe someone had stolen it and Darragh was trying to track it down. After all, it didn't belong to him.

Yesterday she hadn't even noticed this field. Today she knew she owned it, and there was something odd going on, but she had no idea what it might be. She really should get back to Sullivan's and pretend everything was normal.

The sun had fallen below the horizon when she arrived back in Leap, although it wasn't dark yet. The lights inside Sullivan's looked warm and welcoming, but there didn't seem to be a lot of people inside. Just as well this evening. She didn't know much, but she was afraid to think about what might have happened to Darragh. She felt stupid, but she was pretty sure there was something more. Damn those fairies.

Mick, behind the bar, looked up when she walked in, and then looked again. She walked quickly over to the bar. "News?" he asked quietly.

"Nothing official, but it doesn't feel right. Darragh's nowhere around, and nobody knows where he went. Ciara and Ronan may come by later, but don't count on it. You haven't by any chance seen Darragh or heard someone mention him?"

"No. You want a pint?"

"I'd better not — I don't know if anything else is going to happen tonight. Does Billy need another?"

"He might."

"Oh, did Susan go home?"

"Helen came by an hour or more ago to take her back to the hotel. Susan said she'd be back tomorrow, and Helen mentioned she had some secondhand appliances that might do fer the kitchen."

"That's good. Will the wiring and drains hold up?"

"It may do, but if not, we can fix it." Mick looked over at Billy and exchanged signals, which apparently translated to *Yes, I'd like another pint, thank you very much.*

"I'll take his pint over," Maura volunteered. Remember, if someone comes in and asks about Darragh, we don't know anything. You can talk to Sean, but don't tell Ciara or Ronan anything unless Sean says you can."

"That is a complicated set of instructions, but I think I can manage. You go talk with Billy."

Maura waited until Billy's glass was ready, then took it over to him. As he did so often, he was dozing by the fireplace, where there were still a few coals burning even in June. He greeted her warmly as he took the glass. "Maura, yeh look tired. Where've yeh been all day?"

"Out with those students you met — they wanted to get some work done on the fairy ring — you know, measurements and such, and whether it lines up with the sun or moon or something. You know, it feels kind of weird to own such a thing. And the land under it. You told me that for a lot of his later life, Old Mick didn't do anything like farming. Why'd he keep the land if it was useless to him?"

"Ah, Maura, my dear, land has always been important to the Irish. It's been well over a hundred years since the English let them have any of it, and then it was rarely the good land — barely enough to feed a small family. But still it mattered to them."

"How much does it take to feed one cow?"

"About an acre," Billy said promptly, "if the grass is good."

"Really. You know, I couldn't tell you how big any piece actually is, so I wouldn't know if that looked like a lot. Did Mick keep a garden at all? I mean, should I be looking for a potato plot?"

"That I can't say. It's been many years since I've been out to Knockskagh. It's a wonder Mick found enough food up there, since he was always here, but I believe he had friends who helped him out."

"Are any of them still around?"

"Could be one or two, but their memory may be failin'. I knew him, and so did Bridget, once. And yer gran."

"That still surprises me. We never got much mail, beyond bills, and I'd bet she never called back here just to chat."

"Have yeh searched yer place?"

"No. It never really felt like mine — I almost expected someone to come by and tell me to pack up. And I don't know of any places he could have kept old letters and stuff."

"Could be he kept some here," Billy said.

"In the pub, you mean? You really think

so? So much of this building is old, and made of stone. I don't know where he'd keep anything. But you're saying he might have been the type?"

Billy smiled gently. "Could be, not that he ever talked about any such thing. And before yeh ask, he never asked me to hold anythin' fer him."

"People just remembered, right?"

"That's often true. But many people left as well and never returned."

"So these fairy forts or whatever they're called — how did they ever survive for a thousand years? I mean, the people who lived near them had to have taken care of them, preserved them, but why?"

"Ah, Maura, it's important to stay on the right side of the fairies."

Maura looked up to see Sean Murphy arriving — alone. "Billy, I need to talk to Sean, if you don't mind."

Billy smiled. "I'm ready fer me nap, so you go on."

Sean had walked across the room to the bar, where Maura joined him. "You still on duty?"

"Much as I'd love a pint, I've a report to write and plans to make," Sean said. "What've yeh told Mick?"

"As much as I know, which isn't a lot. Did

Ciara and Ronan go back to where they're staying?"

"They have, but there's still no sign of their friend."

"How much did you tell them?"

"Nothin' to tell, since we found nothin'."

"Is there anything I should do?"

"Yeh might want to look at the maps Ciara brought that show Old Mick's land. Might be some good places to hide things, if nobody's usin' those plots."

"You didn't ask Ciara?"

"She seemed too upset. Tomorrow will do."

"Do you want me to come along?"

"Up to you, I'd guess. Yeh don't know where the plots are, but yeh're the official owner."

And what a great introduction *she* was getting to this added property, Maura reflected sourly. "Let me know what you decide, if you want me there. But I doubt I can add any information."

"I'll do that. I'd best be off to Skib," Sean said.

"I'll see you out." Maura followed him out the door, but in front of the pub she stopped him. "What do you think happened? I know you don't have a lot of facts. Deaths are pretty rare around here, aren't they? So how likely is it that somebody would have killed a stranger from Cork city?"

"Maura, I can't answer those questions. I don't think it's wise to jump to the conclusion that someone's killed him, especially if he's no more than a student at university. The man is still missin', and I'm hopin' we'll know more by tomorrow. If I don't see you early in the day, I'll stop by here after and update you."

"Thanks, Sean. Good luck."

When he was out of sight, Maura drifted back into the pub. She had to admit she was depressed, which seemed kind of odd, because she hadn't even known she owned that patch of land until the day before, and she'd barely met Darragh. But she wished she hadn't known either — the land or the man.

When she returned to the bar, Mick asked, "Would yeh rather go home?"

"I don't think so. All I'll do there is worry about things I don't know. Are there things that will warn off fairies? I don't want to annoy them. Or maybe they're trying to protect me from something. Maybe Sean will go searching on his computer and find out that Darragh is a world-renowned criminal and Ciara and Ronan are his accomplices. Although what they could possibly want isn't clear to me. There's not much to steal up north of here, and from what I've been hearing, it's not likely there's any treasure in the fairy rings."

"Well, think about seein' yer mother and yer sister in the morning, and maybe a new old stove." Mick's comment made her smile. "What a thing to look forward to! And Sean's a good man. Will yeh be wanting company tonight?"

"I think I will. And thank you, Mick. Every time I think I have a handle of Ireland and the people around here, something weird happens. I hope there's a simple explanation for whatever happened to Darragh."

CHAPTER TWELVE

It was another slow evening, and once again Maura and Mick made an early night of it. Maura waved to Old Billy as he hauled himself out of his favorite chair and tottered his way to the door. Her phone did not ring, with either good or bad news, which she took to mean that neither Sean nor the rest of the gardaí had found Darragh, dead or alive. Ciara and Ronan did not appear, looking either for sympathy or for a drink or three. The whole situation was odd: a peaceful fairy fort in a field that looked the way it must have looked for hundreds of years, a missing archaeologist, and an equally missing ground-penetrating radar machine. Sean had said he would get in touch with the university archaeology department to see if the little group was legitimate and doing recognized research. But it seemed unlikely that they weren't. What other explanation was there — they just wanted to take a quick vacation and dig in the dirt? From what little she knew, Maura was pretty sure they weren't going to find a trove of gold and jewels in a fairy fort.

Oddly enough, when she and Mick reached her cottage after closing, she felt restless. They didn't go inside right away but sat on a crumbling stone wall in the front of the cottage and spoke in quiet tones. "Do you know, this business with the land made me realize how much I haven't even thought about or looked at around here," Maura said.

"What do yeh mean?" Mick asked quietly.

"Well, my grandmother died, and when I got here I found out I'd inherited this place, and a pub came with it. I got very busy trying to find out what was what and who was who, and signing legal papers, and learning the business — and Irish pubs are definitely not the same as Boston pubs, no matter what the ads say. Anyway, bottom line is, I just kept trying to keep my head above water. I had a place to sleep and a job to go to, and a whole lot of people to meet. But there were things I kind of didn't notice — like the rest of the land I'd inherited. Maybe I didn't have the time, or maybe it never occurred to me there was anything more, and I wouldn't have known what to do with it anyway. I never figured I'd own anything, so it didn't much matter."

"And?" Mick prompted.

"Now all in the course of a couple of days I've discovered I have more land than I thought, and some of it may be historic — but I didn't even know fairy forts existed — and other people are interested in it for the history, not because the grass tastes good to cows, and then this bunch of students about my age show up and ask if they can check it out, and of course I say yes. And then one of them just disappears without a trace. Is any part of this normal?"

"Parts of it, mebbe. Nobody gives lectures on fairies in West Cork to newcomers like yerself, but they are a part of modern life around here. In a quiet way, at least. Yeh can choose to believe or not, but there are those that do. But whatever happened to Darragh — now that's not normal. The fairies may bring bad luck with them, but they seldom kill someone. Or if they do, yeh'll find a body. Havin' a guy simply disappear is different."

"That's a relief," Maura told him. "And Sean took it seriously. I mean, he didn't arrive at the field and tell us to let the fairies work things out. That makes me feel better. There's nothing more I'm supposed to do about all this, is there?"

"Fer now, I'd say no. You've got yer mother and yer sister to think about, and yeh want to finish buildin' the kitchen, which is a grand idea, and there's still the music. Runnin' around looking fer missing people is not on your task list. Is it?"

"I hope not, Mick. I've only just gotten used to all the rest of it. Are there any laws that apply to fairies? Like if they decide to take up a bit of vandalism, or steal cattle, or scare children?"

"Not lately."

"Anything I should be on the lookout for?"

"Just me. Do yeh mind if I protect yeh?"

"No, not as long as you don't get hurt or disappear. Where should I look if you do?"

"Under a hawthorn tree?"

Maura checked to see if Mick was joking. It looked like he was, which was obscurely reassuring. "Anything I need to do to keep them away?"

"Ask Bridget — she's more likely to know. But give the gardaí a while to see if they can find Darragh. Maybe there's a simple explanation for his whereabouts."

"I hope so. Ready for bed?"

"I am."

Maura woke early again the next morning,

worrying about what had happened to Darragh. Had Darragh been injured in an accident, hitting his head and bleeding a lot? Or had someone hit him? Had he been dragged away by someone, or had he woken up and realized he needed help? Or woken up and forgotten who he was, and then wandered off? No, that last was the kind of thing Maura thought she'd seen on bad television, and not in Ireland.

And what the heck had happened to the radar device? That had to be expensive, at least for a student. Had Darragh hidden it, figuring he'd come back and get it later, or that he could tell Ciara where to find it? Or was someone else trying to sell it at this very moment?

"Yeh're worryin', aren't yeh," Mick stated, his voice muffled by his pillow.

"Shouldn't I? Okay, I didn't know the guy, or the fairy fort, or the land, or much of anything else, but I feel weirdly responsible because it happened on what turns out to be my land, which I didn't even know. We'd better drum up some business to distract me."

"Fair enough. Remember, yer mother and Susan were plannin' to come by this mornin'."

"True. I assume they aren't bringing three

ovens and a fridge along to see how they fit."

"Not likely. But they might want to measure. Susan seems a nice enough girl. She and Rose have fun, and I think Rose could keep her in line. I'd hate to see Susan get bored after no more than a few days and start sulkin'."

"Sounds like she got thrown into all this without any warning. I don't think it's anything like she expected."

"No more than you did."

Maura turned onto her back and pulled the blankets up. "I meant to tell people who remembered my gran that she had passed on. I thought I'd spend a week here, tops. Didn't quite work out that way," she said quietly.

"Do yeh regret it now?" Mick asked.

"No. How could I? It was a gift, and unexpected. I had no reason to go back to Boston, and I don't miss it. I'm still learning about this place, and now I've got friends here. And you."

Whatever Mick might have answered was interrupted by a knocking at the door. Ciara? Sean? Or the wandering Darragh? "I'd better go see who that is," Maura told Mick. She pulled on some clothes, then hurried down the stairs.

She opened the door to find Sean. "Good morning! You're here early. Any news?"

"None to speak of. We waited for the sun this morning to take a closer look at yer field, but we found no sign of the man."

"Can you come in and have some coffee?"

"If it doesn't take long. But we're done searchin' fer now."

"Then sit down," Maura ordered him, "and I'll boil some water." She filled a kettle and set it on the stove, then took a chair across from Sean. At the sound of footsteps above his head, he said, "Mick?"

"Yes, Mick. So, you haven't found Darragh, you haven't found a trail, you haven't found the radar equipment, you haven't had a ransom note. Is that right?"

"As far as it goes. And Ciara hasn't heard from him, and there's no one reported injured at a hospital."

"What do you make of that?"

Sean shook his head. "I've no idea. Nor does anyone at the department — I asked when I stopped by late in the day. And you've had no contact with him, have you?"

"No, not here, and not at the pub, by the time we left last night. And Ciara and Ronan didn't stop by either." She stood up abruptly as the water boiled and poured it over coffee grounds. "This is ridiculous,

Sean. An ordinary guy shows up with a couple of his friends in a small town in the country, then disappears. For no apparent reason. Why?"

"That I can't tell yeh, Maura."

"Is there anything you want me to do?"

"Do yeh have any more fairy forts on yer land?"

"Sean, I don't even know where the other pieces of my land are, much less if they have ring forts on them. You thinking that maybe Darragh got bored and went looking for more, and something happened to him there?"

"It's only a guess. But yeh have no maps to show?"

"Ciara has all of those — you can ask her. Or you can look up land records online, I'm told, or go to the library. I can't help you there — I barely know how to turn a computer on, and I wouldn't know what records to look at."

"Someone around here might know — I'll look into it." Sean looked up as Mick came down the stairs. "Mornin', Mick."

"Sean. I'm thinkin' yeh might spend some time talkin' to my gran Bridget down the lane, or to Old Billy at Sullivan's. They're old enough to have long memories about the townlands."

"And why would I be needin' that?" Sean asked. "The man's been missing less than a day."

"Just a thought, Sean," Mick replied. "There's places up in the hills where people go to hide things, though mebbe not lost archaeologists."

Maura spoke up then. "Mick, can you pour the coffee? One other thing, Sean — the radar machine would have been meant to look under the ground. Was there any sign that anyone was poking around in the middle of my circle, or anywhere else? You know, holes in the dirt, or a dip that showed something had been buried there some-time?"

"Yeh're thinking of treasure hunters?" Sean smiled. "We were waitin' for the mornin' sun to look fer signs of diggin' — better angle to the light. But nobody's mentioned seein' anything like that."

"Tell me this, then," Maura went on. "The older folk around here used to be scared of messing with the rings, right? So they wouldn't have gone poking around looking for treasure or burying someone, would they?"

"Not that I've heard," Sean admitted. "Why?"

"I'm just throwing ideas around. If there

was a dip, if somebody was buried there, it would have to have been either a long time ago, or pretty recently — not this week, but in the past century, maybe. But if somebody wanted to dig now, they'd have to have a reason, like they know something. Or they're looking for something they've heard of, which is why they might have a radar machine."

"An interestin' idea," Sean agreed, "but so far there's no evidence. But it's no problem to take another look at your field, and any others we come across." Sean drained his coffee cup. "I'd best go to Skib and make my report, but I may be back. You'll be at the pub?"

"I will," Maura said. "My mother's supposed to be coming back to tell us about used stoves she has handy, and I'd hate to miss that."

"And her girl?" Sean said, smiling.

"Susan? She may work for us a bit this summer, or she may get bored by the end of the week and find something else to do. I don't know her well enough to say, so we're taking this one day at a time."

"Best of luck to yeh, then. I'll stop by later."

"Thanks for keeping us up-to-date, Sean. See you later."

Maura saw him out the door, then closed it behind her.

"He knows about us?" Mick asked.

"Of course — he's a garda, and not stupid. Besides, I think he's more interested in Rose right now. They make a nice couple."

"And she's how much younger than Sean?"

"Not too much. And I'm not going to meddle. I kind of like having a garda to talk with, since we seem to keep running into problems. You ready to head for Leap?"

"It's early yet, and I'm worried about some of the things you and Sean were talkin' about. About the fairy ring, I mean."

"What? And why?"

"It's true they've been there fer a long time, and the people who live with 'em respect them and leave them alone — that's an old custom. But what if someone — a group, a family, a single person — who didn't come from around here decided that ring would be a good place to hide something? Sean may understand the idea of it, but how hard did he look inside the circle? Would there be something there?"

"You're asking me?" Maura asked, with a half smile. "But I guess, logically, if whatever it was was put in the ground a century ago, the dirt would long since have settled. I mean, the cemeteries around here are like that, unless someone was buried not long ago. But why are you asking? You think Ciara and her friends should dig holes in every circle they find, just in case there's something there? Might give other people the wrong idea, and then what? Those things that have been there a thousand years will be a big mess."

"I get yer point, Maura. And we've plenty to keep us busy workin' without running around digging holes. But I agree with Sean that we should look at that ring fort again."

"If we don't have any answers by then, and the weather holds, we can do that," Maura said. "Not that I think we'd find anything that Sean didn't. But right now we need to get to the pub."

Chapter Thirteen

Maura was surprised and kind of pleased to find her mother and Susan at the pub when she arrived. Rose was busy entertaining them, since there were no more customers to be seen. Maybe come the weekend things would pick up?

"Hey, Helen, Susan," Maura greeted them. "You're here early."

"We are," Helen said. "But I don't have any meetings or appointments for a couple of hours, and I promised Susan I'd bring her back today, so here we are. And I wanted to get some measurements for appliances for your kitchen."

"Rose said you mentioned that. But keep in mind that our kitchen is really small — can't be anywhere near the size of the hotel kitchen. So I won't get my hopes up, but I appreciate the thought. You two had breakfast?"

"Of course. One of the perks of working

at the hotel — there's always plenty of food available," Helen said. "Come on — show me what you've got to work with. Susan, you can hold the other end of the measuring tape."

Susan led the way, and Maura considered asking Rose to join them, until she realized that with four people in the small room, no one would be able to see anything, much less measure.

"Rose, do you mind keeping an eye on things out here?" she said instead. "You can take a look at whatever Helen suggests later."

"That's fine, Maura," Rose said. "I spend enough time in there as it is these days. We can compare our ideas once everyone has seen the space."

"Thank you!" Maura followed Susan and Helen into the back.

When Maura entered the kitchen, Helen was standing in the middle of the not-large room, turning around and studying it. "You're right — it's small. How many covers are you thinking of for each meal?"

"Covers?" Maura looked blankly at her.

"Meals, per hour, or for the evening. What hours do you plan to serve? Will the menu change, depending on the time, or the day of the week — as in, more or longer meals on weekends? Or will it be a more or less fixed menu?"

"You've lost me already. Maybe I should just let Rose listen to you — she's doing most of the planning."

"No," Helen said firmly. "This is your place, and you need to understand how it works. You don't have to cook — Rose is doing a fine job of that, from what I've seen, and you have other help. But you need to know things like quantities and the cost of ingredients. Don't worry — you don't have to know all this today — but right now you do need to know how much space you have to work with, both for storage and for staff. You've got plenty of time."

"If you say so," Maura muttered.

Helen went back to studying the layout of the room. A few cabinets remained, although Maura couldn't guess how old they were. Billy might know. The windows were set high in the outer wall, which made the space dark, but if they had been lower there would have been less room for a refrigerator or a stove and oven and ventilation, Maura had to admit. Which probably meant they'd need a brighter light fixture. "What do you think we're going to need?"

"I'd go with a six-burner stove, or maybe four burners with a central grill. A good-size combination refrigerator and freezer. A bigger sink, definitely. Were you thinking of a dishwasher?"

"Human or mechanical?" Maura asked with a smile. "Actually, I haven't thought much about it at all. When Gran and I lived in Boston, I think the kitchen was usually smaller than this, and the appliances didn't work well most of the time. Plus, Gran wanted to have a table in the kitchen. You probably remember she kept bringing home some recent arrivals from Ireland, and she wanted to be able to talk to them while she cooked. I'm sorry — is that an unhappy memory?"

"In a way. Not your fault, of course — you were only a baby. And I think your grandmother wanted something to keep her busy when she wasn't working, so she didn't have to dwell on the death of her son. Tom. Do you know, I seldom refer to him by name? Since I've been here, I've been wondering what his life — *our* life — would have been like if he hadn't died so early. I had no plan, no idea what I wanted to do, and I had you to take care of. It was a difficult time for all of us, I think."

"So you walked away?" Susan spoke for the first time.

Helen turned toward her. "Yes, love, I did.

I wasn't that much older than you are now, and younger than Maura. I'm not proud of it, but I didn't know what to do. Do you remember me at all, Maura?"

Maura shook her head slowly. "Not really. I think I remember a woman who hugged me, but I wouldn't have known you in a crowd. Gran did her best to make up for it after you left. And she never said anything bad about you, to her credit."

"I'm glad to know that. We got along fairly well. We might have done better if we both hadn't been so busy all the time. I have to say, I think she was a stronger woman than I was, and also a kinder one."

"Hey, you two," Susan interrupted. "Can't you wait on your old-time stories until after we measure this room? Having a table to sit at or work on in the room makes sense, even though it would be crowded. But if the cooking gets crazy, it'd be another work surface if you need it. How about storage for pots and pans and plates and glasses?"

Maura resisted the temptation to throw up her hands. "I have no idea how many I'd need or how often we'd have to wash them. Helen, maybe you can help with that. Or talk to Rose — did she tell you she's taking cooking classes in Skibbereen?"

"Not only did she tell us, she told us we

had to eat lunch there when we had time. Right in the center of town, isn't it?"

"It is, on a main intersection. And while you're there, check out Fields, which is the big supermarket. I don't know who supplies your hotel, but if you're cooking at home or at a small place like this, they've got great food."

Helen smiled. "Susan, you'd better start making a list."

"Got it. Rose said she'd take me there to pick up supplies."

"The cakes and breads are terrific," Maura said. "So, is there anything else I need to think about? And if you don't have any leftover machines that don't fit, I won't mind. There's an appliance place in Drinagh, not far from here, which has about everything we could need. Plus cow-milking equipment."

"I'm sure you need that," Helen said wryly, and then she and Susan burst out laughing.

It surprised Maura that they seemed to be happy to be with her, with each other, in Leap. She never would have expected it only a few months earlier, but it felt good. What would Gran have said if she could see this? West Cork had been her home, where she'd married, where her son had been born. And then her life had changed, and not for the better. Yet Maura had come full circle: here she was, where it had all begun.

"Helen, I asked you before — how long do you think you'll be around?"

"What? Oh, in Ireland. It's kind of open-ended, and it depends on what kind of progress I can make at the hotel. It's still possible that it will be too difficult or too expensive to try, but it is a beautiful place, with a long history and a good reputation, so I'm not ready to give up on it. And maybe when I've done as much as I could, and this kid here needs to go back to school" — Helen smiled at Susan, who returned her smile — "we could take a week off and see a bit more of the country? The three of us?"

"I'd like that," Maura said, to her own surprise. She had no idea what state her business would be in by then, or how much time she could take off, but she'd rather say yes than no now.

"Good," Helen said. "Now, Susan, we need some measurements for appliances, and then I have to get back for another meeting. But you can stay here if you want. When you get back to the hotel, we can get an inventory of what's lurking in the hotel basement, and I'll bring you back in the morning to see what will fit. Okay?"

"Deal," Susan said cheerfully. "And Rose said she'd show me how to make a few dishes, which might help my cooking. And it would show us the best ways to arrange supplies and stuff. Thanks, Mom."

A few minutes later Maura watched them go. What had just happened? Was her brain turning to mush?

"Yeh look happy, Maura," Rose said from behind the bar. "Yeh think the kitchen will work out?"

"I'd like to say yes, but you're the one who will be using it. I give you permission to veto anything you think won't work. When's your next cooking class?"

"In the mornin', but it won't be a long one. I think Susan's getting the hang of things."

"Looks like she's enjoying herself, which I didn't expect. I thought she'd stay mad at her mother longer than this."

"Ah, Maura, surely yeh've noticed that Ireland has a way of making things better."

"Most of the time," Maura told her. She decided not to add *between bodies and crimes.* They all should enjoy the moment.

Late in the afternoon customers started drifting in — a mix of familiar local faces and a few clusters of tourists.

Seamus and some of his buddies wandered in later in the afternoon. "Hey, Seamus," Maura called out. "I haven't seen much of you lately. You keeping busy?"

"That I am. It's the cows wantin' my attention. But I'm parched, so some of us sneaked over here, but we can't stay long."

"Pints all around?" Maura asked.

"Please," Seamus said.

Maura started pulling a row of pints. "While I've got your attention, can I ask you a question?"

"Yeh're more than welcome to," he said.

"What can you tell me about fairy forts?"

Seamus stared at her for a moment, then burst out laughing. "That's the last thing I expected to hear from yeh. Why on earth are yeh askin'?"

"Because I just found out there's one on a piece of land that I didn't know I had, and now I'm curious. Believe me, there aren't any in Boston."

"There's plenty around here, if yeh know where to look. Particularly along the coast. I'm sure yeh'll be finding more near yer place."

"Some people have been telling me they're bad luck. Is that true?"

"Let's say yeh don't want to mess with 'em, even if yer tryin' to graze yer cattle near 'em."

"Seamus, I don't have any cattle, and I'm not planning on getting any. I've got another question for you: do you believe in fairies?"

Seamus grinned. "Yeh mean the ones that live in the fairy forts? Nah, I'm just kidding. I've never met one, though I've talked to people who claim they have. But it's safer to leave the forts alone, just in case."

"Okay. Are there good fairies, or are they all out to get you?"

"Maura, whatever got yeh started on this?"

"Finding out I have one, I guess, and the land that comes with it. What if I'd decided to plant in that field and dug the whole thing up?"

"Yeh might've been found crushed under a tractor. Best leave them alone."

"Right." Maura topped off the pints and slid a tray of glasses across the bar to Seamus. "So I'll leave mine alone. You wouldn't happen to have a few on your land, would you?"

"And why're yeh askin' that?"

"I'd just like to compare them. Unless you're hiding a still or a drug lab inside one."

"Would I do that?" Seamus asked. He winked at her and carried the full tray to his buddies at a table.

Mick appeared from the back room. "What was that about?"

"I was just asking Seamus about fairy forts. I might as well know what I'm dealing with."

"I think the best plan is to leave them alone."

"I suppose. What's on our calendar? Rose has a class in Skib tomorrow morning, and Helen said she'd be back with some more information about what equipment she could give us, or maybe she'll send Susan. And weren't we talking about taking another look at my fairy fort, to see if anyone has been poking around in it lately?"

"If the sun is right, it's a good plan. No further word from Sean or the students?"

"No, and I'm not going to hunt down Ciara and friends. I really don't have much to add to solving Ciara's problems. Let's just hope somebody's found Darragh and the Cork students can finish what they started."

Maura went home alone that night, which was a bit of a relief. She admitted she had strong feelings for Mick, although she was reluctant to label them. But at the same time, she spent most of her time at the pub, surrounded by people, and she craved just a little time alone. She had come to realize that she liked living in the country, without noise or artificial lights or passing cars. What she hadn't known was how much the noise and lights and passing cars — and drunken pedestrians — in Boston had kept her on edge. Rural Ireland was a pleasant change, and she had found that she enjoyed it more and more as time passed.

CHAPTER FOURTEEN

Mick arrived early at her cottage the next morning so they could make the short trip to the fairy ring together. She didn't think she'd find much there, but she wanted to check one more thing off her to-do list. *Look for disturbed soil in a fairy ring* was not typical, but it should be quick. She didn't really expect results, because she knew Sean had already searched it, but under different conditions — late in the day, in waning light. If she and Mick didn't find anything, she wouldn't even mention it to Sean.

Again it took only a few minutes to reach the field with the ring. They didn't pass any farmers, although one lonely cow stared at them over a hedge as they passed. It was another lovely day, with wisps of mist in low-lying parts of the land that would burn off quickly when the sun hit them. Mick was driving, and he pulled into the same dirt lane where she had parked before.

"What is it we're looking for?" Maura asked him. "It's so pretty, I almost hate to disturb it here."

"We agreed we wanted to see if there was any sign of someone digging, when the sun hits the soil at the right angle. If there's nothing to be seen, we can head for the pub."

"Got it. Is it going to be bad luck if we climb over the edge of the ring? Is there a prayer I should say?"

"Are yeh serious, Maura?" He regarded her quizzically.

"I don't know. I don't think so, but there's a lot of this that I don't understand."

"Let's start, then," Mick told her, as he opened his door and climbed out of the car, while Maura climbed out the other side.

It was even lovelier outside of the car: the air was fresh, and drops of dew twinkled on the foliage, which Maura couldn't begin to identify. An occasional bird flew past, ignoring them. She could hear a cow lowing in the distance. With some regret, she told Mick, "Might as well get it done."

He led the way across the field toward the ring. The structure was no taller than he was, but tall enough that he couldn't see over it into the interior.

"Did this place ever have an entrance?"

Maura asked.

"Probably, but I don't think anyone bothered to maintain it. And I suppose fairies don't need a door or gate."

"Can I climb to the top, or will they throw things at me?"

"I wouldn't worry. Just don't fall off."

Maura looked for a section of the perimeter with easy footholds and carefully made her way up to the top. She pivoted so that she was looking at the interior of the ring. She saw grass and weeds, but they were spread evenly over the surface, which was level. The sun was rising behind her, and hitting the interior of the ring at a sharp angle . . . and then she realized there was an elongated, curved shadow in the center. She shut her eyes and opened them again, but it was still there — although at the rate the sun was rising, it might not be visible for long. "Mick?" she said.

"What?" he answered.

"Come look at this and tell me if I'm imagining things."

He clambered up quickly and settled beside her. "What am I lookin' at?"

Maura pointed. "There. In the center."

It took Mick a moment to figure out what she saw, and then he straightened abruptly. "There's a depression in the grass, right?

It's been there a while, because the grass is grown, although I can't say how long. Could be weeks, could be years."

"Do you think Ciara or Darragh saw it?"

"I wouldn't be sure, since the light has to be right. Are we goin' to get closer?"

"I guess. That's why we're here, isn't it?"

Maura felt a weird sense of foreboding as she slid down the interior side of the ring. She chided herself: she was just being silly. It could be almost anything, or nothing at all. And she didn't see any fairies.

Mick followed behind her. "Do yeh want to do the honors?"

"What do you mean?"

"Is this thing a figment of our imaginations, or is there something real there?"

Maura had reached a spot maybe a foot from the dip, but she wasn't ready to poke it. She walked slowly around it, but it didn't disappear. It didn't look disturbed, but it was definitely there. "Do you think some animal took a nap there, or just rolled around?"

"Unlikely, I'd say. Do you want me to see if there's anything there?"

"I guess. Do you have a penknife or something? Or are you just going to dig with your hands?"

"Hands." He knelt at the edge of the dip

and poked gently. "Feels like the rest of the dirt here, so the hole is probably not very new."

"Can you get this over with? Either there's something there, or there's nothing and we can go find breakfast."

She watched Mick's hands prodding the soil and grass. Finally he started working his fingers gently into a section of it — and then he stopped abruptly and looked up at Maura. "There's something."

"What is it?"

"Sean'll have my hide if I disturb anything important."

"And he'll do the same thing if we call him out here to look at mud. Go ahead, unless you want me to do it."

"Be my guest." He stood up, then took a step back.

Maura took his place. Her hands were smaller than his and slid easily into the dirt. It seemed to have been disturbed recently and the top layer felt fairly soft, though she found the edge of the dip and thought it was harder in texture. Finally she gathered her courage and worked her hand into a spot different than the one Mick had tried. A couple of inches down she encountered something. Not a rock, because it wasn't that hard. Not a newly dead body, which would be squishy, so it couldn't be Darragh. It felt more like leather, with some harder bits mixed in. Part of her wanted to squeal like a terrified child. A bigger part wanted to know what the heck it was, so she began to scrape away the surface soil barehanded.

After a couple more inches she found something that felt both soft and hard. She took a deep breath and pushed aside the dirt that covered it, then took a hard look at it. And another one, to be sure she wasn't wrong. Then, without turning, she said, "Mick, I think you need to see this."

He knelt beside her. "It's human. It looks like a hand, and it's been here for a while. The skin's all but gone, but the bones seem to be intact."

Maura caught the flicker of movement out of the corner of her eye, and when she turned to look, she saw an animal she didn't recognize, about the size of a small dog. She elbowed Mick in the ribs. "What the heck is that?" she hissed.

He turned to follow her gaze. "Looks to be a badger."

"There are badgers around here?" Maura asked, keeping as still as possible. "Are they dangerous?"

"They're not meat eaters, if that's what yeh're askin'. Mostly they're nocturnal, and they live in small hollows or caves. This one might still have young, although they'd be a couple of months old by now."

"Okay, so what do they eat?" Maura's heart rate was dropping gradually.

"By choice, earthworms. Mebbe beetles. Not humans."

Maura realized what that meant. "You're saying that whatever messed up the soil in that patch in the middle was more likely a badger than a person?"

"That'd be my guess. It wasn't looking for bones, I'd wager. Probably hunting for worms."

"Great. Now I've got a badger in a fairy fort that has found a corpse. Should I call Sean?"

"It's a safe bet that the hand — and whatever's left of the rest — does not belong to Darragh. You can tell Sean about it, and he'll probably need to do something, but it's not urgent. The body's been there a long time."

"Centuries?" Maura asked.

Mick shook his head. "More like less than a century but more than a day. It's not Darragh, as I said."

Maura pulled her hands away from the pit, rubbing the damp dirt off on her jeans. "I think you're right." Mick reached into his pocket for his phone, but Maura stopped him. "I should do it. It's my land."

"If that's what you want," Mick said.

"It is." She retrieved her own phone and walked across the ring, turning her back on Mick. Once again she hit Sean's number, and when he answered, she said, "It's Maura. Mick and I have found something else at the ring fort. No, it's not Darragh, but it is a body — an old one, and it's been there a while. But not a thousand years. I imagine the gardaí will have to do something about it? Or we could all forget we've seen it. Oh, and it looks like I have a badger family, and they found it first."

Sean sighed. "I should have known things went too smoothly with yeh. I'll come out there and look it over. But yeh can go ahead into Leap. I'll talk to yeh there when I know more." Sean ended the call.

Maura walked back to where Mick was standing, staring at whoever it was who lay at his feet, or what little could be seen of him. Or her. "He's coming?" Mick asked.

"On his way. He said we could go on to Sullivan's. Nice that he doesn't believe we would have killed someone a few hundred years ago."

"I'm sorry, Maura."

"Don't be, Mick. You thought we should

179

take a last look at this place, and I agreed. Or maybe the fairies called to me. Damn, that sounds stupid. Look, I'm happy it's not Darragh, and I can't begin to guess who it is. Let Sean take care of all that. It's not Old Mick, is it?"

"No, it can't be — I went to his funeral. So unless somebody dug him up and planted him here, it won't be him. And what's left looks too old anyways."

"Then who? Any guesses?"

"No, but there've been many deaths in this area, going back a long way. Maybe Sean will have an idea, or at least an old list of people who've gone missing. Probably before his time, though. Do yeh think Ciara and her friends found this?"

"Well, nobody was talking about it. But then, they didn't mention seeing any badgers either, although I guess they'd be likely to hide. And Ciara seemed honestly excited about doing this research. You think that was just a cover story that would let her hunt for a body? And she's my age. Could she have known this . . . what? Man? Woman? She claimed she'd never even been to this part of Cork — she'd only seen maps. But even if she knew what or who she was looking for, *how* would she have known?"

"Maura, I've no idea. Shall we get ourselves to Leap?"

"I suppose. Oh, and one good thing has come of this."

"And that would be?" Mick asked.

"I've found I have my own badger. I've never seen one. Do I have to do anything with it? Feed it? Start an earthworm colony for it? Or just leave it be?"

"I think it would rather be alone, Maura. Yeh can come out here now and then and see if yeh catch a glimpse of it. And the family. Or more — sometimes they live in colonies, and it's a big ring fort. It's probably been a home to badgers for a long time. You ready to go?"

Maura thought for a moment. "If you don't mind, I think I'd like to talk to Sean when he gets here. Let's sit on the wall and wait for him."

Maura and Mick were waiting side by side on the top of the ring fort wall when Sean's car pulled up. He climbed out and crossed the field to where they sat. "What've yeh got, Maura?"

"We've found a burial inside the ring fort."

"Who is it?"

"We don't know, but there's a body, and we figure it's been there too long to be Darragh. Once we found it, we left it alone. Are you missing any people?"

Sean straightened, and his expression grew hard. "Let me take a look. In the circle, you say?"

"Yes, pretty much in the middle."

"Wait here, both of yiz."

Mick stood and offered Maura a hand to pull her up. They remained standing on the edge of the fort's wall, watching as Sean carefully approached the small hole they'd dug to reveal part of the body. Sean found it easily enough, then spent a couple of minutes staring down at what the hole held. Then he knelt to look at it more carefully. Finally he stood up again, pulled out his phone, and made a call. Maura assumed he was calling the garda station and requesting more people to identify the body and what had happened to him. Or her.

Finally he came back to where Maura was standing. "I'd hoped you were pullin' my leg, but yeh were right. There's a body in there, or at least some of one, and it's human. I won't investigate any further — there are others better suited to that. It's safe to say it's not the man we were lookin' for. Is there anythin' more yeh know?"

"Sean," Maura began, then swallowed and tried again. "I'm not from here, remember? I didn't know I owned this piece of land until this week. I don't know the history of the townland or the county or even Ireland — it's nothing they teach back in Boston. Mick and I, we came out here this morning to see if we'd missed anything. Clearly we did. And now we're handing the whole mess over to you. Can we go to Leap now? You know where to find us."

"That's fine. I'll come by later when we know more. And try not to talk about it yet. Nobody saw you come out here this mornin' or noticed you pokin' around in the dirt?"

"I didn't see anyone," Maura told him. "Mick?"

"Nor did I. It's been a quiet mornin'."

"Then go to the pub, and I'll be round later."

"Thanks, Sean," Maura said, then turned to climb out of the ring. Mick followed, and they remained silent until they reached his car.

"Will I drive you in, or do yeh want yer car?"

"I hate to sound like a wimp, but I don't really want to be alone. Do you mind taking me?"

"And bringin' yeh home. Not a problem."

"And when we get to Sullivan's, remind me to wash my hands — it was kind of creepy, finding somebody else's hand."

"I understand."

CHAPTER FIFTEEN

As they drove toward Leap, Mick said, "Yeh're quiet."

"What do you expect?" she snapped at him. "We just found a body. On my property. I've never dug up a body before, not even in Boston. Blood on the pavement maybe, but not someone dead. And we don't know who he is. It's unsettling. Though the badger helped."

"Don't bite my head off. And remember that badgers aren't very friendly, so don't go thinkin' of pettin' one."

"Mick, Gran and I never even had a kitten, so I guess I'm not into animals, and I sure wouldn't go petting wild ones. Anyway, would you be happier if I burst into tears?" Maura demanded.

Mick pulled over abruptly by the side of the road. "I'm not judgin' you, Maura. I don't expect you to go all girlish, or start cryin' on my shoulder. If yeh don't want to look upset, that's up to you. Might be better, in fact, if Sean doesn't want us to go around blabbing about what we've found."

Maura turned in her seat to look at him. "Why should we not talk about it?"

"I keep fergettin' yeh're not from around here. There's a long history of violence between different groups in West Cork. I don't expect yeh learned about it in yer schools in Boston, but many men died here once the Troubles began. On both sides. Which makes me think that's where our man in the ring fort might come from, and that Old Mick might've known something about it. Leave it to Sean to look into it."

"You still haven't told me why not to talk about it."

"Because odds are the man — I'm guessin' it was a man — is related to someone, or known to someone around here."

"But that means he could have died as much as a century ago," Maura protested. "Who's going to remember? And if they do, why shouldn't they tell the gardaí?"

"I'm guessin' it's less time than that, but the conflict goes on. Yeh've already found that memories are long around here. And people in this county have lost a lot of family, one way or another — people were killed, they emigrated, they went to prison.

Or they just disappeared, and nobody said anythin' about it."

Maura thought for a moment. "Okay, so we don't want to dig up any sad memories. But I still don't see why we can't talk about it with other people. How are we supposed to find out who it might have been?"

"Let Sean and the gardaí figger it out. Or at least start lookin'."

Maura glanced at her watch. "Damn, I'm supposed to be meeting with Helen and Susan back at the pub, to see what they've turned up in the way of appliances. So, fine, I'm not saying anything to anyone. It's not like I knew the dead guy, and I'm not looking to find out who he was. Maybe he has nothing to do with me, or us, or with anyone else around here." She was silent while Mick started up the car again. "One more thing . . ."

Mick kept his eyes on the road. "What?"

"Do you think there was any chance Ciara and the guys knew anything about this? I mean, this was the first circle they picked to look at, and it wasn't by chance: they had to find maps and then find me in order to get there. I can't say whether it's the biggest or the most important monument they could choose, but it's a real coincidence. I guess we'll have to wait to see if Sean's found them, or found out anything about them. I've already told him all I know. Anyway, I hope I haven't kept Helen waiting."

"How's it goin' with her?"

"Good, I guess. I think the hotel stuff keeps her busy, which makes sense if she's trying to save the place, but at least she trusts me with Susan. I'm kind of surprised Susan doesn't hate me, but she seems to be happy to spend time with me. But it's all pretty new for all of us — I'm taking it one day at a time."

"The girl seems to be enjoyin' herself."

"I think you're right, Mick. I hope it lasts."

"Why wouldn't it?"

"Maybe she thinks I'm taking Helen's attention away from her."

"Or maybe she likes you." Mick smiled.

It was just past nine when they parked up the street from the pub. The front door was open, and as they walked toward it, Maura could hear the noise of Rose clanging around, cleaning up. When Rose walked in the door to the bar Maura said, "Don't you have a class this morning?"

"I do, yes, but I was worried when you weren't here."

"We got sidetracked at the old ring fort. It seems a badger family lives there, and I'd never seen one, so I wanted to watch it. Mick, can she use your car to get to Skib? Or one of us could drive her over."

"No worries," he said. "We've enough to keep us busy fer a while, so take the car, Rose. Is anything new here?"

"Uh, Helen said she'd be here by ten, with Susan. That's all I know."

"Well, enjoy your class. I'll keep an eye out for Helen and Susan."

"Thanks, Maura. I'll be back by noon. Mebbe if we're lucky we can get some more done on the kitchen."

Mick handed Rose the car keys, and Maura called out, "See you later!" as Rose left.

Opening time was ten thirty, but Helen and Susan arrived closer to ten. "I can't stay long," Helen said, somewhat breathlessly, "but Susan and I measured what appliances were stashed in the hotel basement, so you can look to see what fits. They don't exactly match each other, but they won't be visible to your patrons, so I guess it doesn't matter what they look like. I'm told they all still work, and I won't charge you for them, if any of them are right for you."

"Helen, you don't have to do that!" Maura protested.

"It's fine, really. They're no good to us,

and we need to clear out our own storage area at the hotel. Rose'll be doing the cooking?"

"Mostly. She'll need some help, but we'll have to see how it goes before we think about hiring somebody else. Sophie and her brother Niall — I don't think you've met them yet — are possible employees, but they only just arrived in Ireland, and they may want to see more of it. I found out earlier this year that it's hard to find people to hire around here — mostly younger people leave for someplace more exciting. I'm glad we have Rose, but I won't stop her if she finds a better job, or one in a better place."

"I like her," Susan volunteered suddenly. "I mean, she's not much older than me, but she works hard, she knows this business, and she really is a good cook. You should try to keep her around."

Maura smiled at her. "Believe me, I will, but I won't stand in her way. Did the two of you have plans for today? She just left for her class, but she'll be back before lunch."

"Just working on the kitchen. You know when you want to start serving food?"

"When the kitchen is ready to cook in. Hey, you haven't been to the farmers market, right?" When Susan shook her head, Maura explained, "It takes place every

Saturday in the middle of Skibbereen, and you can find just about anything there. I go looking for used cookware and china, because I know we'll need them soon, and they're cheap at the market. The food is as fresh as it can get, usually picked in the morning. And there are nonfood things too, like used clothes and old books and a guy who sells live chickens and ducks. It's fun to wander around and look at stuff."

Susan turned to her mother. "You mind if I go on Saturday, Mom?"

"It sounds great! I might want to go myself, to see what's available — but you can go your own way without me."

"Thanks. You want me to start something, Maura?"

"Let's go measure."

Half an hour later Helen had penciled in measurements next to rough sketches of appliances in a notebook she was carrying. Maura wished she could give her more information about what the Sullivan's kitchen needed, but she had no idea — Helen was likely to know more than she did.

"I really appreciate your doing this, Helen," Maura said.

"You don't really have to thank me, you know. The stuff is just going to waste in the storage rooms, and I'd be happy if you have a use for it. And you don't have to pay for it. Just tell some of your customers to eat dinner at the hotel and I'll be happy."

Rose arrived then, and Susan volunteered to show her what they were thinking about for the kitchen. Maura enjoyed watching the two girls — they seemed so young! — talking about kitchens and what they might need. She was left alone with Helen in the main bar — she could catch up with Rose later.

"How's it going with the hotel, Helen?"

"Inconclusive. I know you haven't been here long, and you aren't exactly an expert on 'fine dining' " — Helen made air quotes — "but I'm not sure which way the economy's going around here. I've been told things are better than they used to be, but that's not the only issue. Skibbereen is a nice town, and more upscale than I expected, but that doesn't mean many people go searching for a high-end meal, or even a hotel, and I know there are a couple of decent hotels in town, like the West Cork Inn or the Eldon. So I'm feeling my way along, talking to the current staff, things like that. But I'm getting mixed responses, from both staff and patrons. I'd hate to see the place shut down, or turn into a private hospital or investment firm or something like that, but I don't know if it will survive as a hotel. And since I'm not particularly familiar with how to promote places in Ireland, I'm a bit lost. Do you have any suggestions?"

Maura did her best not to snort in amusement. "Helen, I am *so* not the person to ask. I haven't been here long, and pubs have their own traditions and patterns, so I didn't really have to change much. Well, except to clean the place up. That was not Old Mick's strong point. But my experience with fancier places is nil. How long have you got, this trip?"

"I haven't really decided, except to get Susan back to school. Would it make a difference?"

"I think so. Look, this is supposed to be prime tourist season, and Skibbereen is one of the main towns in this area. If I was you, I wouldn't decide anything too quickly. Stick around, get to know how the hotel and the kitchen work, watch who comes in and how they react. Talk to the staff and ask questions. What works? What doesn't work? The board doesn't need a decision tomorrow, do they?"

"No. They left it up to me to make a recommendation. You aren't just saying this because you want to get to know me better, are you?"

"Well, I do, but it's a business suggestion, based on what little I know about the area and the market. And I'd like to get to know Susan. How's she handling having a big sister?"

Helen looked around before answering, but clearly Rose and Susan were having fun in the kitchen space and not paying any attention to Helen and Maura. "I wish I'd told her more and sooner. But she's a teenager and she's lived a very different life compared to rural Ireland. I didn't know how she'd react. Or if she'd be mad at me for hiding my past from her for so long."

"She isn't?"

"She was at first, but I think she's used to the idea now. In a strange way I think it's made me more interesting to her, the fact that I had a different life before she was even born."

"Does your husband know all the details?"

"More or less. He's never been all that interested. But we get along fairly well, even with the kids."

"Good to know. Will he be visiting here?"

"Depends on a lot of things."

Maura hesitated for a minute before saying, "Helen, I'd like to know more about my father, if that's all right with you. Gran never talked about him. She didn't talk about Ireland, or Leap, or the people she'd known here. I figured she was mourning her past life, and I didn't want to pry. But you knew my father. I'm not saying we have to do it now — pick a time that works for you, and we can find some privacy somewhere. Is that okay?"

"I'd like that, I think. I loved your father, and then I was angry that he died and left me with few choices. Not that I resented having you so young, because we both wanted you, but then I was left alone to take care of you. I didn't feel I had a lot of options, and I needed to make money just to support myself. I know it wasn't fair to dump you on your grandmother — she had enough to worry about without my adding that. But I was desperate. I apologize, to you, and to her memory. I've been trying to make up for it ever since. I guess coming here, getting to know you, and letting my daughter get to know you, is the last step in apologizing. And I really appreciate your not throwing us both out at the sight of us. I know it's going to take time, but I want to try."

"That works for me. Look, I'm still learning how to run this business. I really like it, but I know I can do better. So maybe we can work together. I know we're talking about very different places, but we're in the same neighborhood, so at least we can compare notes. So, are we going to have appliances?"

Helen smiled. "I think we can make things work. But you do keep pretty busy here."

"I know, and I've tried to find more staff, but it's not easy around here. You'll probably find the same thing. But I'm sure we can figure something out."

"Uh, you mind if I ask where Mick fits? Not that I mean to pry."

"We're taking things slow, but I think we're in a good place together. Not that it hasn't taken a while. He's a big help here, even though he's qualified to do more and different things. But I'm not telling him to go."

"I'm glad to hear it. You two seem comfortable with each other."

"Thanks. I guess." Things would probably be even better if they didn't keep tripping over crimes, but she wasn't going to complain. It was nice to have someone to lean on — something she'd missed for much of her life. "Why don't we go see how Susan and Rose are doing, before they redesign the whole kitchen?"

"Good idea. And I have to be back at the

hotel by one, but that should be enough time."

"Sounds like a plan."

Chapter Sixteen

It was past noon when Sean Murphy came in the front door of Sullivan's. Helen had just left for her midday meeting, and Rose and Susan had headed up the street to find some lunch. They seemed to be having a good time, and Maura didn't begrudge them some fun. That left Maura and Mick to handle the small crowd of customers — and Sean.

He did not look happy. "A word wit' yeh, Maura?" he said.

"Sure. Back room?" she told him.

"That'll do."

Maura led the way into the back room and pulled the door closed. "No news or bad news?" Maura asked.

"More like none, I'd say. The gardaí recovered the body from yer fairy fort and took him to Cork for an evaluation. From what we've seen, he appears to have been male, around fifty years in age, Irish rather than foreign or dark-skinned, and the cause of death was a combination of strangulation and a broken neck."

"No ID on him?"

"None. His clothes were ordinary, not new, and with no identifying features. He had brown hair and was clean-shaven. Nothing in his pockets. No scars or other obvious injuries."

"Do you know how long he's been dead?" Maura asked.

"Hard to say, what with the damp soil, but we'd guess mebbe twenty, twenty-five years? Could be longer."

"So, he's been dead for a while," Maura said, more to herself than to Sean. "He was killed well after the whole Irish Independence thing, so he's not exactly ancient. And with the way you describe his neck, he was killed — I mean, it wasn't an accident. It's kind of hard to fall down and break your neck, isn't it? Any idea who buried him, and why there?"

Sean slumped on a bar stool. "Hard to say. There's plenty of folk around here who won't go near a fairy fort, and there could well have been more of 'em that long ago. Else they felt sure nobody else would be looking there, so they thought it was a good hiding place. There's plenty of other places to hide a dead man — wooded areas or open land. Odd that he was found in the center of the ring, though."

"Do the gardaí know of anyone missing from that time? There aren't a lot of families or houses out in Knockskagh."

"There's no official record, but there's plenty that disappeared in the past."

"So what do you do now?" Maura asked, with some sympathy.

"I don't know," Sean said.

"I'm sorry," Maura told him. "Should I have left him alone there and not mentioned the body?"

"Nah, I'm glad yeh didn't do that. That wouldn't have been right. Yeh said it's yer land?"

"That's what the deed says. I didn't know until Ciara and friends showed up with an old map. Have you seen anything more of them? Or did they go back to the university? At least we know the body we found isn't Darragh's, but none of us seem to have heard from him."

"The university claims they're registered, but that's all they know. A lot of people are gone for the summer, and I wouldn't know who else there to ask. I hate to keep askin' around here, since there's no crime that we know of and I'm busy enough already. But no one's seen them around here. Did they mention if they'd brought any camping gear?"

"No, they were staying at the hostel. Do you think they just got fed up and went back to Cork?"

"That I don't know. Mebbe they took off for Dingle or some other place to look at forts there, since this one seems to have turned out so poorly."

"Ciara seemed more worried about finding Darragh than learning something about the archaeology of the place, last time I saw her. And you know that body's not Darragh's, but Ciara wouldn't be thinking about that, because she doesn't even know about the body. And I can't imagine she's imagining something awful happened to him. She's probably ticked off that he's just wandered off without telling her."

"Ah, Maura, I could've phoned all this in to yeh. Don't know who it is, don't know who put him there, don't know when or why. All we know fer sure is that he's dead."

"Can I talk about it now with people who come in here, or would you rather I didn't?"

"Hold off on it fer a bit longer, if yeh don't mind. Mebbe if we get an identity fer him, it'd help."

"Do you guys do DNA stuff around here?"

"Depends. Fer a stranger this long dead, it's unlikely there'd be anyone to match him to."

"I'm sorry, Sean."

"Why? You probably weren't even alive when he died, whenever that might've been."

"I know, but it's one more problem that you have to solve. You can't just fill out a form that says 'Unknown' and leave it at that, can you?"

"That's not a choice." He stood up. "Just thought I'd let you know that we don't know anything. Sorry."

"Hey, you tried. I wish I could tell you anything, but it's all new to me."

"I understand." Sean managed a brief smile. "I'll let yeh know if I learn anything. Ta."

He left, and Maura slid behind the bar in the front room.

"Anythin'?" Mick asked.

"Nope. We all seem to agree that the guy in the fairy fort was male and he's dead, but that doesn't help much. Oh, and we agree he's not Darragh, which you probably already guessed. This whole mess is ridiculous! People appear and then disappear again, without a trace. A body pops up from the ground, on land I didn't know I owned, in a monument that's hundreds of years old. Nothing makes sense. I mean, you don't find bodies every day around here, do you?"

"More often a dead cow. There's not much yeh can do, Maura."

"Yeah, I know. Hey, aren't we getting near a solstice or something?"

"End of the month. Why are yeh askin'?"

"Because things are just weird, and I'd like to know if there's a reason. Will there be fairies dancing in the meadows by moonlight?"

"Not that I've ever seen. But I won't say no."

"You're not helping, Mick," Maura told him.

Business picked up after lunch. Rose and Susan came back, loaded with a hodgepodge of food, which they handed out to Maura and Mick, then disappeared into the kitchen again. Maura admired their enthusiasm but was beginning to wonder if the improvements would ever be finished. But it wasn't as though they needed them, since there weren't a lot of people asking for food. Yet. She reminded herself to talk to Rose about creating some publicity, whenever the kitchen was ready.

There was no further word from Sean, but Maura wasn't surprised. He was too young to have any memory of a missing man now found dead. He'd done all he could with the body they'd found, but there was little to work with to identify him. No one who had come in for a pint had asked any questions about finding a body, and true to her word, Maura wasn't going to bring it up.

Past midafternoon, Rose and Susan emerged from the back of the building. Rose slid behind the bar to do her shift. Susan, on the other hand, made a beeline for Maura. "Mom said she'd be back this afternoon to pick me up, and she's found a guy at the hotel who has a truck and who's going to bring over whatever appliances Mom thinks will fit."

"Susan, that's great. Are we actually ready to install anything?"

Susan dimpled. "You're asking me? I've never done anything like wiring or plumbing in my life. I'm okay with painting and washing windows. But I think Rose and I are going to need some help. Let's see what the guy says later — he should know, and he'd probably like to suck up to Mom if he wants to keep his job."

Maura wanted to tell her that sounded crude, but it wasn't exactly her responsibility. "Are they losing staff at the hotel?"

"I don't know. I don't know how many

people work there, or if any have left. I'm pretty sure everybody there is nervous, since nobody knows if Mom's company is going to sell the place or make it into something that isn't a hotel. Or just keep it the way it is, only better."

"What do you think of it?" Maura asked.

"Me? I don't go to a whole lot of hotels. Sometimes with Mom, when she doesn't know what else to do with me. Seems nice, and it's kind of interesting. The gardens and stuff are really cool, and the food I've had there was good. What kind of people are they trying to attract?"

"To stay there, you mean? I don't know. I'm not much of a hotel person. I've worked in a few bars in Boston, but that's not the same. And Boston is a big city that thinks it's important, so some places are really fancy. And expensive. This is kind of more country. Have you seen the grounds at the hotel?"

"Not all of them, not yet. The brochure says there are some really odd things there, like this big hole in the ground that somebody dug. And there are lots of big trees."

"Then you know as much as I know."

Maura turned away to fill a pint for a customer who had wandered in. She didn't recognize him, but she wasn't about to turn him away.

The next person to arrive was Ciara. Maura did a double take to make sure of what she was seeing. "Ciara? Welcome. Where've you been? Where are your friends?"

"Hey, Maura," Ciara said, sliding onto a bar stool. "I've been looking for Darragh, but no luck. He's just vanished. No call, no note. No sign of his car or that expensive radar machine he borrowed. Can I have a pint, please?"

"Sure. Were you looking around here, or did you go back to Cork city?"

"A bit of each, I guess. But no one's seen him anywhere."

"Where's Ronan?"

"He's in Cork. He says this area kind of spooks him. He's more into flying the drones than looking at what the drones can show him."

"Did he know Darragh well, or was Darragh your friend?" Maura asked, as she topped off a pint of Guinness.

"I'm not sure how well he knew Darragh before we decided to come out this way. We'd been in a few of the same classes, Ronan and me. I did know Darragh before — I saw him at the university now and then, but not often. This whole thing is so messed up!" She grabbed her pint and drank down a large portion of the glass. "Maybe all those stories about fairies haunting places are true. I'd rather not find out the hard way."

"You mind if I ask you something?" Maura asked her. Ciara just shrugged — she looked drained. "Did you ask the gardaí in Skibbereen to help you find him?"

"Why would I do that? He hasn't done anything wrong. Except disappear without telling me or Ronan. Or anyone else." Ciara looked near tears.

"Did he have any enemies in Cork?" Maura felt stupid asking, but she thought she should check.

"Maura, he's a student! He hasn't committed any crimes. He doesn't deal drugs. He likes his research. Why would he have enemies? And why would I need the gardaí?"

"Aren't you worried about Darragh? I mean, how often does he disappear like this?"

"How'm I supposed to know? We aren't a couple or anything. We happen to share classes and like the same kind of research. I told him what I was thinking of for a summer research project, and he volunteered to come along. He said he could get a ground-penetrating radar from the department and he wanted to see if it was a useful tool. That's all." Ciara drained her glass and pushed it toward Maura for a refill. "And that's how I connected with him and I saw the radar thing. And now both are missing."

"So is he on the trail of something that he didn't want to tell you about? Did he get gored by a bull in a field somewhere? Ciara, what happened?"

"I don't know," she said, and burst out crying.

Clearly she cared more about Darragh than she was willing to admit. Maura wavered only half a minute. Then she took Ciara's arm and carefully led her into the back room for some privacy. And then went back to the front, pulled her mobile phone from her pocket, and called Sean. When he answered, she said quickly, "Sean, I've got Ciara here. I think you'd better talk with her while you can. And no, Darragh isn't here, and Ciara says she still doesn't know where he is."

"On my way," Sean said, before he hung up.

Maura walked back to the second bar, where Ciara was leaning on the surface and sniffing. "Ciara? I asked Sean Murphy to come talk to you about anything you've learned since the last time you spoke. He'll be here soon. He's a good guy, and you can trust him. He's trying to help."

Ciara blew her nose. "Sure, why not? Things can't get any worse, can they?"

Only if we find Darragh's body. Maura shook her head, more for herself than for Ciara. "Things will be fine." She hoped.

CHAPTER SEVENTEEN

Dealing with Ciara, Maura realized how bad she was at comforting a sobbing woman, but there wasn't much she could do about it. She didn't want to leave Ciara alone, especially since there was more than one way to get out of the back room, which meant Ciara could disappear again. But Maura wasn't about to let Ciara slip away. Not without getting some answers. If there were any, which she was beginning to doubt.

Mick poked his head in the door, and Maura slipped over to see what he wanted. "Sean's out front," Mick said. "Should I send him back here?"

"Please."

A minute later Sean let himself into the room quietly and pulled the door shut behind him. Ciara didn't seem to notice his arrival.

"Miss McCarthy? Mind if we talk?"

Ciara looked up, her eyes bleary. "Sure,

fine. Sit down. But I don't know what I can tell you."

"Can yeh stay while I talk with her?" Sean asked, looking anxiously at Maura. "Yeh're more of a friend to her."

"Sure, why not?" Maura wasn't sure how to define her relationship with Ciara, but it was more than a pair of strangers. Maybe having another woman in the room would make things easier for Ciara. Or not. This whole situation was far outside Maura's experience, and she was making it up as she went.

Maura put on her public voice. "Sit down, Ciara, Sean. Anybody want coffee or tea?"

"We should get started," Sean said. "I don't want to keep yeh long, Ciara, but I'm glad yeh came in today. Maura's told me a bit about yer background, but I'd like to be sure of the details. Could we go through what yeh've told me before, to be sure I got it right? You're a student in Cork?"

"Graduate student," Ciara corrected him quickly. "In archaeology, particular in Ireland. I'm working on a project involving fairy forts . . ."

Once she started talking, she didn't stop. Maura paid attention to what Ciara said, but found herself wondering what she'd been doing for the past couple of days —

and whether she actually did know where Darragh was. Unless, of course, he was dead. Would Ciara know? But Maura couldn't find any reason he'd be dead, and she didn't dare interrupt Sean's careful interrogation. She hoped Ciara was telling the truth.

It didn't take Ciara long to outline how they had come to choose County Cork, and what their timetable was supposed to be. By the time Ciara's voice slowed, Maura had noticed there were details she hadn't mentioned. She glanced at Sean, who gave her a small nod to go ahead.

Maura cleared her throat. "Ciara, you said you knew Darragh before you came here, right?"

"I told you as much. We weren't close, but we both knew quite a bit about prehistoric rural monuments. Plus, he knew he could borrow a radar device. He and Ronan arrived after I did. They stopped here first, looking for me. Remember?"

"Yes, I do. And I know you were all at the fairy fort yesterday morning," Maura said. "I was there with you, but I left early to get to work. You called and told me that Darragh wasn't there, and he hadn't told anyone where he was going. Is that right?"

Ciara nodded. "Ronan and I went into

Skibbereen to get some food for lunch, and when we came back, Darrah was gone. We didn't find him there anywhere around the fairy fort. And he took the radar unit with him." Nothing Maura hadn't heard before. Ciara went on. "Ronan and I looked around for him, but we didn't find anything — no note, and no sign of the things he had brought. Maura and Mick helped look too. No one's seen him since — is that right, Garda Murphy?"

"It is, Miss McCarthy. He's not appeared at the place where you three were stayin'?"

"No, not since he left the fairy ring that morning, with us."

"Would he have gone back to Cork?" Maura asked.

"Not without telling us," Ciara said firmly. "And we wouldn't have minded, if only he'd let us know. We're just beginning our research."

"He looked kind of older than you. Had he been a student longer?" Maura asked.

"He never said," Ciara told her. "I think he'd skipped a semester now and then, so he was taking his time."

"Did he know much about the fairy forts?"

"More than Ronan and I did, but I think he was most familiar with those in West Cork."

"Was he from here?" Sean asked.

"No, or not lately. Maybe he knew there were more monuments around here than in other regions. There's quite a few along the coastline, and we were looking for distribution patterns."

"Do yeh think somethin's happened to him?"

"Like what? He fell off a cliff? We weren't close to any. He fell into a lake? Same thing, and someone would have noticed, would they not? He's hiding out in an abandoned house? Maybe no one would see him, but why would he do it? Or he simply got bored with Ronan and me and went back to Cork city."

"Did he have a girlfriend there? Or a boyfriend?" Maura asked suddenly.

Ciara turned toward her. "Not that he ever mentioned. And he made no personal calls once we arrived here. He preferred to be alone, as near as I could tell. He worked hard, but he kept to himself."

"So we've nothin' more to work with," Sean said, sounding depressed. "There's not much more I can do, seein' as there's no crime."

"This kind of thing doesn't happen in the country!" Ciara protested. "He had few friends *or* enemies. We decided to go exploring West Cork while the weather was fine, and then he disappeared. Maybe he'll turn up in some other place, or maybe he's dead in a hole in the ground. We don't know!" She was beginning to sound hysterical.

"He doesn't do drugs, does he?" Maura added. She had to admit she was grasping at straws. "Or does he have some kind of disease that would knock him out?"

Ciara shook her head. "Not that I know about. I do hope he's all right."

"We'll keep our eyes open for him," Sean told her gently. "If you should hear from him, please let me know. Will you be staying around here any longer?"

"Maybe," Ciara snuffled. "A few days."

"That's grand. Don't worry, we'll find him. Do yeh want to stay here fer now, or shall I take you back to where yer staying?"

"I'll go now, but I have my car. I just stopped in here to see if Maura had heard any news."

"Then drive safely, and let me know if you learn anythin'," Sean said.

Once Ciara had gone out the front, Maura sighed. "This is getting ridiculous. Nobody's seen the guy, dead or alive? He's just a student! And I can't imagine that the radar machine thing could have been worth enough to kill him for, but that would mean he took it with him. None of this makes sense."

"I'd have to agree wit' yeh, Maura. It may be that someone did him harm, but why? And what did they do with his remains?"

"You're supposed to have the answers to that, not me, Sean. And why of all the places in West Cork did they land on my property? There must be other examples of these rings that are easier to see and get to. And I certainly don't know a thing about the history of fairy forts. Or much else around here, either."

"Don't worry yerself, Maura. I'd best be on my way back to Skib, on the chance that the man will pop up somewhere. Dead or alive."

"Good luck with that, Sean. But thanks for coming by."

She led Sean to the front door and watched him walk down the street. Then she turned and scanned the room. There were a few patrons, some clearly local, others tourists. It wasn't exactly bustling, but it didn't look empty either. Mick looked at her from behind the bar. "Did Sean have anythin' to add?"

"No. Ciara was a soggy mess. She said — again — that she didn't know Darragh well. She says they aren't a couple, but I'm not convinced. Not that it matters — she doesn't seem to have any ideas about how to find him, and she claims she hasn't seen him since before lunch yesterday. I think she said Ronan went back to Cork city, and she didn't know if or when he's coming back here. And that is all I know. Not much help, is it?"

"All too little," Mick agreed. "And Sean had nothing more?"

"Nope. Maybe it's hard to hunt for someone you've never seen, who doesn't know the area and could have gone anywhere, or left entirely. Are we making too much of this?"

"There's still the dead man to think of."

"True. Sean didn't mention that to Ciara. But from what you and I saw, he has nothing to do with Darragh. Tell me this, Mick — do you think they were looking to see if any or all fairy forts had burials in them, or were they looking for this specific one, whoever he is?"

"I can't say, Maura. From what I know, they're fairy portals, and the fairies wouldn't welcome a human corpse on their doorstep. So your dead man would be the exception."

"I'm not sure if that makes me feel better or not, but I suppose it improves the odds that somebody will know who is he and why he's there. What will they do with the body, if nobody can identify him?"

"I've never had reason to ask that. But yeh must know there are more bodies than stones in many of the burying grounds around here. Do yeh know where yer grandfather was buried?"

"Gran never talked about it, and I didn't ask. I know Gran didn't have much money and moved to Boston as fast as she could after he died, so maybe she couldn't afford a marker — all her money went to boat tickets for herself and her son. I don't think Helen would have asked her. I'm not sure Helen even knows where my father is buried. And I'm guessing it's not worth looking for Donovans around here, because half the people I meet are Donovans. You knew Old Mick, right?"

"I worked fer him, fer a few years. Why do yeh ask?"

Maura ignored his question, since she wasn't sure herself. "Were you friends? I mean, did you sit around and talk on slow days?"

"No. He was much older than me, and I wasn't feelin' very talkative then, as you know. But he didn't pry. He knew my gran, bein' neighbors, but they weren't close. Mostly polite, and they'd do favors for each other now and then, after my grandfather passed on. He's buried in Leap, if yeh're wonderin'."

"Old Mick's buried here in Leap? At the church up the road? Nobody's mentioned that."

"That he is. People all but forgot that he had a house somewhere else — he spent a lot of nights upstairs here, and there was no one to go home to. If I recall, it was Old Billy who settled where to put him in the end, and nobody complained. They'd been friends a long time."

"They weren't related?"

"They never said, but I'd guess no. They were old men with no family to turn to, no more. Never married."

Maura digested that for a moment. "And then somehow I ended up in the mix, and I'm not related to either of them. That I know of, at least. Lots of people around here seem to keep secrets."

"You've already said yer gran fixed it with Old Mick that you'd end up with the pub and the cottage. And yer gran knew Bridget, who lived down the lane from him. It's no more complicated than that. If they'd had children, yeh might never have come here."

"Old Mick had a pretty good amount of land, if you add it all up. Didn't someone around here want it?"

"I'd never heard, if it's true. Old Mick was a man who didn't talk much about himself. I'd be guessin' he inherited it from his family back a ways. Yeh could look it up if yeh wanted. There'd be records in Skibbereen."

Maura was getting more and more frustrated. "Mick, I'm happy with the cottage. I don't need any more land, and I wouldn't know what to do with it. Just finding out about the fairy fort has been confusing enough. If Old Mick had no family around here, who's in the circle? Did Mick put him there, or didn't he even know anyone was buried there? It sounds like a dumb question, but people have been telling me that most folk won't go near a fairy fort, much less bury someone in it."

"That I can't tell yeh, Maura. Like we've been sayin', nobody ever talked about it."

"Do I have to do an exorcism or something to clean it up?"

"Leave the site alone fer now — nobody's goin' to disturb it."

"Not even the gardaí?"

"No more than Sean and his lot have already done."

"And what if no one ever figures out who it was?"

"It wouldn't be the first time. Don't worry yerself about it — yeh had nothing to do with the man."

"I hope that's true."

CHAPTER EIGHTEEN

The conversation with Ciara and Sean had eaten up a chunk of Maura's afternoon. Not that she'd had any specific plans for the time, but she wished somebody would come up with some information about the dead man. It wasn't that she was bothered by bodies, but this one had come with so many attachments: a piece of land — one of several? — she hadn't known she owned; a group of eager archaeologists exploring that land and its singular monument; the disappearance of one of those people beyond even Sean's ability to locate him; the semi-disappearance of the other two people, although now Ciara had reappeared and reported that Ronan had bailed and gone back to Cork. Still no sign of the third person, Darragh, dead or alive. The body from the ring fort had been excavated, and Sean had said the gardaí had shipped it to Cork Hospital for a professional examination. Sean's guess was that the body had been buried for quite a few years, though it was hard to be exact, and he guessed the man had been around forty at the time he died and he didn't think it was worth doing more than the required minimal autopsy. That was all anyone seemed to know.

Maura had a suspicion Old Mick had had something to do with it, but she had never met him and he'd left no evidence behind. *Physical* evidence, she reminded herself. There were still a few people around who had known him personally, but they seemed to agree that Old Mick hadn't been one for sharing information. Or maybe he had shared it, all those years ago, and they had all clammed up since, or anyone who had known him was dead. What could have led everyone to remain silent? Her best guess was that something illegal had happened, but those people who knew about it didn't think they needed to report it to the gardaí, then or now. It seemed to her that the only way to find out anything was to ask those people of the right age, but she didn't feel she had the right to do that. She was the outsider, the newcomer, and she knew squat about local history or families.

Her thoughts were interrupted by Helen's arrival. Maura was surprised that Rose and

Susan hadn't been making much noise. Or maybe they'd left while she was in the back talking to Ciara and Sean. After all, there wasn't much to be done with the kitchen space until the questions about appliances and utilities were answered.

"Mick?" she called out. "Are Rose and Susan still here, or did they go somewhere?"

"They went out fer a bit but promised to be back when Helen was expected. Good afternoon, Helen. Can I get yeh anything?"

"Coffee would be good, thanks. How's the kitchen coming along?"

"Sit, please. And I can't say because I haven't seen it today," Maura told her. "Do you have anything to add?"

"Maybe. Let's wait until the girls are here so I don't have to repeat everything."

"No hurry. You may have noticed that things don't move fast around here. How's the hotel doing?"

"I think the staff is getting used to me, and I'm not pushing too hard. I'm still getting used to the place, and I don't want to rush on making changes or spend a lot of money only to find the place has been sold yet again. I hear that happens a lot."

Mick brought by a mug of coffee and set it in front of Helen. "Anythin' else you'll be needin'?" he asked.

"We're fine for now, I think," Maura said. "Maybe when the girls get back, we can think about food. Thanks."

When Mick had returned to the bar, leaving them in a quiet corner, Maura said, "Can I ask you something?"

"Of course. What is it?"

"Have you heard that a body was found near my cottage? On land I didn't even know I owned?"

"There've been comments from the staff, who seem to know everything that's going on around here, but no details. Who is it?"

"That's part of the problem: no one seems to know." Maura looked around, but nobody in the room was paying them any attention. "My garda friend Sean made some guesses about how long the body had been buried, and how old the man was when he was buried, but there's no ID."

"How very odd," Helen commented. "How long has it been?"

"His first guess was maybe thirty years, but it's hard to say, and it could have been longer. He's having an autopsy done in Cork."

"So, well before your time. But the place you own now used to belong to the man who owned and ran this place, right?"

"Yes, but I only learned that when I ar-

225

rived here. It seems Gran knew him, but she never mentioned him to me — just set up the whole inheritance thing without telling me. I wanted to ask you if she'd ever said anything to you about what went on around here when you were all living together."

Helen shook her head. "I respected her, but we were never close, even though I was married to her son. Your father. And then he died and everything seemed to fall apart. I can see why she was devastated by his death, after she'd left Ireland and raised him in Boston, but we never talked about it. Partly that was my fault, I suppose. I thought I had my life worked out, but when Tom died . . . Well, you know what happened. I couldn't handle it, so I left, and it took me a while to pick up the pieces of my life."

Maura was beginning to get frustrated. Sure, Helen had walked out — and away from her. But Maura was working hard to forgive her and to get to know her. And beyond that, she wanted to give Susan a chance. "Helen, you don't have to keep apologizing to me. I don't know that I would have done anything different. Gran left a letter saying that I should come here to Leap, but she didn't explain why. She kind of pretended that I was supposed to know. So I came, and I was going to leave in maybe a week, and then things started happening — like inheriting this place, and the cottage — and I just sort of went along with it. Besides, I had no reason to go back to Boston. So I can see why it was hard for you.

"What I want to know now is whether Gran ever said anything about her life here, before she left. Friends, family, land — anything. But nobody's said anything, although she's been gone a long time, so maybe nobody knew anything then or remembers her. Except Bridget. I know Mick's grandmother was a friend of hers, but I haven't asked for many details. I suppose I should now, because if anybody knows who the dead man was, Bridget would be the best person to ask."

Helen was silent for a moment. Finally she said, "Thank you for not beating me up over what I did. I was young and stupid, and I hope I've outgrown it."

"Does Susan know the whole story?"

"Pretty much, now. I said before, I only told her about you after I went back home last time, and that was only the outline. I filled in some of the blanks when I decided we should come here together, and she should learn about her family in Ireland. Do you know if your grandfather had any family left over here?"

"Not that Gran ever mentioned, and I haven't gone looking. Out of respect for her, I guess — I figured if she wanted me to know, she would have told me. And she didn't. She used to entertain a lot of Irish immigrants, help them get on their feet in Boston, but nobody ever said, 'Aha! We're related.' " And I haven't stumbled over any relatives here, but I haven't really been looking. There's been a lot to learn."

"I can understand that," Helen said, smiling. "And it looks like you're doing well. Not only do you own property, but you've got people working for you, and friends outside of work, and you're learning all the time. Look, I've got nothing against Boston, but to me it looks like you're enjoying yourself here. Except, of course, for a body now and then, but I gather that's not normal for this part of the world. You aren't in any rush to make changes, are you?"

"Well, like I said, I'm still learning. And I do like the place. I didn't have any relatives back in Boston, but here half the people I meet think they are related to me or know people who are. I keep forgetting it's a small country, and people don't usually leave or go far these days. It's kind of nice."

Helen smiled. "I'm glad you found something that worked for you. And I did respect your grandmother. I left because of my problems, not because she wanted me to. I was young and stupid and scared. Do you know, I think you're older than I ever was at that age."

Maura summoned a smile. "Look, Helen, let's not beat this into the ground. It looks like it took you a while, but you've finally done something with your life. You seem to be on good terms with Susan, although I haven't seen the two of you together much. So maybe it just took you a while to figure things out. Me, I'm still working on it."

"Thank you, Maura." Helen drained her coffee cup. "So what's the story about this dead man?"

"So far, nobody knows. These three students from Cork were working on a summer research project, and the first place they started looking turned out to be on a piece of land I inherited, though I didn't know that until they showed up and told me. As far as I know, they didn't find anything the first time they were looking. The next day one of them disappeared, and nobody's seen him since. But then Mick and I went out there the next morning and noticed sort of a dip in the ground, so we started poking around and discovered there was someone buried there. Of course we backed off fast, and I called Sean Murphy and the gardaí. Sean was here earlier today, and he says they haven't identified the body and they don't even have any guesses."

"Wow," Helen said. "This was — what do you call it? — a fairy fort? People don't usually get buried there, do they?"

"Yes and no. There are lots around, but most people seem to think they're either cattle fields or entrances to the fairy world. They're not usually used as burial grounds. Doesn't help much, does it? The body we found was definitely human, not a dead cow. But he'd been buried for a while, not just a day or two."

"You think there are more around? Bodies, I mean."

"I'm not the person who would know, and right now we're trying to keep it quiet so everybody doesn't go running out and start digging. If you happen to stumble over a body at the hotel, tell Sean first, okay?"

"I wasn't planning on looking, but I'll keep that in mind." Helen's face lit up. "Ah, there's Susan and Rose. Susan looks so happy! I was worried she'd spend the time here sulking and not speaking to me. I'm glad she's found a friend."

"Rose is older in spirit than she looks — she's been working most of her life. I guess I'm glad she's found a friend closer to her own age — she looks happy too. Are we going to go look at the kitchen?"

"Yes, please. I've got some diagrams and pictures from my phone, and we can see what works in the space you've got. It's pretty small, but it's not like you're planning on cooking dinner for twenty people every night. Are you?"

Maura laughed. "Ask Rose. I'm lucky if I can boil water."

Susan spotted her mother as she walked in. "Oh good, you're here. Did you bring the information on what's at the hotel?"

"Of course I did. And you have the measurements for the kitchen space, right?"

"Yup. Rose and I finished before lunch. Want to see what will work?"

"Sure. You coming, Maura?"

Maura grinned. "You really think all of us can fit in that room?"

"Let's find out. You know there will be more than one person in there at a time."

"Well, yeah, I guess. Have you seen the back of this place, Helen?"

"Just a quick look. What do I need to know?"

"Well, for one thing, there's a back door, which should be good for deliveries, but I guess we've got to be careful not to put the fridge in front of the door."

"See? You're already thinking. Come on, girls — let's check this out," Helen said, and Rose led the way.

It was good to see them all looking happy. Rose knew the room best, and was most likely the best cook. Helen had professional experience in setting up working spaces, but Maura had no idea whether she could cook. And Susan had more enthusiasm than knowledge, but she seemed eager to learn. Too bad she wouldn't be around long, because she was in an odd way a good influence on Rose. But Susan was young and still had to finish school, so she couldn't stay. Maybe Helen would let her visit on vacations?

"It's coming along, isn't it?" Mick said quietly as he stood in the doorway and watched the group.

"It is. This kitchen may actually happen. Too bad only Rose will be around to do the cooking."

"What of Sophie? Will she stick around?"

"We still haven't had that conversation. But she's getting good experience in Skib, and it would be nice to have more staff to call on. Which would mean more food to offer our customers."

"Take it step by step, Maura," Mick cautioned.

"Don't worry, I will. Can I ask you something?" She led him back into the front bar.

"Of course."

"Do you think Old Billy or your gran would know something more about the body in the field? I haven't wanted to ask them, first because I didn't want to spread the word around unless Sean said it was all right, and then because if they did happen to know who it was and why he was dead, it might make them sad, and I didn't want to do that. But Sean hasn't found out anything useful yet, and Bridget must know the land out there. Do you think it's a bad idea?"

"Let me see if me gran has anything to say. You can talk to Old Billy, since he knew Old Mick well. But don't be surprised if they don't share what they do know."

"Believe me, I understand. A lot of people around here keep secrets. But does that mean they're hiding something? We know the man was killed — would they know who did it? And would they tell us if they did?"

"Maura, I can't say. Tread gently."

"I'll try. Thanks."

CHAPTER NINETEEN

"Maura? You coming?" Susan called out from the back of the building.

Maura grimaced at Mick before turning and heading for the back room. With three people already standing around in it, it was crowded, so she stopped at the doorway. "So, what do I need to know?"

Rose took the lead. "Yeh know I've been takin' classes not just fer cooking but fer organization and layout management, so I'll start. Helen can fill in if she wants."

"I'm listening," Maura said.

"First, it's not a big room, and we've no plans fer making it any bigger. It might be nice, but it's not essential, given the number of people we expect to want to eat here. I'm sure yeh've already figgered out that we need a fridge to keep things cold, a fairly big stove to cook on — more than one dish at a time — and storage space for food and tools and dishes and the like."

Maura nodded. "Yes, that much I know — I've worked around kitchens before, even if I can't cook. Is there really enough room for all of that?"

"I'd say yes," Helen jumped in. "Fresh food matters around here, so you don't need a giant refrigerator or freezer. For the stove, Now that I've seen more of the place, I'd go with four burners and a central grill. You'll also need a larger sink. And you'll have to sit down and figure out how to divide up the products you'll be using and the cooking pots and the plates and glasses. I know it sounds like a lot to think about, but I'd bet you'll find out what works quickly enough, once you start using the kitchen."

"How many staff would it take?" Maura asked.

"Two to three, I'd guess. One or two to cook, and another to serve and clean up. You haven't the space for a modern dishwasher, so someone will have to keep up with the dirty stuff. Look, it may take a while to work out the rhythms among you while you're cooking, but I think you can do it. Just let your customers know you're still figuring out the details."

"What about how much food to buy? How much to charge?"

"Yeh're gettin' ahead of yerself, Maura,"

Rose told her. "First we need the space, and everythin' has to work. Once that's set, we'll be sittin' down a couple of times a week to figure out menus and costs and such. I've learned a lot about that already."

Maura was beginning to feel overwhelmed. Why was it she had decided to do this? Maybe to make a bit more money by attracting more people? Or to keep Rose around by giving her more responsibility? Or because she was trying to keep up with the times? "Rose, I think it sounds wonderful. How long will it take to pull everything together?"

Rose glanced at Helen. "A coupla weeks, mebbe? There's still the wiring and plumbing to work out. And we'll have to get the word out if we want customers."

"Do we need licenses or anything?"

"I'll check into that," Helen told her.

"Great. Now for the last question: if any of the hotel's appliances will work, do you know any people who can install them? and make them work?"

"I think so," Helen said firmly. "I'll let you know in a day or so. And you should expect to pay the installers, though I don't know how much they charge. Maybe you can pay them off with free meals, over time."

"So we're done?" Maura asked. "You have

any pictures? You said you've got measurements, but should we lay out what goes where? Make tape outlines on the floor? There's a small fridge there now, but do we need more?"

"We can check. I think this will all work out, Maura. Rose and Susan are handling it well. You go back to work out front, and let us handle measuring and such."

"Right," Maura said, feeling an odd mix of enthusiasm and disappointment. She wondered if Mick would want to be involved, but somebody had to stay out front and fill pints.

There was no sign of Old Billy in his usual chair by the fire. Should she be worried? "Mick, have you seen Billy today? Or yesterday?"

"Not today, but he was around fer a bit yesterday. Why are yeh askin'?"

"I guess because I want to talk to him about the body, but I don't want to bother him at his place. Like I said earlier, he was a friend of Old Mick's, and he's one of the oldest people I know around here, so he's my best chance of finding out any details. Could be Mick never shared any with him. Or Billy swore an oath to Old Mick that he'd never say anything to anyone. I'd just like to ask him. If he says he doesn't know anything or doesn't remember or something like that, I won't pry. I certainly won't say anything to Sean, although he may think of it himself. You think that's okay?"

"Just be careful. Billy's a good man and an honest one, and if he says he can't speak of it or doesn't know anything, yeh'll have to take him at his word. And if yeh tell him yer not gonna hand it to the gardaí, he'll trust you. There are some secrets that are personal."

"Fair enough. I hope he's all right."

"Go and see, then."

Maura stepped outside, then hesitated. Why was she worried? She was very fond of Billy, and she didn't want to upset him. She wasn't just being nosy about the body she'd found; if it had been found anywhere other than on her property, she wouldn't have thought much about it. And she'd more or less promised Mick that if Billy didn't admit to knowing anything, she'd drop the whole thing. After all, the man in the fairy fort had been dead longer than she'd been alive, so it had nothing to do with her.

She walked to the end of the building that housed Billy's rooms and knocked. "Billy? It's Maura. Can I talk to you for a minute?"

"Give me half a moment, my dear," he

called out, his voice muffled by the thick walls.

It took him maybe thirty seconds to arrive at the door, but he welcomed Maura with a smile when he managed to wrestle it open. "Come in, come in, please."

"Billy, good to see you. You haven't been around Sullivan's much, and I was worried. Are you feeling all right?"

"Just old. Happens to the best of us, they say. Are yeh keepin' busy?" Billy shut the door behind her. "Have a seat."

"Thanks." She settled into a battered upholstered chair and waited until Billy had taken another one. "There haven't been a whole lot of customers lately. I wish I knew why. I mean, this is tourist season, right? Has someone else stolen them?"

"Ah, these things come and go. They'll be back, I don't doubt. Yer mother and sister have been around a lot."

"They have, and I'm glad we've had a chance to talk. Do you know, Helen never talked about her first marriage to the rest of her family? Susan didn't even know I existed until recently."

"How's she takin' it?"

"Pretty well, I think. She and Rose seem to have hit it off, and they're busy remodeling the kitchen, so she's got something to keep her busy. Helen has offered to find us some used equipment for the kitchen, which will save us money. Now, if only I was sure any of us could cook . . . Apart from Rose, of course."

"Yeh'll be fine."

"I hope so." Maura paused for a moment to gather her thoughts. "Billy, can I ask you about something? I don't know if you can answer it, or whether you'll want to answer, and I understand if you don't."

"And what would yeh be wanting to know?" Billy was watching her face, but he didn't look troubled.

Maura took a deep breath. "You and Mick Sullivan were friends, right?"

"That we were."

"For a long time, you've said. And he ran Sullivan's for years. When did you move in at this end?"

"Hard to say, now. Thirty years, mebbe? Neither of us had family, so he let me use this place. Never asked me to pay. He had plenty of friends who'd come by fer a pint, evenings. He was never worried about makin' any money — he just liked the company. Didn't like tourists much, though, and after a while they stopped comin, so it was mostly friends."

"You mean it wasn't because he never

240

cleaned the place?" Maura asked, smiling.

"Might have been. It was mainly men — farmers from outside the village. They didn't much care about it bein' clean."

Now came the hard part. "Billy, have you heard about the body that was found in the fairy fort this week?"

He didn't answer quickly. "I might have done. Where was he found?"

"On a piece of property north of Knockskagh. That Mick used to own. Where the fairy fort is. Now I own it, but I've never really explored all the bits and pieces of fields that he left me."

"Ah. And yeh're wonderin' if I might know who it was?"

Billy was a very perceptive man, Maura thought, not for the first time. "Well, yes, I am. I hope you don't mind my asking. It was because of those students from Cork University — they went looking at that place first, trying to plan their research. Then they came back the next morning, but one of them kind of disappeared in the afternoon. At least, nobody's seen him since then, and he doesn't seem to have gone back to Cork. Mick and I went up there the next morning to see if they'd missed anything, and if it might be visible in the light of early morning."

"And yeh found something?" Billy's smile had faded.

"We found what looked like a burial, and I started poking around to see if it was just a hole in the ground. Except then I found part of a skeleton, and it was human. I called Sean Murphy right away."

"What did Sean do?"

"He sent whatever was left to Cork for a quick autopsy, and then he asked that Mick and I wouldn't say anything until he knew more. And we haven't. But Sean was guessing that it was a man who was maybe forty or fifty, and he'd been buried for a couple of decades. Sean's too young to have been around when the man died. And then he said the man didn't die a natural death. So I was wondering if you were around then and knew anything. Or Mick was, and did he ever say anything. And that's all I know."

Billy didn't say anything for a couple of minutes, and Maura waited. "That's a long time ago now, Maura," Billy finally said quietly. "Mebbe Mick said something, mebbe he didn't. I'll have to think back. My memory's not what it once was, and I don't recall anybody askin' about a man gone missin' back then. There were fewer gardaí then — years back Leap had a station with only the one garda, but that's been gone fer a while. Mebbe nobody ever missed the man. I'm sorry if that's no help to yeh."

Maura had to admit to herself that she was disappointed — either he didn't remember anything, or he was being careful to hide what he knew. "Don't worry about it, Billy. I certainly don't know anything. I wouldn't worry except that it's on my land, which was a surprise." Maura stood up. "That's all I wanted to ask. Will you be stopping by the pub later? I can guarantee you it won't be crowded. I don't know where everyone is, and I'm hoping that serving food will improve things, bring more people in."

"Sounds like a grand idea. I'll stop by in a bit."

"Good. I'll be looking for you. And thanks for the information."

She left Billy's apartment feeling dissatisfied, and angry at herself for feeling that way. She'd promised herself that she would accept whatever Billy told her — she liked and trusted him, and didn't want to think he wasn't telling the truth. But at the same time, she'd sensed something vague about what he said. Okay, he was old, and probably forgetful. He hadn't left his own lodgings in Leap for more than a couple of days for a long time. Would seeing the fairy fort jog his memory? But was there anything about his memory that needed jogging?

The whole situation was a mess. Nobody seemed to admit to knowing anything. Did it matter? The man was dead. Most likely whoever had killed him was also dead. Old Mick, who had owned that patch of land, was definitely dead. Why should she care? Either Sean would find something or he wouldn't — it didn't affect her.

When she walked back into Sullivan's, nothing much had changed. Helen and Susan were gone, and Rose was still clattering around in the soon-to-be kitchen. Mick looked up. "Did he have anything to say?" he asked her.

"No, not really. I don't know why I care. The man died, he was buried by someone, and however many years later we found him and Sean took him away. End of story. Billy says he'll come by later for his pint, but there's nothing he wants to share. And that's where we are."

CHAPTER TWENTY

It was nearly closing time when Maura asked Mick, "Is tomorrow Sunday?"

"So I've heard. Why do yeh ask?"

"It means we don't have to come in early in the morning."

"Right so. I was thinking of stoppin' by to see Bridget — it's been a few days now."

"I haven't seen her either, and I'm sorry. I can't even claim I've been too busy to stop by. Have you told her about the man in the fairy fort?"

"That I haven't. Are yeh sayin' I should?"

"I don't know. Billy couldn't remember anything useful, but I wasn't sure whether his memory was failing or there was nothing to remember. Or if he was hiding something."

"And why would he be doin' that?"

"I'm not sure. And I'm only guessing. Remember, I don't know much about Irish history, so I certainly don't know what was going on around here before I was born. Was there a lot of crime or violence?"

"Yeh're talking about the 1960s? Before my time as well, although there always seemed to be something going on, even in West Cork."

"Sometimes I wish I'd talked more with my grandmother, although she didn't seem to want to talk about her early life. Made me wonder what she was hiding, or if it just made her sad. She had plenty of friends and coworkers in Boston, and I've told you before she used to invite new arrivals in, and feed them and help them find a job and a place to live. But none of them stuck around for long. And she never got, well, involved with anyone new. I suppose we were both lonely, but we were so busy just trying to make ends meet that we didn't have time to think about it. I wish she'd said more about Leap and Knockskagh too — not that there are many people around there now, and probably fewer when she lived here. I know she and Bridget wrote back and forth sometimes — I found the letters after Gran died. And she wanted me to meet Bridget when I got here."

"Bridget spoke of her now and then," Mick said. "Not often, though. Happened a lot around here, in the past — people would emigrate, lookin' for work or a better life, and they'd never return. They might write now and then, and send some money, but things would be different without 'em."

"Sad," Maura said. "Do you know, I have no idea where my grandfather was buried? Did he have a headstone?"

"Hard to say. People couldn't always afford one, but the family would remember where the burials were, and honor them. There aren't so many cemeteries — the one in Leap, down the street, Kilmacabea, Drinagh, and the older Drinagh West."

"What about your family? Where are they?"

"My parents and sister are still living, though not near here. I'm not sure about me grandfather — Bridget would know. But like you, I hate to ask her."

Funny, Maura thought. It wasn't the stone that mattered to people — it was the family memories. No one was forgotten.

"When do you think you'll be at Bridget's in the morning? We could have breakfast together, since we'll have time."

"Say, nine o'clock? I've some things to do at my place — do yeh mind if I don't come over tonight?"

Maura smiled. "I think I'll survive. Maybe I should have Susan come spend a night or

247

something. You'd think we'd have a lot to talk about, if Helen doesn't mind. Shoot, I don't know anything about Helen's parents either, and they'd be my other grand-parents. How did I manage to miss so many details of my own life?"

"Very un-Irish of yeh, Maura Donovan. But yeh're learnin'."

"Can we shut down now?"

"Since there's no one in the place, I think it's safe."

Maura drove slowly back to her cottage after they'd locked up. The sun had set, but the sky was still a milky color. She thought she saw a rabbit — or were they hares? She could never tell the difference. Few lights were on in the houses, and there were no cars on the roads. It was kind of nice, now that she knew the way and didn't get lost.

She'd never given much thought to the local history. Some houses she passed were clearly old, although they'd been kept in good shape. Others were new. Did people really come back to family land here? Or were they — what did people call them? Blow-ins? Looking for a change of scene, a quieter, simpler way of life? She'd met few of them, but she hadn't made a point of go-ing around and introducing herself. Most of her waking time was spent at the pub, so she didn't really know who her neighbors were. Or how many there were. No more than she'd known about Old Mick's jumble of small pieces of land. Had he had a herd of cows, back before he started running the pub?

Where did she come from? And where did she belong? She'd always thought she was from Boston, but only because she didn't know anywhere else. Gran had seemed determined to be American, and she'd never mentioned the idea of going back to Ireland. Had she missed it? Or was there no one left behind to miss?

She parked beside her cottage. Outside the car she paused, inhaling the sweet summer air. Nothing like Boston's! Once inside she decided she might as well go to bed. She could get up early in the morning and maybe make some scones or biscuits or something. She really did need to learn how to make a few basic things to eat, and she could bring them down to Bridget's for breakfast. And Bridget could tell her how she'd gone wrong that she knew so few people, either in Boston or in West Cork.

She checked her supplies: flour, eggs, butter, milk, and sugar. She should be able to make something edible from those. She stuffed them into her bread box — she'd learned quickly that there were always a few hungry mice or beetles that would find their way to flour. Then she turned off the lights and went up the stairs.

The rising sun woke her early the next morning. It wasn't even six yet, but she felt rested, and she still had to find a recipe for her . . . baked whatever. She should start by turning on the oven before she started mixing things. Downstairs it was delightfully cool, so she put some water on to boil and opened the front door. It was nice not to have to rush anywhere, and she decided to walk up the hill to admire the view — unless she ran into the pig stink, in which case she might want to walk in the opposite direction. Luckily what little breeze there was was at her back, and maybe all the pigs were still home in bed.

She'd mentioned to Ciara the fairy fort at the top of the hill, just past the pig farm. The road had crumbled away, once the last owner had passed away, and she was reluctant to drive on it. All she could see was the perimeter of the fairy fort, but it was clearly large. A single cow looked up when she leaned on the gate, then went back to chewing its grass. It occurred to her that she hadn't seen her friend Gillian for a while, even though she lived just over the hill.

Although Gillian was busy with her baby and was trying to get back into painting as well, so Sunday at dawn was probably not the best time to drop by — and today Maura was planning to see Bridget for breakfast anyway. But soon. With a sigh, Maura turned around and headed back down the hill.

She admired the view of Bridget's cottage against the rolling landscape. There was no sign of Mick's car, and no smoke coming from Bridget's chimney, so she turned to the left toward her cottage. Then she stopped: there was a man sitting on the crumbling pier that had once held up a gate. He stood up when he saw her approaching, and she realized she recognized him.

"Darragh? Where the hell have you been? Half the village and the gardaí in Skibbereen have been looking for you. Are you all right?"

"Can we take this inside?" he asked. His voice was hoarse, Maura noted, and he looked tired and not very clean.

"Sure. You want coffee or anything? Have you eaten? I'm having breakfast with my neighbor in a while and I was going to try to bake something. Have you talked to Ciara? She was worried when you just disappeared."

"She staying here?"

"In my place? No, she went back to where the three of you were staying, some hostel. She said Ronan went back to Cork, but she's still around. What happened with your research project?"

"I learned what I wanted to know. Can we go inside now?"

Maura thought he sounded pissed off. Why? He barely knew her. She'd offered to feed him. What did he want?

"Darragh, what are you doing here? And where have you been for the past couple of days? Hiding from the gardaí?"

He pulled the door shut behind them. "I need to talk to you. Sit down."

"Why do you want to talk to me? You barely know me."

"Just listen, will you?"

Maura stared at him. What was his problem? Had he been bitten by some rabid wolf or something while he was hiding out? No, there weren't wolves around here, as far as she knew. Had he drunk some poisoned water? This whole scene was getting more and more weird.

"This was Mick Sullivan's place, right?" he demanded.

"That's what I was told, when I inherited it."

"Are you related to him?"

"Not that I know of. I grew up in Boston, in the States. I didn't see Ireland until a last year. Why? I don't know squat about Old Mick. He's dead. That's why I'm here — he left it to me."

"He's dead?" Darragh said. He sounded surprised.

"Yeah, dead."

"And you're not family?"

"No. From what I was told, he never married or had any children. That's why this place looks like crap — he never did much with it, and I haven't either. Why do you care? You think you're his long-lost something-or-other?"

"God, I hope not. Where's that coffee you mentioned?"

"I'll make it." Maura stood up quickly, dumped some coffee grounds into a battered aluminum coffeepot, and poured the water over the grounds while she tried to sort out why Darragh was here. How did he know Old Mick?

"The man was past eighty when he died. What's he to you?"

"A killer."

Well, that certainly clears things up, Maura thought to herself. "Darragh," she began carefully, "does this have anything to do with the man in the fairy fort?"

"So you found him. Yes, it does."

"Do you know who he was?"

"Do you?" Darragh spat back.

"No, I don't. I didn't know Mick Sullivan. I haven't been living here long. I didn't know I had extra land, and I certainly didn't know about that fairy fort because I didn't know what one was. I'm not even sure I was born when that man was buried there, and I'd never been to Ireland then. Oh, and the gardaí don't know who he was either. What is it you want me to tell you?"

"What happened to the man?"

"Well, I don't know!" Maura protested. "I'm the new kid here, remember? And why are you asking about him? You're not old enough to have known him. Why do you even know he exists? Was that why you started this research? By the way, where's your radar thing?"

Once again Darragh ignored her questions. "It's safely stowed. Anyways, someone around here must know about him."

"I don't know a heck of a lot of people around here, and I certainly never talked to any of them about a fairy fort and a body in it." Maura stood up abruptly, grabbed two mugs, and took them and the pot over to the table. "So, why are you here this early, glaring at me, and asking me questions I couldn't possibly know the answers to?"

Darragh stared at the coffeepot as if hoping it would give him a sign that the coffee was ready. Or maybe he hadn't slept for days and was totally spaced out, Maura thought. But it was clear he was angry about something, and she couldn't figure out why he'd be angry at her.

"Darragh," she said carefully, "did you know there was a body there?"

He filled a mug with coffee. "I suspected. There or somewhere close by."

"Did you think it was in any random fairy fort, or this one in particular?"

"I knew that if the body existed, and had survived being buried for years, it would be somewhere in West Cork. And I guessed that it had some connection with Mick Sullivan. That's one reason I was taking classes in Cork — so I'd have a chance of finding him."

"And why would you want to do that? After so many years?"

"Because I think that body was my grandfather."

CHAPTER TWENTY-ONE

That was the last thing Maura had expected to hear, but then she'd known about the fairy fort less than a week, and known there had been a body there less than that. And why was Darragh so angry? He must have been a child when his grandfather — if that was really who the body was — had been buried in an obscure corner of West Cork. And why here? And what did any of it have to do with Mick Sullivan?

She took a deep breath. "Okay, Darragh — you're going to have to explain. Have you told the gardaí what you suspect?"

"No!" he said sharply. "It's none of their business."

"Why do you say that? Who knows he's dead? Do you know who killed him, and why? Who buried him way out here? Did his killer hope no one would ever find him? Did your family know? Did the gardaí ever look for him, or did nobody ever report him missing? And why do you care so much now?"

Darragh began shaking his head as if to clear it. "Shut up, will you? This is my family you're talking about! It's part of my history, and I want to get it straight. All I've got now is bits and pieces of the story, because my relatives would never talk about it. Like they were embarrassed, or angry. You don't have any stake in this — you're an outsider, with no family here, and no history."

"You're wrong about that, Darragh," Maura said. She had as much right as he did to get angry, and she was getting tired of being lectured to by a person she barely knew, who clearly knew even less about her. "My grandmother was born here, and her husband. Their son — my father — was born here. That's all the family there was, so it's not like I've got sixteen cousins up the hill. But I'm not some silly tourist who thought a cottage in the country sounded like a cool idea. I've never lived here before, and my grandmother never talked much about it. My father died before I was old enough to remember him. Look, I don't have any problem with you. I'm sorry you think it's your grandfather you found. Are you planning to tell the gardaí? Reclaim the body? Bury him in a family plot?"

"No. Because it's not as simple as that. The man was murdered."

That was not what Maura had expected to hear from him. She already knew from Sean that the man had been killed, but why would Darragh know? "Oh. Well, maybe that's different, but it was a long time ago."

"Not long enough."

"Darragh, what is it you want? You want to arrest someone for killing your grand-father? How likely is it that he would still be alive? Do you want to rebury him? Do you want to go back to doing research on fairy forts? Or Irish history? Or lay the whole thing to rest and do something different with your life? What about Ciara? Is she part of this, or does she just hope to be? Or is she a cousin or something and she's just faking it and trying to help you out?" Maura was babbling and she knew it, but she wanted answers.

"It's none of your business, Maura."

A body on her land wasn't her business? "Then go do something else. This isn't my problem."

"I think Mick Sullivan was part of this, and I want to know if he left any kind of proof behind."

"You mean here, in this cottage? Go ahead

258

and look, as long as you don't knock down any walls or break anything. I didn't arrive with much, and I haven't added much. He left me this place because he had no one else to leave it to, but he certainly didn't fancy it up before he died. By the way, I was told he died in this house — nothing like a clinic or hospital. But I haven't found any letters or records of what happened. Maybe he'd simply gotten into a fight and hit your grandfather too hard and that was the end of it. I only know that he spent more time at the pub than here toward the end of his life, and he was buried in Leap. Maybe he thought this place was haunted, although I haven't run into any fairies."

"Wherever it happened, how and why did he haul the body out to that field and bury him?" Darragh demanded.

"Hey, Darragh, I really don't know. I barely know what a fairy fort is, and people have told me most people find them unlucky and stay away. They don't come back in the dark and bury bodies in them, although if it was Mick who killed him, maybe he thought no one would look for the body there, because they all thought the place was haunted. You know anything different?"

Darragh shook his head. "No. Like I said, nobody talked about it. But my grandfather left and never came back. All I remember is a rough old man with gray hair. I've never even seen a picture of him."

"Well, I'm very sorry, and I do know something about losing people, but I don't know anything about your family's past. Are you leaving anytime soon?"

"What, West Cork? Your cottage? I haven't decided. You tell me, Maura Donovan: how many people are there around here who are old enough to remember what happened?"

"I don't know. I don't go looking for people or asking questions, because I'm in the pub all day and half the night. If somebody comes into the pub, they don't start talking about old crimes and people who are gone. You might talk to Old Billy. You met him at Sullivan's — he lives at one end of the pub building, and he was a friend of Old Mick's. For years. He's the right age, but he's never talked about his past that much. But I think he's the closest thing to a local historian that we've got. Unless you want to go back to the university and find some professor to ask."

Maura was beginning to think Darragh had calmed down, or maybe he was just tired, when there was a knocking at the door. "Maura, you there?" Mick's voice. It must be time for breakfast with Bridget.

But Darragh had gone tense. "Who's that?"

"Mick Nolan. He works with me at the pub. You must have seen him there. His grandmother Bridget lives just down the hill, in that yellow house."

"She's a Nolan?"

"She married one. I think she was born a Sullivan, but only a cousin or something to Old Mick. But she's lived in the same house most of her life, so she knew him." Before Darragh could decide what he should do, Maura went over to open the door for Mick.

"Are we still plannin' on breakfast?" he asked. And then he spied Darragh.

Mick stiffened. Was he worried about Darragh being there? Did he believe Darragh was there to rob the place? Which was silly, since there was nothing of value in the cottage and Mick knew it.

"You met Darragh, right, Mick? At the pub, and the fairy fort? He just showed up, with some interesting stories. About his past, or his family's past, anyway. I'll let him tell you about it, because it's not my story." Mick's gaze hadn't left Darragh's face, and Darragh returned the stare. Maura was losing patience. "Mick, isn't Bridget waiting for us?" she asked.

Now Mick glanced briefly at her. "Yeh're

right — she is. I'm sure she'd love to see Darragh. I think she knew his family, years ago."

Out of the corner of her eye, Maura saw Darragh straighten up and freeze. Interesting. "Would you like to join us, Darragh?" Maura asked. "I'm sure Bridget could tell us some interesting stories about her life here." She knew she sounded phony, but somebody had to do something.

Mick didn't say anything, but he cocked an eyebrow at Maura. She wasn't about to explain her rather odd request, but she definitely wanted to be there, and Mick as well. And she was pretty sure she wanted to hear what Darragh knew about the history of the neighborhood, and his grandfather, and Old Mick. There was clearly a hidden story there.

She stood up quickly and turned off the oven. "Sorry, Mick — I didn't get around to baking anything. Will that be all right? I know Bridget's scones would be better than mine."

"I'm sure she'll be fine with it. Are yeh ready to go? Darragh, what about you?"

"I'm looking a bit scruffy," he said dubiously.

"Ah, Bridget won't mind. Come on then, or we'll meet ourselves eatin' lunch."

Mick waited until Maura and Darragh had gone outside, then pulled the door shut behind them. Darragh had stopped in the unpaved lane outside Maura's cottage. "Grand view, isn't it?" he said, almost to himself.

"Does it look familiar, Darragh?" Maura said, coming up behind him.

Darragh shrugged. "It looks like Ireland, and I don't mean Cork city. Bridget's in the yellow cottage, Mick?"

"That she is. She'll be waitin' fer us."

As they neared Bridget's home, Mick took the lead and knocked on her door. Bridget must have been waiting, for the door opened quickly, and Bridget smiled at her guests. "Come in, come in. Maura, I thought you might have gotten lost, it's such a long way from yer home."

Maura smiled at her joke. "Sorry, Bridget, but I had an unexpected guest of my own, and then Mick arrived, so we invited Darragh as well. I hope you don't mind."

"Of course I don't, Maura." Bridget stepped into the sunshine to greet Darragh. "*Fáilte* — Darragh, is it?" Then she stopped and took a closer look. "Ah, yeh're the spittin' image of your father. You'd be a Hegarty, would you not?"

By now Darragh was gaping at Bridget.

Finally he found his voice. "That I would. You knew my father? Would he have come from near here?"

"Down the road, maybe a kilometer, toward Leap. But the Hegartys moved away many years ago, as you may know. Please, come in, sit down. Maura, can you pour the tea?"

"I'd be happy to, Bridget. I'm sorry I haven't been to see you lately, but we're building a new kitchen at the pub and it seems to have kept everyone busy lately. And my mother's come back, and this time she brought my half sister with her, so things have been very interesting."

"I'd love to hear more. This grandson of mine here doesn't share the details with me. Mick, will yeh bring the brown bread and butter to the table, please?"

While Mick and Maura were sorting out the tea and food, Darragh had all but fallen into a chair and was staring at Bridget. It was highly unlikely that he would remember her, but maybe the sound of her voice and her accent were familiar. How did it happen that he'd never come to West Cork looking for the fragments of his past until now? Old Mick had always been here, and so had Bridget. They both had good minds and sharp memories. Except that nobody had ever mentioned the fairy fort to her. Did they not want her to know about it? Or were they trying to keep prying eyes away from it?

Maura set about filling teacups from the pot. "Are you feeling all right?"

"I am. This is the best time of year for those of us whose joints are gettin' stiff with time. And I've nowhere I have to be. My grandson here asked if I wanted him to take me to church today, but I told him I'd rather wait till yer opening yer grand new kitchen."

Maura smiled. "We haven't set a date yet, and it's not exactly new, but I'm pretty sure all the parts will work. So you want us to have a party?"

"Wouldn't that be a fine thing?"

"It could be, if we get any more customers. They seem to be avoiding us this summer."

"Ah, it's a busy year fer them. Yeh might recall the snow we had a few months ago — it did serious harm to many of the fields, and the dairy farmers are trying to make up fer the grass they lost. Don't take it personal."

"Thank you — I'm glad to know it's not something I did. Will the grass come back before the end of the year?"

"It might, but there's some that's lost, and it won't. Farmin's not easy work."

"Has Gillian brought the baby by?"

"Now and then. He's a lovely boy, isn't he? And she seems to be a good mother, although she's said she'd like a few more hours in her days because she's back to painting again."

The conversation drifted along on what was going on around Knockskagh. Maura avoided talking about her mother and her new sister, mainly because she wanted to talk to Bridget alone, without the guys getting bored. Bridget was the last person who had known her gran, and Maura wanted to hear her memories.

And whatever memories hadn't come up as well, like the fairy fort and the body in it that no one had mentioned before now. She glanced at Darragh, who hadn't said a word but stared consistently at Bridget. Bridget had noticed, and once she'd collected all of Maura's and Mick's news, she turned her Darragh. "And what's brought you to West Cork, Darragh Hegarty?"

"I, uh, well, I'm getting a degree in archaeology at University of Cork, and I'm working with a couple of other people surveying the local fairy forts."

Bridget nodded. "Ah, I see. And is there

266

nothin' more than the history of the sites that yeh were lookin' fer?"

Darragh shot panicky glances at Maura and Mick, and then seemed to make a decision. "Well, yes and no, yeh might say. You knew who I was, soon as yeh saw me, but my parents never talked much about this part of Cork, and I'm beginning to learn why. My parents left the place when I was very young and never came back. They rarely talked about it, and never when there were us children around, and they didn't answer any of our questions. It took me a long time to put together what pieces of the story I could find. The other people I met at university knew more about how to find where people had lived or owned land in the past, and that's how we found Maura here. And the fairy fort that was on what had been Mick Sullivan's land."

"It's been many years since I've seen that," Bridget said wistfully. "Yeh've heard the old stories, about how they're haunted, or fairies live there. Most people don't care to visit, and Mick Sullivan was one of 'em. Why'd that one interest you?"

Maura watched while Darragh wrestled with what to say next, or whether to say nothing, but she didn't interfere. Bridget was a strong woman, and the odds were that she knew something. Maura decided to let Darragh make up his own mind.

At last he spoke. "I don't mean to upset you, but I believe Mick Sullivan killed my grandfather and buried him in the fairy fort. Maura and Mick found a body there this week."

Bridget didn't answer immediately. Finally she said, "I believe yer right, Darragh Hegarty, though no one's said anything about it for many years." When Mick moved to interrupt, she raised a hand. "He's right to want to hear the story, now that he's come so far. And there's few who remember it. I'll tell him what happened, for it's a bit late fer anyone to pay the price. If you've other things to do, Mick, go on your way."

"We've got time," Mick said stiffly. "And we don't know the story ourselves, though part of it falls on what we know now is Maura's land."

"Mrs. Nolan," Darragh protested, "I don't mind if they hear — and you're right: there's nothing to be done now. But I've heard too much to just let it go. If you don't mind telling it."

"It's time fer it all to come out. Maura, will yeh refill the teacups? This may take a bit of time."

"Of course. I guess I've got a stake in this too."

Chapter Twenty-Two

When she was done pouring, Maura said, "I'll need to make some more tea," in a cheery tone that sounded completely unnatural to her. Was she really that nervous? She checked to see if there was enough water in the kettle and turned on the flame under it.

"That'd be lovely," Bridget said.

"Let me help," Mick said, springing out of his seat and following Maura to the small kitchen.

Maura cleaned out the teapot while Mick hunted for more bread. "I'm sorry," Maura said in a very quiet voice. "Like I said, Darragh just kind of showed up, looking for his past, and it's clear that Bridget knows a lot about it. But I don't know what it is, and she doesn't have to talk about it. I haven't asked half the questions I could have, about Old Mick, and how I ended up with his home. And pub. I have an unhappy feeling that it's connected with Darragh's family, but I'm not sure *I* want to know. You can stop it if you want."

In an equally quiet voice, Mick said, "Bridget seems all right with talkin' about it, and mebbe she wants you to know where yeh fit."

"I've always been afraid to ask much. I didn't want to upset Bridget, and she's a good friend."

"Might be she's afraid of the same thing. Could be there's things about Old Mick and the other people around here that she thinks you'd rather not know."

"Hard to imagine. Maybe it's the fairies who want me to know. I guess when I first got here, I didn't really expect to stay long, so I didn't go looking for family history. I figured if my gran never talked about it, either she didn't have the answers or she didn't think I needed to know. And I didn't nag her."

"But yer gran still sent you here. Knowing that you might find out some things."

"You think Darragh needs to know?" Maura found a clean plate and started slicing bread.

"Bridget can always say she doesn't know," Mick pointed out. "But she's not one to hold a grudge. Though Darragh might, or already does — hard to say. Depends on the story he hears."

"All he's said so far is that his grandfather was killed by Mick Sullivan. Do we want to know more? Or should we end it here and send him on his way?"

"Mebbe we should ask Bridget how much she wants to share. If anything."

"How much time do we have?"

"It's not yet nine."

"Then we'd better go ask. I'm sorry, Mick."

"You've nothing to be sorry for, Maura. Whatever happened, it's long before your time."

When they returned from the kitchen with a fresh pot of tea and a plate full of brown bread, Darragh was all but inhaling the last of the first round. Maura wondered just where he'd been the last couple of days, and if he'd found anything to eat. And why had he been hiding?

As if reading Maura's thoughts, Mick asked, "Where's he been hidin'?"

"He didn't say," Maura replied as quietly as she could. "I think he needed time to think. It's not that he's angry at us, but he wants answers." She picked up the tea tray. "Let's get this out there so we can move on."

"Thank you, Maura, Mick," Bridget said when they returned from her kitchen. "We're well set now."

"I love your bread, Bridget," Maura told her. "One of these days I'll figure out how to make it myself."

"Ah, it's easier than it looks. Yeh'll just have to practice. But be sure yeh get the right flour."

"Well, at least I'll have a better kitchen to work with soon."

After everyone had helped themselves to bread and butter, they all settled in chairs and somehow ended up staring expectantly at Bridget, as she noticed quickly. "Yeh'll be wantin' your story now, I expect," she said.

"Only if you want to tell it, Bridget," Maura said quickly. She didn't want to cause Bridget pain.

Bridget smiled at her. "It's time it was told. It's been a good many years, and most of the people involved have left West Cork or have passed on. There may once have been a crime, but there's no one left to charge fer it. Will yeh let me tell it my way? Mick, I don't think yer father ever told you, and I know yer gran didn't tell you, Maura, so let me spin the tale without interruptin'. Yeh can ask questions later."

"Fair enough, Bridget," Maura said. Mick

only nodded. Darragh said nothing.

Bridget settled herself in her upholstered chair. "It was more than sixty years ago now. Me husband Michael and I were livin' right here, with our children, including Mick's father. Mick Sullivan lived alone in the cottage — he never married and had no children. He was a cousin of mine, and the land between us had been split long before, but there was more than enough. Darragh, you're a Hegarty. Did yer people ever mention where they were from?"

"You mean, more than West Cork? I think they said Bandon originally, but then my father moved to Dublin, or maybe south of there. Carlow's what I first remember. No one ever mentioned why they'd moved, and I always assumed it was for finding a better job, since we never had any money."

"That was before yeh were born, young man. But there were still family here, and yer parents came back to visit now and then."

"So you knew them?" Darragh asked.

"Only to speak to. We weren't related, but neighbors always welcomed neighbors back then."

Maura struggled to remember exactly when her grandmother had grabbed up her son and left for Boston. Had that been for money too? Had they owned a house, or only rented one? Of course, Maura hadn't come along for quite a few years, and many things could have changed by then.

Bridget's eyes looked shrewd, although the smile hadn't left her face. Maura was getting more confused by the minute, but that was her own fault: she'd never paid much attention to recent Irish history, and American schools simply didn't teach anything about it. She struggled to figure out when these events had happened and started trying to do the math in her head. She was in her midtwenties now, and Darragh looked to be about the same age. Gran had left Ireland before Maura was born, nearly thirty-five years earlier, which made it around 1990. And that would have been her parents' generation, so her grandparents must have been adults another twenty-five years earlier, or around the mid-1960s. Why on earth was she supposed to remember anything from that time? Darragh would be in the same boat. Mick was a bit older, but enough to harbor memories of that era?

How had all this come to light now? She'd been minding her own business, just getting used to living in rural Ireland, so different from Boston, and now without warning they were talking about murders that happened before she was born and fairy forts. As she'd been told more than once, memories were long in Ireland, but she had no memories to share. Her grandmother Nora had never shared any, but now Maura was finding out how much she had hidden, and she felt lost.

Bridget interrupted her reverie, almost as though she'd been reading Maura's thoughts. "Maura, I know yer gran never told you about any of this, and she had her reasons. We wrote each other, now and then, but there were things we never mentioned — what would have been the point? What was done, was done, and we'd gone on. Oh, we'd made some changes in our lives, over time, but there was no goin' back."

"I can understand that, Bridget. And we sort of did the same thing, when my father died, when my mother left. We couldn't change a thing, but we had to survive, so we just kept going without looking back. But I never knew that Gran kept in touch with you, and with Old Mick. I didn't even know you existed. Heck, I could barely find Ireland on a map. So whatever you're telling us will be new to me — probably more than to Mick or Darragh. Before we jump into this, can you tell me if anyone is likely to be arrested?"

"Ah, Maura, it's too long in the past now.

If I had to guess, I'd say that Old Mick might have been the one, and it may be that Nora waited until he'd passed to speak of this. If anyone cared at all."

"I did, and do," Darragh spoke up suddenly. "Maybe that sounds foolish. But no one in my family ever shared the details. I assumed there *were* details, since sometimes someone would ask a question and others would fall silent. Not often, but enough to know there was something secret. But I think it's safe to say that no one ever came to our home talking about a killer."

"That's no surprise, if yeh were livin' in Dublin. This place is hardly on their minds, though things might've been different a hundred years ago. West Cork may look peaceful, but there was a time when a lot of people died here — strangers, friends, relatives. They were hard times."

"Hold on a sec, Bridget," Maura interrupted. "I went to school in Boston, remember? I could probably give you a quick history of the American Revolution or the Civil War, but I don't know much of anything about Irish history from any time, except maybe during the Famine. I can say that a lot of the people — men, mainly — that my gran took in and helped might've mentioned why they'd left Ireland and their families

277

behind, but they weren't handing out any details. So I kind of always knew something had happened, but I never knew what."

"And did yeh hear of the IRA?" Bridget asked.

"Sort of. The Irish Republican Army, right? There were — and are — a lot of Irish in Boston. But it always sounded like the IRA changed over time, thanks to politics. We're talking here about one particular time, right?"

"The sixties," Mick volunteered. "One particular phase of the organization. But the IRA had a long history in West Cork, in all its forms."

"Am I going to embarrass myself or upset anybody by asking stupid questions here? Because, like I said, I don't know much of anything. Is it safe to say that what little family I had, had nothing to do with the IRA or the military or anything like that?"

"I'd say yes, Maura," Bridget said. "You know yer gran left here soon after her husband's death, with her son, but that wasn't fer political reasons. If anything, it was to keep herself and her young son safe, in case anyone thought she'd been part of the death."

There was that term again: death. Darragh believed Old Mick had killed his grandfather and hidden the body. But he hadn't said why — why the man was dead, and why Mick would have been responsible. Did Darragh know, or was that one of the things he was trying to find out? And why had he waited so long to come looking?

Maura checked her watch again: it was now approaching ten, and she and Mick were supposed to be opening the pub in about two hours. She truly wanted to hear what Darragh and Bridget had to share about whatever had happened, but somebody had to see to business. She could call Rose and ask her to open, but she hated to rush the discussion. She wanted to talk to Sean Murphy about whatever she learned here, but that would be a private conversation, not a public one. Not that she was reporting a crime or anything like that, but she thought Sean should know, and she wanted his opinion.

How had this gotten so complicated? "Bridget? And the rest of you? I don't want to rush this, and I really want to hear what happened, because it's part of my life too. But I'm supposed to be running the pub, even if it doesn't open as early as usual today. And even if you give me the short versions, I'm going to have questions, and I'm pretty sure Darragh will too. Mick, do you want to be part of this?"

"Yes. Fer my gran here, and fer you. Darragh's his own man, and I can leave him to figure it out. But I'm thinkin' he came to West Cork with a bone to pick with someone, and he may not like what he hears. It's up to me to look after Bridget. I'll stay and we can go through it all now, or we can set a later time when there's no hurry."

"Yeh'll be needing to hear Old Mick's side," Bridget said. "It's up to me to speak fer him, fer he was family, and a friend as well. Still, I know yer all eager to hear the truth. Does anyone have a plan?"

"We've all forgotten Old Billy," Mick announced. "Shouldn't he be part of this too?"

"Did he have a role in whatever it was that happened, or is it only because he's one of the oldest among us?" Maura asked.

"A bit of both," Mick said slowly. "Bridget, how much does he know?"

"More than you'd think. He was my friend, and Mick's, for many years. He knew the facts, but he's never told. He deserves to have his say."

"How about this, then?" Maura offered. "Say we close the pub early tonight, and we get together with Billy and Bridget, wherever it's convenient? I know it will be late, but I don't want to sit on this and stew about it. What do you all think? Bridget, it would be hardest on you, I guess, and you don't have to do it."

"Ah, Maura, I've been living with this story fer more than half my life. If I wait much longer, there'll be no one left to tell. And now, after so long, the tellin' can't hurt anyone. I'd be glad to be part of it."

"Here or in the village?"

"Ask Billy if he's willin' to come, and where he'd like it to be. At least I know I have you and Mick to bring me home, if we're at the pub. Where do yeh think Old Mick would like it to be? Because he's the center of the story."

"We can ask Billy, because Sullivan's has been his home for a long time, and he was Mick's friend. Does that suit you?"

"I believe it does."

CHAPTER TWENTY-THREE

Once they'd established that the details of the story would keep until later in the day, the breakfast at Bridget's wrapped up fairly quickly.

Maura was quick to tell Bridget, "Mick can bring you to the pub later — unless, of course, you change your mind. I won't mind if you do, because we can talk about it all some other time."

"Ah, Maura, yer too kind. I've waiting a long time to see the end of this story, and I don't want to put it off any longer. If anythin' goes wrong, I'll call. But I'm lookin' forward to seein' Billy again — it's been too long, and he has his own pieces of this puzzle to share."

"Thank you, Bridget," Maura said. "I'll be seeing you later."

Maura opened the front door and waited for Darragh to follow her. Outside she said, "Where do you want to go? You can come sit in the pub if you want, or hang out around here. Or you can skip this meeting or party or whatever it is and write us a note. Are you going to invite Ciara?"

"Why would I do that?"

"Because I think she cares for you. If you're going to disappear from her life, it would be polite to let her know. And I'm not volunteering to be the one to tell her, because I don't know either of you well. If whatever it is is over, *you* tell her. Mick and I have got to get to the pub, so make up your mind where you're going to be today. And if you want to take a shower and change clothes, you're welcome to use the cottage."

"What?" Darragh looked confused. "Oh, right — I'm not in any shape for a party, am I? And maybe I could use a nap."

"You still have your car?" Maura asked.

"Yes, but it's out of sight."

"You can drive it to Leap. Like I said, Mick will take care of his grandmother. And if you make her unhappy, I may have to bury you somewhere myself. Which reminds me: assuming the gardaí don't find a reason to charge anybody, what do you want to do with your grandfather, if they'll release the remains?"

"I'll have to give that some thought. My

family won't care, but I do. Look, Maura . . ." Darragh fumbled for words. "I'm sorry if I've messed things up. I really thought it would be simple: find the fairy fort, find the body, if it was there, and be done with it. I never expected to involve so many people. Nor did I think you'd all be connected somehow."

"Hey, that's how it seems to be around here," Maura said, managing a smile. "Look, Mick and I will be leaving. You can hang out here as long as you like. I can tell you there's no money hidden and nothing of any value, and Old Mick didn't leave a journal with all the details of what happened with your grandfather. You're going to have to come and listen to everyone else if you want to know."

"Thanks, Maura. You've been kinder than I had any right to expect."

Maura gave him a curt nod, since she had no idea what to say, then turned and went down the hill to where Mick was waiting next to his car. "Have I screwed this up?"

"Why would yeh say that?"

"I could have kept my mouth shut about all of it. God knows what Sean is going to think, if he hears the whole story. Or I could have told Darragh to go on his way and get out of our lives, and we might never have known. Is Bridget going to be all right about this? I didn't think she'd know about the whole mess from the past. I don't want to make her unhappy."

"I think she's stronger than you give her credit for, Maura. And it's partly her story too. So much of history around here was never written down, and it's the people who were in the thick of it that hold on to the memories."

"I still feel like a fool, now that I've gotten everybody else into this mess. It wasn't my problem to share."

"Yeh might be surprised, Maura."

"Do you know more than I do, Mick?" she asked.

"I'm not sure. Let's give it a rest until later. We'll go to the pub, and you can talk with Billy. I'll pick up Bridget in the afternoon."

"What do I tell Rose? Or Susan and Helen? 'Sorry, but we're settling a family crisis that's more than half a century old and you're not invited'?"

"Yeh might argue that Helen has a connection. It may be what brought her husband — yer father — to the States."

"I don't know her well enough to ask. Heck, if I couldn't ask Gran, how can I ask Helen what she knows or wants to know?"

"Your choice, Maura. Mebbe she won't come by at all."

"And what about Susan?"

"Maura, I don't know. Yeh might have noticed I'm not good at talking about things that are personal, even if they're long past. I can't be tellin' yeh how to deal with yer relatives."

"We are a mess, aren't we? I don't know whether to laugh or cry."

"Then let's go see how yer kitchen's comin' along, and then you can talk to Billy."

"I guess that will have to do. One last thing: does this have anything to do with us? You and me, I mean?"

"It might do. Don't borrow trouble, Maura. We'll be sorting it out later."

Maura surprised herself by getting into Mick's car. Sure, her own was sitting right up the hill, and she might even need it later in the day, but right now she wanted Mick's company. And she was pretty sure she'd want it later.

As a couple they were in fact a mess. She'd known him for well over a year now, and for much of that time she'd been unsure of what her plans were going forward, and reluctant to get involved with anyone. She got the same feeling from

Mick. After all, he was intelligent and educated — and single. What the heck was he doing in a small shabby pub in a village in West Cork? But as far as she knew, he hadn't been looking for anything more. Still, after some time Bridget had pushed him into confessing why he'd lost all ambition and was content just to drift through his life. It had been a shock to her to find out what he'd been hiding, but it had explained a lot.

That train of thought led her to recognize that Bridget was a wise woman. She knew her grandson, and she wasn't lecturing him about getting on with his life. She'd also known Maura's grandmother for years, but she hadn't told Maura what to do next when she arrived. Which led Maura to think that if Bridget believed they needed to get this whole messy business of the body in the rath sorted out, then maybe she was right. And when Bridget and Billy were gone, much of that history would be lost, the story left unfinished. So why was she so upset about it?

Maybe it was the fairies talking to her again. Not that she believed in fairies, but there were an awful lot of unusual things happening in Leap and beyond that she couldn't begin to explain. She was trying to keep an open mind, but when a stranger showed up and started poking around a prehistoric monument in her back yard, or found himself a body that he claimed was his grandfather, she had to figure there was some sort of explanation. She was torn between reluctance and curiosity about hearing what Billy and Bridget had to say, and where Darragh fit.

"Are yeh sleepin'?" Mick's question interrupted her scattered thoughts.

"What? On, no, just thinking. Or trying to. Everything has happened so quickly that I can't make sense of it. Was I being an ostrich, keeping my head in the sand? Or bog, in this case?"

"I'd say there were things you didn't need to know, so you ignored them. Like the boundaries of Old Mick's land. You weren't plannin' to farm, so it didn't matter. Yeh got the forms filled out fer runnin' the pub, and that's kept yeh busy. Most normal people don't go lookin' fer bodies."

"You've got that right. Actually there were plenty of killings in Boston, but none of them had anything to do with me, as far as I know. Can we talk about something else, before I have to explain everything to whoever walks in?"

"Such as?"

"Mostly this kitchen project. This is me, and I don't cook. Rose is a great cook. But does she want to keep working on the business side of things? Should she be looking for a bigger, better job, whether or not it's in a kitchen?"

"Have yeh asked her?"

"No. I wanted to see what she could do, now that her father Jimmy is out of our hair and busy with his new wife's farm. Rose is smart, and she's a good planner. But we haven't tried serving food to more than a couple people at a time. What if we actually get busy?"

"Maura, when we left the place yesterday, yeh didn't even have a working kitchen. Yeh're getting' ahead of yerself."

"When will I have a kitchen?"

"Yeh want a date? If everythin' works out, I'd say in two weeks. Ask Helen if she's found what yeh need, and when we can get hold of it. And we'll find a plumber and an electrician to see that it all works. Are yeh havin' second thoughts?"

"I don't think so. Maybe I'm just feeling overwhelmed, and that was before the body turned up. And that's another question: when do I tell Sean what we seem to know now, or do I say nothing?"

"Wait until we've all met tonight. Yeh'll

know more then."

"I guess." Maura lapsed into silence until they arrived at Sullivan's. Which looked far busier than it had the night before when she had left, and it wasn't even opening time yet. The battered truck parked in front was a giveaway, with Helen standing on the sidewalk beside it issuing orders. Maura concluded that the appliances had arrived.

When Mick had parked his car, Maura clambered out and hurried toward the front of the pub. Helen welcomed her warmly. "I think I've cleared out the entire basement of the hotel, but now you have your choice of appliances. Kevin, my go-to guy from the hotel, is here and he's checking out the plumbing and wiring, and he's got some pals who'd be happy to help install things. I hope you don't mind, but they weren't busy this morning, and I thought you'd like to see how things fit sooner rather than later."

"Uh, yeah, sure, that's great. I was just surprised that it happened so quickly. Is Rose here?"

"Yes, Rose and Susan both. They're in the kitchen."

"So once the plumbing and wiring are set, maybe we can paint. And find some cabinets for storage. I don't know where to look, but Rose can ask some of the people at the cookery school — they're sure to know. Or we can ask some of my secondhand-furniture pals. You really are quite an organizer, Helen. Will you be staying around today, or do you have to get back to the hotel?"

"They'll need me there before noon. I do wish the owners would decide what they want they want to do. If they decide to sell again, I won't be hurt, but I'd like a decision. If they want to make a go of it, there's a lot that can and should be done."

"Which way do you want to go?"

"I could go either way — I just want an answer. Although I have to say, I kind of like having a good excuse to spend time with you. As long as I'm not in your way."

"No, we're good so far. What about Susan? Or your son?"

"Susan's having a grand time, or so she says. Of course, she doesn't have to spend the time with me, which in her eyes is probably a plus. Tommy? I'm not so sure what he'd think. Are there any sports teams or clubs around here that he could join?"

"I am *so* the wrong person to ask that, but you could ask Rose," Maura said, smiling. "How does he feel about horses? Because I know in summer there are various kinds of racing going on."

"I'll have to ask him. So, want to see the kitchen? Kevin is happy to move things around, so most of them are still clogging up your hallway. Feel free to ask him to re-arrange them."

"I will," Maura said politely, although she wondered if she could make a coherent decision about anything. At least appliances were real, solid objects, which had to be better than dead bodies from the past. She'd feel lucky if tonight's group shared what information they had and they could put the whole story to bed and get back to normal life. Whatever that was.

Chapter Twenty-Four

Maura did her best to call up some enthusiasm for her new — or at least improved — pub kitchen. Even from the next room it looked like Rose and Susan were having a good time, although the fact that Kevin was in his twenties and a poster boy for gorgeous young Irishmen might have had something to do with that. She didn't know what she expected now, and she'd never paid much attention to how ovens and dishwashers and such worked. Maybe somebody else would make the choices for her?

She got as far as the door, then stopped. Rose and Susan were leaning against a rough board countertop on the far side of the room and grinning like fools. "What do yeh think?" Rose asked.

Maura took a moment to look around the room. To her surprise, it looked larger and cleaner than she expected. "Does everything work?"

"It will soon enough," Rose said. Susan nodded.

"Are there plugs and pipes and drains and that sort of thing?"

"There are," Rose said triumphantly. "All that's missing is storage space and some shelves, and we'll be ready to go."

"Wow. That was fast." Maura considered for a moment. "Do you like it? I mean, do *you* like it? You didn't just pick stuff because you thought I'd like it?"

"Of course not," Rose said firmly. "If it's me that's doin' most of the cookin', I want to be happy with it. Susan, you're with me on this, aren't you?"

"Yes! Look, if I can fry an egg on the stove all by myself, then it's got to be good. And I like the layout — it's easy to get around with more than one person working, even if you add a worktable in the middle. Anything else will just be fine-tuning. What do you think, Mom?"

Helen had come up behind Maura and was studying the layout. "I think you're both right," she said finally. "Good flow, and the units have good space on top without taking up too much room. Kevin, you promise everything works? And all the attachments are ready to go?"

Kevin grinned, showing off his very white

teeth. "Fer sure. It'll all be ready by tomorrow. Promise."

Helen was looking very pleased with herself, Maura noted. Then she turned to Maura. "The final choice is yours, Maura. Do you like it? Well enough to keep it? Because I can keep looking if it doesn't work for you."

Maura took a deep breath. "I think it's wonderful. Everything fits together well, and I'm guessing it's more practical than fancy, which is exactly what we need here. Are you really giving it to me?"

"Maura, it's been sitting in the basement of the hotel for a few years now. All we've done is clean it up and make sure it all works. You might want to slip Kevin some euros for installing it, but I'm sure he'll be reasonable."

"You've got a deal, and I can't thank you enough. Let's see how the first few days go — we'll have to get used to using it before we start inviting guests — and maybe then we can have a real dinner, all of us."

"That'd be grand, Maura," Rose said. "We can plan a time to discuss what our menus will be like."

"Let's let Kevin get things up and running first, Rose. Tomorrow, maybe? And don't forget that we need pots and pans and plates and such."

"Let Kevin put it all together," Rose said firmly. "We can't fill shelves that aren't there."

"Well, we're way ahead of schedule, so I won't complain. Enjoy yourselves!"

Maura backed out of the kitchen, feeling somehow relieved that something was getting finished. Helen followed her. "You really think it's done right?" Helen asked a bit anxiously.

"It's great! I couldn't have done it. And I really do appreciate the help. Sometimes I forget I'm supposed to be running a business here. Rose knows more about it than I do. She's the one who handles all the computer stuff, including advertising, and it was her idea to take cooking classes. I just watch her and admire."

"You're lucky to have her. I think Susan's still a bit young to do something like this, but she seems to be enjoying it, so maybe it will give her something to think about for her future."

"You aren't going to send her to college?"

"I'll leave that up to her. Sure, we can afford it, and she makes good grades, but there are so many things she could do, and I'm not going to insist. Or maybe she'll take a year off to travel and try different things.

I'm sorry — I know it's not the life you had, and maybe part of that is my fault."

"Helen, I don't hold that against you. You had to pull yourself together and find a life that worked for you. Sure, I could be angry that you just walked away from me. In fact, sometimes I am. But I don't think you were selfish about it. I can't imagine having a child to worry about, and no husband, and having to find work just to get by. The best I could manage, when Gran was still alive, was a bunch of crappy jobs that didn't last long — easier in a big city than in a place like this, but not a lot of future there. I didn't have anything like a plan, and I didn't collect many skills along the way. You did a better job than I did."

"Well, you may not have come looking to run a pub in Ireland, but you've certainly earned it. I think your grandmother would be proud of you."

Kevin came tromping into the main room. "I'll get a bite to eat, and I've some tools and wire and the like to collect, but I'll be back later to start putting the pieces together. If that's all right with you, Maura?"

"Sure. Oh, and we never discussed light fixtures. Could you make it a little brighter in there, while you're wiring? Especially over the stove and in the middle of the room?"

"No problem, Maura. See you later."

Helen glanced at her watch. "Oh, heavens, I've got to get back to my meeting. Is it all right if Susan stays for the afternoon?"

"That's okay. I'm sure she'll enjoy watching Kevin at work."

"I think you're right — he's nice to look at. I'll pick her up later."

Maura took a moment to collect herself. Kitchen build-out: all planned and ready to start. Check. Now she needed to talk with Billy, which wasn't going to be quite as easy. If he didn't like the plan they'd sketched out for the evening, she wasn't going to pressure him. He could think about it for a while. And she had no wish to criticize anyone who'd had a hand in whatever had happened in the past. She just wanted a few more details to file away.

She waved to Mick, behind the bar restocking, and gestured toward the end of the building where Billy's rooms were. He nodded wordlessly. Helen had left, and the girls were still having fun in the soon-to-be kitchen, so she went out the front door and turned up the street toward Billy's door. When she reached it, she didn't hear anything, so she knocked softly. It took him half a minute to open the door.

"Ah, Maura, *Dia dhuit*! I haven't overslept,

have I?"

"Not at all, Billy, and you know you're welcome anytime, early or late. But there's something I need to talk to you about, and I don't want to do it in the middle of a bunch of people. Do you mind?"

"Not at all." He stepped back to let her enter. "Yeh look worried."

"I am, sort of, but it's not even really about me. Or you, I guess. Can we sit?"

"Where are me manners? Too few people come callin'. So, please sit and tell me what's troubling yeh."

Maura sat. "You've been living in these rooms for quite a while, haven't you?"

"Quite a few years, back when Mick was alive."

"And you and Mick were good friends, right? He wasn't just letting you use his empty space?"

"We were friends, or as friendly as a pair of old men can be. I'd known him fer a long time, and we got on well. Not that I was his only friend."

"When did he start staying here, instead of the cottage in Knockskagh?"

"Ah, I'd have to think about that. A good many years. When he was runnin' this place, it was easier on him to stay in the village, and he had no one to go back to at night.

Any more than I did."

Maura took a deep breath. "Billy, there's something I have to ask you about, and I don't mean to pry. If you don't want to answer, that's all right." She swallowed. "You know about the dead man that was found in Mick's fairy fort?"

Maura watched Billy's expression change, and he didn't answer quickly. "Where the university kids were pokin' around, right?"

"Yes. They're studying archaeology, but that wasn't the only reason they chose that site to look at. At least, not for Darragh. You met him at the pub, right?"

"I did, as well as the others. They seemed like nice young people."

Maura went on, "That was after the first time they'd looked around the site, and they took me to see it. They went back the next day, but I didn't stay. Later in the day, Ciara was still there, but she told me she couldn't find Darragh. Nobody had seen him. Mick Nolan and I went back to the site and looked carefully at it, and . . ." Maura wasn't sure how to describe what she'd found, and how and why.

"Yeh found yer dead man."

Maura nodded. "Yes. I was curious about why the students seemed so interested, and why they'd brought fancy equipment with them. I thought if we looked carefully when the sun was at the right angle, we might notice something, without machines. And we did. There was a dip in the earth, and when I looked closely at it, I found the dead man. And he wasn't a thousand years old."

"More like thirty-some years dead, I'd reckon," Billy said.

"You knew about him? And who he was?"

"I did. I have done since Mick dug the hole up there and laid him in it."

"Billy, this is the hard part, for me, at least. When we found the body, I called the gardaí, and they took it to Cork to examine. Last I talked to Sean Murphy, nobody had figured out who it was, only that it had been buried up there for a long time. You're telling me you know who it was?"

Billy nodded, and looked like he was starting to speak. Maura held up a hand. "I'm not worried about what the gardaí know or don't know. I'm guessing that anybody who was directly involved in the man's death is gone now. But then Darragh appeared at my place this morning, and he told me some troubling things. We had breakfast with Bridget, and she gave some hints that she knows the story too. I didn't ask for any details, but it seems that a lot of people up there know what happened, and it's personal, not just some guy who got kicked in the head by a bull. But I didn't feel right asking a lot of questions. So we — the four of us — talked about getting together later today and sharing what we all know. I know the least of anybody, and I don't feel I have the right to push too hard, but even Bridget said she thought it was time the story came out, because somehow it affected all of us."

"And she agreed?" Billy asked softly.

"Yes, but she didn't share any details. And we said we'd ask you if you wanted to be part of this. Like I said, it's not a garda investigation, but the death is somehow involved with all our lives, including Darragh's and mine. Look, you don't have to be there. You were Mick's friend, and if he had anything to do with this, you might think you're letting him down. And I gather everyone has stayed quiet about it since the man died. That doesn't have to change. What do you think?"

Billy didn't speak immediately. Finally he said, "I think Bridget's right, about the story comin' out. And she was one who was part of it, years ago. As was yer grandmother. And Darragh's family — the Hegartys — who left this part of Cork a long time ago. And I wouldn't say that Mick's role was all bad, which is why some of the others — like myself — protected him. So, Maura Donovan, I'd be glad to join your gatherin' today. Will yeh be closin' to the public?"

"I think so. We're moving fast on rebuilding the kitchen, and it might be kind of dusty and loud for a meeting. We can put up a sign explaining, and then we can use the back room, where no one will notice. Does that work? It shouldn't take us long. Should we ask Rose to stay?"

"Her family was never a part of this, but there's no harm done if she wants to hear what's said. Have yeh told yer mother?"

"No. She was born in America, and I doubt Gran ever said anything to her. Heck, Gran didn't tell *me* anything. But I don't think Helen's a snoop, so if she wants to stay, I might let her. And Susan, although she's not related by blood to the last generations. Only to me, I guess."

"Ah, Maura . . . I'll come by later and see what's happenin'. If nobody's interested, I'll have me pint and call it a day. But there are few of us who remember what happened, and if we say nothin', the story will be lost. Let's see how it goes."

Maura stood up. "Thank you, Billy. I'm still finding my way through local history, and who's who. It's not like anything I've known before. Some people might tell me this doesn't involve me, but others have given some hints that it may. I'll just wait and see. And I'll see you later, I hope."

"For a while, at least."

CHAPTER TWENTY-FIVE

Maura couldn't figure out how she felt as she walked slowly back to the entrance of Sullivan's. Billy hadn't bitten her head off, or pretended that he didn't know what she was talking about, not that she had really expected him to — he was basically an honest man as well as being a friend. After talking to Bridget, who was Billy's age, she could tell it was a story that had been important to both of them, and possibly their extended family and friends, but that they'd been reluctant to share. But she was pretty sure there was no one left to accuse of murdering the man. She wasn't going to say anything to Garda Sean until she knew more. On the other hand, if he managed to find any information about a suspicious death that had happened that long ago, she wouldn't lie to him.

She'd found the small clutch of letters between her grandmother and Bridget before she left Boston and skimmed them, but there had been no mention of a long-ago crime. She couldn't recall seeing any letters to or from Mick Sullivan, although maybe Bridget had passed on information. Or maybe everyone had been content to forget what had happened, whatever it was.

It was another beautiful day, and church had already let out. No one seemed interested in stopping by the pub, and most likely the cows needed them, given the welcome weather. She wasn't surprised to see Mick come out when he spotted her. "It's quiet today. Yeh want to sit fer a while and enjoy the day?"

"Sure, why not?" She settled on the garden bench she'd bought several months earlier, and Mick joined her.

"Did yeh talk to Billy?" he asked.

"I did."

"Will he be comin' later?"

"I think so. It was kind of like talking with Bridget earlier. He'd say things, but in a sort of roundabout way, without all the details. But I think he agrees with her — the story needs to be told, though not necessarily to the gardaí or the rest of the world. If it was something that only the pair of them knew about, I doubt we'd ever hear a thing about it. But since both of them seem willing to share what they know with me and with Darragh, I have to think there's something more complicated going on. Or there was, years ago. I'm not sure I want to know what happened — I kind of like things the way they are. We don't have to share whatever we learn with the rest of Leap, do we?"

"Not on my account. It's old history now." Mick fell silent for a bit, then said, "So yeh never learned anythin' about Irish history in school?"

"Maybe a few sentences about the Potato Famine. Why?"

"Because there's much of our local history that comes from conflicts in the past. You might call it all part of the same conflict, since they seemed to keep sprouting anew, or you might say the Irish love to fight about something, and every few years they find something else to quarrel about. And, occasionally, kill each other about."

"And I know squat about most of them. I saw the movie *Michael Collins* on some TV channel, and if you lived in Boston, you heard a lot about Whitey Bulger. And that was about all."

"Sam's Cross, where Collins was born, isn't far from yer cottage. It's a small country, remember? And he died not far

307

from Bandon."

"So why is this supposed to matter to me?" Maura demanded.

"Because yeh've probably already seen that most people in places like Cork are related to each other. That cuts both ways, depending on whether yeh know them or not. And whether you believe they've cheated yeh in some way. Like stealin' yer cattle. Or done harm to a relative."

"So how does all that figure in what we're trying to learn about the dead man in the rath?"

"I'd wager yeh've already guessed that he was known to one or more of the families who lived near yer cottage, years back, and may still. Like Bridget and yer gran."

Maura stared out at the harbor. "I don't like it."

"Nor should you, but it did happen, back in the day."

"So how do I talk with Bridget and Billy?"

"Let them talk. They mean yeh no harm. More likely they've tried to protect yeh, or they're afraid of hurting yeh."

"Mick, I'm going to have to think about this for a while. Are you going to go pick up Bridget?"

"That I am. I spoke with her on the phone while you were talkin' to Billy. Tell Rose to make a sign fer the front saying we're closed for renovations or something and tidy up the back room, while I go pick up me gran."

"Yes, sir. Whatever you say, sir. Do we need to feed anybody? I'm never sure either Billy or Bridget gets enough to eat."

"If yeh must, send Rose to get somethin' they can eat. Not a meal, mind yeh, but somethin'." He stood up and headed for his parked car.

Maura couldn't summon enough energy to move, so she sat and thought. She'd been in Ireland over a year now. It had taken a bit of getting used to, after living in Boston all her life, but after a while she had found she enjoyed it, and she liked many of the people. And she had a home and a business, thanks to Old Mick, whom she'd never even met. But it was beginning to seem like any time anything happened, it was like scraping off the present to see pieces of the past. And the past wasn't too far below the surface, only most of the time she didn't recognize it at all, even though most people she knew here did.

She knew Bridget and Billy as well as anybody around, but apparently that was less well than she had thought. They'd been good to her, and Bridget was the closest link to her past that she knew. Clearly

Bridget had chosen her stories carefully, but now they seemed to be cropping up unexpectedly.

But Maura had a choice: shut down the conversation before it got started, or find out what they *hadn't* said since she'd arrived. She had a feeling it had something to do with why her gran had packed up and headed for Boston with her son so quickly, and then never talked about where she had come from. Which in a way had helped make Maura who she was today. She might not like what she heard, but she needed to know the truth about the past. Her past, somehow.

Back inside, she cornered Rose. "Rose, would you mind making a sign for the front window? I'm planning a meeting with a few people in a bit, and I don't want to be interrupted. Mick's going to pick up Bridget, probably around six, and Old Billy will be coming too. And Darragh Hegarty. Don't worry — no real problems, just some details about the body we found in Knockskagh. And if Sean Murphy comes looking for us, I don't think we'll be ready to talk to him, but I will tomorrow if he wants."

"Sounds serious, Maura," Rose said, looking concerned. "Is everything all right?"

"It is. Don't worry. We're just trying to tie

up a few loose ends about something that happened a long time ago."

"About the dead man, yeh mean?"

"Exactly. But he's been dead a long time. This is just to settle some things from the past."

"Am I invited?"

"If you like. I don't really know what we'll be talking about, but you know these people better than I do, and Old Mick hired you and Jimmy, so you knew him too. And you're not supposed to be serving us — just be part of the group. But please don't tell Jimmy about any of it. If he knows already, fine, but if he doesn't, he'd probably spread it all over West Cork."

Rose smiled. "I hear what yer sayin'. And I'd be guessin' I should get some food in?"

"Shoot, I almost forgot. Please get enough to feed us all, but sandwiches would do. Oh, and one other thing: thanks for keeping Susan busy. She seems to be enjoying herself. I'm so glad she wasn't stuck following her mother around at the hotel — she's getting to know a bit more about Ireland this way."

"I think she may be havin' a good time. Sounds like she doesn't get much chance to try out new things back home. And she says it's a relief not to have to deal with her brother. Will she be coming back again, do yeh think?"

"I think her mother's willing, but even if the hotel survives, I don't know what Helen's schedule will be. And I guess I'm not sure how long Susan will be interested, or if she finds something else she enjoys, but I'd be happy to have her. And the kitchen looks great."

"We're almost ready to make a go of it. We can talk about staffing later. And menus."

"Sure. Mick's just gone to pick up his gran — we invited her this morning. And Darragh Hegarty, although I'm not sure he'll come — he's part of the story too. I don't know how long we'll have, since our main guests are well past eighty and need their sleep, and we have to get Bridget home."

"I understand," Rose said, smiling. "I'll get to work on that sign, then pick up some stuff fer supper."

"Thanks, Rose."

One more thing done. Maura was forced to realize that apart from running a pub — a public house, where the public was expected to show up — she had little experience with entertaining a small group of people or throwing a small party. And she was nervous, which was ridiculous. She knew all these people, and they were her friends. Except for Darragh, but he might get some closure out of their gathering. Unless he was looking for vengeance or something, and they'd probably be finding out soon enough how his grandfather had died and nobody had ever explained how or why. If Mick knew anything about that, he hadn't said — he was pretty protective of his grandmother. And Maura had to wonder if she really wanted to know what had happened. Her own grandmother had kept her secret well. Why?

Rose disappeared for a short while and returned triumphantly waving a couple of bags from Costcutter up the street. "I've bought some cake, if that's all right. Will we be wantin' tea? Or coffee?"

"Either one's fine with me," Maura told her. "Billy might want his pint, but I don't think this is an event for drink. We can play it by ear. At least if we're in the back, we won't look like we're all sitting in a fishbowl. I'd rather not have outsides barging in tonight."

"Yeh haven't talked to Sean, have yeh?"

"No, I want to know more first. And I didn't invite Helen and Susan. If Helen is connected, it's not closely. And she's not Irish. Do you think I'm Irish, Rose?"

"More each day. It was there hidin' all the while."

"Thanks. I think," Maura said, and went back to cleaning off the tables in the back.

Mick returned half an hour later, escorting Bridget and handling her like she was made of china. Bridget looked calm and happy — maybe she didn't get out very often anymore, although Mick brought her to church regularly. She certainly didn't seem worried about the coming talk.

Bridget greeted Maura warmly, even though they'd seen each other only a few hours earlier. "Thank yeh, Maura. I hope our gathering won't upset yeh, and I think yer gran Nora would approve. Is Billy comin'?"

"He is," Maura told her. "You and Billy share this story, don't you?"

"We do, though it happened a long time ago. And as yeh know, we both knew Mick Sullivan well. You've done him proud with this place."

"And I'm grateful to have it, Bridget. I thought we could sit in the back room — more private. Would you like some tea? Coffee? And Rose brought cake."

"I'll wait fer Billy, if yeh don't mind."

"Then please sit. Did you spend any more time with Darragh?"

314

"Only a bit. I'm not sure we'll be seein' him here. He's a troubled young man, but he knows very little of this story — only enough to make him angry. I believe it's because he was raised near a city, by a family who kept silent. I think livin' here all these years has helped us. Ah, Billy, there yeh are. When did we last meet?"

Billy was beaming as he walked in and saw Bridget. "Must've been after Christmas? Or nearer Lá Fhéile Pádraig."

"Billy, that's too big a party fer me. Call it Christmas. Half a year, then."

"I'm happy to see yeh, even if it's for an unhappy reason."

"Maura deserved to know, and if the Hegarty lad comes, he needs to hear it. Fer you and me, it's ancient history."

"Maybe we should move to the back room and get comfortable," Maura said. "Rose put up a sign to warn other patrons we'd be closed to work on the kitchen — not that we've had many people in here of late, and it's Sunday. And we have tea or coffee — or a pint, Billy, if you want."

"Let's begin and we'll see how we feel. I'd like to stay awake fer this, which isn't an easy thing at my age."

Maura smiled at him. "I understand. Rose, can you stay out here a little longer and see if Darragh shows up? If not, you can turn out the lights and join us."

"No worries, Maura."

"Then let's get started," Maura said, and led the way to the quiet back room.

CHAPTER TWENTY-SIX

The back room seemed strangely quiet to Maura, with no people in it except their small group. She'd gotten used to the music nights there, when it was impossible to hear a conversation with a person sitting next to you. But in that case, whatever the volume, people seemed to enjoy the setting and the company — and the music too. It had been a good idea to open it up to something new like that — or to revive what had once been new but had faded away under Old Mick Sullivan.

She hadn't made a plan before shepherding her friends together. When she started to form a plan, the door opened to reveal Rose leading Darragh into the back room. Rose followed him, then closed the door behind her.

Darragh looked anxiously around the room. "Sorry I'm late. I wasn't sure I wanted to come, but then I told myself, it's kind of the reason why I was here, outside Leap. I had only shreds of a story about what had happened to my grandfather, but I couldn't just leave without knowing what there was to know. If that makes people here uncomfortable, you can tell me to go."

"Ah, lad, none of that," Billy said. "You may not like the story, but yeh're family to us in a way. Bridget and me" — Billy glanced at his longtime friend — "we're the last people who know what really happened. Maura's grandmother Nora knew the truth, but she made the choice not to share it, and left here for Boston with her young son. Maura here has told us that her gran never told her anythin' about where she'd come from and why she'd left. We plan to change that tonight, if yeh're all willin'."

Nobody seemed to object. Maura cleared her throat anxiously. "This meeting came about only yesterday," she began, "because Mick Nolan and I found a body buried inside the fairy fort on land which is mine now, but which belonged to Mick Sullivan before. I inherited the land and his cottage and this pub because he and my gran kept in touch, and she fixed it that it should be mine. I never met him, and my gran never said anything about what she'd set up, but told me I had to come here and say her good-byes to her old friends. That was more than a year ago now. But it was finding the body that brought about this meeting to-night. Before you ask, I can tell you that the gardaí don't know who the dead man was. I certainly didn't, and if Mick Nolan did, he didn't tell me. That leaves you, Billy, and Bridget as the only ones who know who he was and what happened to him."

Darragh cleared his throat and spoke. "I've met you all now. I came here under false pretenses, or sort of false. We were all at the university, studying archaeology, and like Ciara told Maura, she and her friends were students doing research on fairy forts, and would she mind showing us the one on her land? Maura didn't know it existed, so we all looked at it together to start. We said we'd be back the next day, and Maura came with us again, then left to come here. Then she and Mick Nolan came back to the ring fort, but I wasn't there at the time. I guess she got curious and started poking around, and that's when she found there was a body buried there. She didn't look any farther, but called the gardaí in Skibbereen and told them what she'd found, and they came and gathered up the body and sent it to Cork to examine. And that's where things stood for a bit."

He took a deep breath, as if to prepare himself. "I didn't grow up here, but I'm pretty sure I know who the man was: my grandfather, Cornelius Hegarty. He died before I was old enough to remember him, and my family moved closer to Dublin. They never talked about him, at least not when I could overhear, but there were always a few odd comments about him. Somehow the name of this village — Leap — and the name of the pub came up. Bridget told me that my parents sometimes came back for a visit, and she met with them — and with me — now and then. She was always friendly to us.

"I know you must be wondering why I'm going on like this," he went on. "Really it's because of a couple of odd comments over the years, about why my grandfather Cornelius died, and who might have killed him. I remembered those comments mainly because of mention of a fairy fort, which stuck in my head, and when I got interested in archaeology at university, I did some research and found how many there were. But the last clue I came cross was the way my family members would mention a man named Mick Sullivan, especially after a few rounds in one pub or another. They never said why, but they hated the very name of the man. So when I was looking at old maps for the county and came across a map that showed a fairy fort on land owned by Mick Sullivan, I knew I had to come looking here. Once I saw the place, I was pretty sure I'd found a body, but I couldn't look more closely just then, so I left for a while, and Maura showed up while I was gone.

"And that's all I know. Her land was Mick's, and he died only recently, so I couldn't talk to him, and Maura knew nothing. I didn't know what to do, but I thought about it a bit and decided I needed to talk to Maura and ask her who around here would be old enough to remember when my grandfather died and what happened. And now here I am. I'd be grateful if you tell me what you know."

"Will yeh be tellin' your people?" Billy asked.

"My father and his brothers, you mean? Depends on what I learn. I think they're still angry."

"And do yeh know why they're angry?" Billy went on.

"If I had to guess, I'd say it was political," Darragh told him.

"And odds are you'd be right," Billy replied. "This woulda been in the sixties, and I'll wager not all of you — includin'

Maura — know much about what was goin'
on in Cork back then. Yeh'll have heard of
the IRA, I'm thinkin'?"

"Yes," Maura said. "But where do they fit
in this mess?"

"I won't tell yeh the whole history of the
war for independence from England," Billy
said, "save that Cork was always a very ac-
tive place. But times changed, groups
changed, and so did their leaders and even
their goals. In the sixties, the IRA, which
held on to its name, moved to the left and
found new battles to fight. I won't tell yeh
that Old Mick or the Hegartys were leaders
or any such thing, but there were strong
feelings among many hereabouts. Mick Sullivan had taken over this place a few years
earlier, and yeh might guess that seein' as it
was a pub then, there were plenty of rowdy
evenin's, and more than a few people were
thrown out. And that's where this story
began."

"Wait," Maura interrupted. "You're saying
they were IRA members back then?"

"Let's say they were sympathetic," Billy
corrected her. "And add to that, hot tem-
pered. The Hegartys still lived out in the
townlands, and Mick had settled in that cottage. Yeh never woulda known yer grandfather James, Maura, but the man had a

temper. He and yer gran Nora lived near Mick — on parts of the Sullivan land that had been split up — and yer father was a small child. One Saturday night things got a bit out of hand and Mick threw the both of them — Corny Hegarty and James Donovan — out of the pub and told them to walk it off. They left, but they didn't cool down, and by the time they'd made it to Knockskagh, even the neighbors could hear the argument. Without dressin' it up, the two men commenced fightin', and James Donovan ended up dead."

"Wait — what? Wasn't he my grandfather?"

"He was that. A good man, but he had a temper. The men were drunk and it was late and they were angry. Coulda gone either way, but it was James who died. Past midnight, it was, and Old Mick was just arrivin' home after closin' and found them. Hegarty was still angry and blamed Tom fer the ruckus. Mebbe he didn't know he'd killed him, but Mick knew, and when he tried to settle Hegarty, said he'd report him to the gardaí, Hegarty turned on him, and it was Hegarty who got the worst of it from Mick. But the fact of it is, they'd killed each other, there in the dark. Have I got it right so far, Bridget?"

"You do, Billy. I was still awake, and came out to see what all the fuss was about, and found Mick standing over the two men on the ground. He explained to me what had happened, but he wasn't sure what to do next. Mick wasn't a violent man, or no more than any publican needed to be, and he hadn't started the fight. If anythin', he'd tried to end it, but the men were dead, and Mick had had some troubles with the gardaí before. There was even a garda station in Leap back then, though it's been closed fer years."

"What did you do, Bridget?" Maura asked softly.

"Mick and I, we stood there in the dark tryin' to figure out what was right. Hegarty had been in trouble long before, but Mick didn't want to have to explain to the gardaí, and they weren't all his friends. So I told Mick that I'd tell Nora that her husband James had met with an accident — hit his head — and was beyond help. And I said it so she'd know there was a bit more of the story, but it wasn't Tom's fault. We wanted him to have a proper burial, and Mick and I believed most of the people around Leap would accept our story and would support Mick's side."

"And my grandfather?" Darragh spoke up

for the first time in a while.

"Mick buried him that very night, where yeh found him. He told me that if the gardaí came askin' after him, we'd say he'd gone his own way, we didn't know where. And not many, save his sons, came lookin' fer him. I'm thinkin' that's when the family left the townlands."

Darragh nodded once. "So you're saying it wasn't political, or even personal — it was simply a stupid accident between two drunken men in the dark?"

"Which was the truth, lad," Billy reminded him. "It was only what came after that we changed the story a bit, and nobody was really to blame. Mind yeh, nobody ever questioned the story, neither the gardaí nor the neighbors. Forgive me fer sayin' it, but yer grandfather didn't have many friends around here, not like James Donovan did."

Maura felt stunned. Why had her grandmother never shared any of this? Maura had always wondered about her abrupt departure to Boston with her young son, where she had no friends or relatives or even contacts. And now it was too late to ask. "Bridget," she said carefully, "where is my grandfather buried? Gran never said."

"In the old Kilmacabea cemetery — you may not have seen it, but it's between here and your home. She couldn't afford a stone, but we gave him a proper funeral, and we raised enough money to let her buy a ticket to the States fer herself and her son."

"Can you show me sometime? I guess I'd like to pay my respects."

"Of course, love. Nora would be pleased. Is she buried with yer father?"

"She is, just outside the city. They share a very simple stone — it was all I could afford when . . . she passed on."

"Don't worry yerself about it, Maura," Bridget said kindly. The she turned to Darragh, who looked like he was trying to digest what he'd just heard. "Will yeh be telling yer people?"

"I . . . don't know. I think the anger, or at least the high feelings, run in the family. I do know there are pubs who won't serve my uncles. And there's no vengeance to be taken, no restitution to be made. Are there Hegartys buried around here? Since the gardaí know where he was found, we can't exactly put him back there. And other people might object."

"You can tell yer family yeh never found the man, and we can lay him to rest locally, if yeh want," Billy said.

"Might be a more peaceful solution. Do we need to tell the gardaí?"

Maura looked around at the small group, and nobody seemed enthusiastic about the idea. "If everybody is okay with it, I can tell Sean Murphy, off the record, like. The man's gone unknown and unnoticed for a long time, so him telling the other gardaí that no one can identify him probably won't raise any questions."

Billy nodded. "That might do. Sean's a good young man, and trustworthy. If he isn't satisfied with what you say, send him to me."

"Thank you, Billy," Maura said quietly. "Is there anything else that needs to be said? Or are you all ready for something to drink? Or would you rather all go home to bed?"

"It's been a long day, though we've done what we came to do."

"I'll take yeh home then, if yeh're ready to go," Mick told her. "But I have one suggestion, before we all go our ways. There's plenty of people who know what we found, even if they'll never know the 'who.' Might we consider giving the man a wake? It seems better than just forgettin' him. Darragh? Is that a problem fer yeh?"

"Let me think about it, but I'd say it sounds good. I hold no grudge against anyone for what happened, and I'm not about to tell people the story. Old Mick's gone, but this was his place, and now it's Maura's. Keeps it all in the family, sort of. But we don't have to decide right now, do we?"

"No," Maura said firmly. "We're tired, and this was tough, since it's personal for most of us. Let's all think about it before we decide."

CHAPTER TWENTY-SEVEN

"See yeh in a bit?" Mick asked quietly, when the others had left and they were alone.

"Yes. I guess," Maura said. "Sorry — that's not fair. I can't make up my mind whether I want to be alone or I need company. Come over anyway, once you've got Bridget settled."

"I will," he replied, then helped Bridget gather up her things.

When they were gone, Rose came up beside her. "You were quiet tonight," Maura told her.

"I'm not related to anybody who was in the room, though I've known some of 'em all my life. I felt a bit like an outsider, but I thought I needed to know what was goin' on."

"You mean, so you know what the problem is when we're all acting like depressed idiots?"

Rose gave her a small smile. "Exactly. Did

yeh know none of this?"

"None. I loved my grandmother, and she was a good, kind, decent person. It was just that she never talked about the past. It was kind of like she just showed up as a full-blown adult in Boston, with no history at all. Which is ridiculous, but still . . . I don't even remember my father. Maybe him dying in a stupid construction accident was the last straw and she just erased all her Irish memories. When he was gone, and my mother left, she didn't talk about either of them. I wonder what she'd think of Helen now? Helen pretty much knew what she was doing was wrong, but she was desperate, and I can understand that. I'm not that different, but I didn't want to leave Gran alone or I might have split too. We were one great family, weren't we? What's the right term? Dysfunctional?"

"You survived, Maura. Yer gran made it possible. And it's like she gave yeh Ireland, only it was after she was gone."

"I guess she did. I hadn't looked at it that way. What about you, Rose? How well do you remember your mother?"

"She was sick a lot, toward the end. Jimmy was no help — he has no patience for anyone who's ill. As yeh well know, I had to grow up fast."

"You're doing fine. I'm glad to have you here. But if you find something better, take it. I won't hold it against you. You've got brains and you work hard. Tell me if you want me to recommend you."

"I'll remember that. But right now we're havin' a grand time with the kitchen. What about your Mick?"

"Is he mine? We're kind of a work in progress. Did he ever tell you about his past?"

"No, but he's a good bit older than me. Why would he?"

"I suppose he wouldn't — it's pretty personal, and it took him a while to tell me anything. He's good to Bridget, though." Maura shut her eyes for a moment. "I'm exhausted."

"So go home to Mick then," Rose told her.

"If I can find the energy. Do you know, I'm not even sure where he lives."

"I could show yeh, but it really doesn't have an address."

"Neither does my place. So far it's 'the cottage halfway up the hill, past the yellow cottage. If you reach the piggery you've gone too far.' This is all *so* not like Boston."

"Do yeh miss the big city?"

"Not really. I mean, there's lots to do there and it's interesting, but all I ever had was a bunch of dead-end jobs and no money. I didn't have many friends at school, and after we graduated, I didn't see any of them. So I can't say I lost anything by coming here, and I did gain a lot. Like my own pub, and a house, and friends. Things I'd never even hoped for. But I still miss Gran."

"Go home, Maura. I'll come in early in the mornin' and clean up, but there's not much needs doing."

"Thank you, Rose. That would be a big help. And I'll ask Sean to come over and tell him the details, and he can decide if he needs to do anything about it all. I can't see that he'd try — there's nobody to charge with the crime, if there even was one. Darragh's found out what he came looking for. Bridget and Billy have passed on the history to us, and now it's ours to do with what we think is best. But I still say we should have some sort of event, even if we don't tell people why. Maybe an opening celebration for the new and improved kitchen? And we'll be the only ones who know it's more than that."

"I like that idea. We can talk more about it tomorrow. Good night, Maura."

"Good night. And thanks for everything, Rose."

Outside the night air hadn't cooled much,

but it felt good. There was no one on the street, and no cars moving. And she was going home, to Mick. How many parts of that sentence had she never expected to say? She'd never had a true home — too many shabby apartments instead. And she'd never had a real lasting relation with any guy. Would Mick stick around? He was smart and educated, and he could do better than fill pints in a country pub. Would she try to hang on to him if he did finally wake up and go back to a life he was better suited for? She had no idea. Could she see herself filling pints behind a bar twenty or thirty years from now? That idea made her smile: she'd never planned that far ahead in her life.

Driving back along the unlit narrow road, the only sign of life she saw was a fox that darted across the road in front of her, its eyes gleaming briefly in her headlights. It took no more than a few minutes to reach her cottage. Bridget's cottage was dark, but the evening must have been hard for her, in more ways than one. Mick's car was parked in front of Maura's cottage, and there was a single light shining in her front room.

She turned off her engine and was startled by the silence that followed. She closed her car door as quietly as possible, then walked into the cottage. Mick rose to greet her. "You all right?"

"I wish I knew. Too much to process. Do you realize that I gained a grandfather and lost him, all in the same day? I don't know how to deal with that. I do know I'd like to visit his grave, if Bridget will tell me where to find it. Is she all right?"

"She is. Tired, of course, but she feels she's done her duty. Do yeh know, she wouldn't have told yeh if she didn't think you were ready to hear it."

"I understand, and I'll thank her for it. Listen, Rose said she'd be at the pub early tomorrow, so we don't have to rush to get there. And I told her I'd get in touch with Sean and ask him to stop by so I can tell him more of the story. I don't think he'll make much of it, and what would be the point? I'd say we could close the book on all this, but that's not really true, because it's kind of still going on: I'm here. Darragh will go back to wherever he came from, but I live here. I work here. I'm the last part of any of those families who's still here, apart from Bridget. I can see why Gran couldn't deal with it, but I don't want to run from it. Does that make sense to you?"

"It does, in fact. Funny how many different ways the past catches up with yeh.

Ready to go up?"

"I am."

The next morning Maura refused to open her eyes until she'd sorted out at least most of the events of the day before. Mick was already downstairs, and there might even be breakfast soon. Rose would get the pub ready for the day. Darragh? She wasn't sure what his plans were. Was he really doing research, or had that been a handy excuse as he combed through fairy forts looking for an old unmarked grave? She'd told Rose she thought they ought to have a party of some sort, and she still liked the idea by the light of day. Maybe it would jump-start the flow of customers to the pub, especially when they learned how good a cook Rose was. Maybe there would have been enough whispering about the unknown dead man that people would be curious and come in looking for an answer — which she hoped no one would give. *What body? Who was it? In a fairy fort? What's a fairy fort? What, nobody knows?* It was almost a game. Poor man. She should stop in and see Bridget before she left for Leap, to make sure she was really all right. And to thank her, or try.

Phooey! The sun was shining, and Mick was downstairs, and they'd solved a murder that had waited for nearly forty years (except nobody had known the man was dead or where to look for him, so nobody had even been trying to solve his murder), and she'd added a new member to her family tree, even though she'd never have a chance to meet him. This was about as good as it would get. Time to get up.

She pulled on jeans and a T-shirt and headed down the stairs. Mick was in front of the elderly stove Maura had inherited from Old Mick, cooking something, so she called out, "Good morning. Whatever that is, it smells good."

He turned toward her and smiled. "I won't tell you what to call it. At least it had no mold growing on it. When are yeh goin' to start eating like a normal person?"

"I'm saving myself for Rose's food. And Bridget's bread. Do I look like I'm wasting away?"

"I'd say not. And Rose's cookin' is worth the wait. Are yeh gonna go into Skib to talk to Sean?"

"I thought it might be easier to have him stop by the pub — no chance that anyone will overhear. I'd hate to see the gardaí start up some big investigation, and what's the point? I'm hoping Sean can end it before it starts."

"Odds are good. Coffee?"

"Please."

Mick filled plates with bacon, eggs and bread, doled out coffee mugs, and settled across from Maura at the table.

"You raided Bridget's pantry?" Maura asked.

"How did yeh guess? Yeh said yeh liked her bread."

"This is nice," Maura said.

"What, the food? The weather? The company?"

"All of the above. It's nice to have you here," she said, then added, "Want to try it full-time?"

Where had that come from? Maura wondered. Was she awake yet? But she found she meant it. Life was too short, with too many unexpected twists and turns, to wait for the one perfect moment, if there even was such a thing. That was one thing this past week had taught her.

"Are yeh invitin' me?" Mick said.

"I think I am. Too much, too soon? Or do you have other plans? Or would we decide we hated each other after a couple of weeks?" She realized her heart was pounding, Why, oh why, had she started this now?

After a surprisingly long moment of silence, Mick said, without smiling, "Maura

Donovan, I would be happy to share a home with you, with all that means."

Something inside her chest loosened. "Good, because I don't have a script for the rest of this conversation. And I'm very glad. Because you know there's never been anybody important in my life, so I'm going to make mistakes. And there will be times when I'll want to be alone, or maybe just not talk. Is that okay?"

"I think I can manage, thank you."

And thank you, Mick, she thought to herself. If he'd said no, she wasn't sure what she would have done.

They sat smiling at each other until Maura said, "My bacon's getting cold."

"So eat it. And don't expect me to cook all the time — yeh'll have to learn herself."

"What, you're making demands already? I'll have to watch and see what Rose does."

"It's a good start."

It took them half an hour to finish eating, clean up the few dishes and pans in the kitchen, shower, dress, and be ready to go to Leap. "We'll have to figure out the car situation. I mean, we have kind of different schedules. One car or two?"

"We can manage two," Mick said. "Or take it day by day. Two cars today? Yeh might need to drive to Skibbereen, if Sean wants to meet yeh there."

"True. Two cars it is."

Mick went down the hill to check on Bridget, and Maura called Sean's direct number on her cell phone. Luckily it wasn't too early, and he answered quickly. "Good mornin', Maura," he greeted her cheerfully. "What can I do fer yeh this fine day?"

"I need to talk with you. No problems, but I'd rather it was sooner than later. Are you free this morning?"

"I think I can manage. Are yeh at the pub?"

"No, I'm still at the cottage, but I'm leaving for the pub as soon as I hang up. But I'd prefer to talk to you at Sullivan's — more private than your garda station."

"I can be there in half an hour, if that suits."

"Fine. See you then."

Mick reappeared then. "Bridget's fine. I should be headin' out."

"I just talked to Sean — he'll meet me at the pub. You want to sit in? There's no way you were ever involved in all this, except when we found the body."

"We'll see how it goes, when we get there."

"Then let's go."

CHAPTER TWENTY-EIGHT

As she drove toward the village, Maura tried to sort out what to say to Sean, or how to introduce the difficult subject of the dead man without giving away too much immediately. Seth had been a good friend to her from the beginning, and while he was young and relatively new to his job as a garda, he was smart and used good judgment. Maura was banking on the hope that he'd make this quietly go away. Cornelius Hegarty had died a long time ago. Only his relatives near Dublin mourned him, and she couldn't picture them or anyone else storming the village searching for vengeance now. She had a suspicion Darragh wouldn't even tell them.

What the heck had happened with Ciara? And where the heck was the ground-penetrating radar device? She could see that Darragh would have wanted something like that, but she doubted he had planned to keep it. Maybe she should ask Sean about that. Maybe she should ask Sean about a lot of things, but she still wasn't sure where to start.

She parked her car and let herself into the pub. Rose was still busy polishing things, and the place did look good. Maybe she should think about hiring a full-time cleaner? Or maybe patrons liked the grimy authentic feel of the place? She knew she didn't want to create some plastic Ye Olde Pub. She also reminded herself to ask Rose again whether there were any regulations about food service they'd have to comply with, and who they should ask, and what forms they would have to fill out, and whether it would cost them anything. Maybe Rose had already looked into all that. Or maybe she should talk to Helen, who did this kind of thing professionally.

Too many questions.

Rose came out from the kitchen space, talking with Mick. "Oh hi, Maura," she said. "Mick and I were talkin' about building shelves and such. Sounds easy enough, but do the shelves go in before or after the appliances? How do we figure how many linear feet? What materials — other than somethin' that's easy to keep clean? Do we

341

have a ladder we can use, if it's over all our heads?"

Maura suppressed a laugh. "Don't ask me. But you're right — make sure whatever finish is on the shelves can stand up to cleaning. Rose, I talked to Sean Murphy, and he's on his way over here. You can guess what we'll be talking about, but I'm hoping there's nothing more that needs to be done, legally at least. Is there anything else we need to think about for this week?"

"We'd best check our supplies, in case we need to order more. I know it's been slow fer a while, but that could change. If yer mother stops by, I want to ask her if Susan'll be around fer a bit longer. She's been a great help, but she's young yet and I won't hold it against her if she gets bored with our lot here. But it's nothin' like she knows back in the States, and she'll have plenty to talk about when she goes home."

"I'll ask when I see Helen again — she hasn't told me what her plans are." Or if the hotel was going to survive at all. Maura was hoping it would, for both her and Helen's sake, and because it had a nice foothold in Skibbereen and was good for business there.

Sean appeared at the front door, knocking before entering. Maura gestured him in.

"That was fast, Sean. Must be a slow day for crime in Skib?"

"It's early yet. Yeh said yeh wanted to talk with me?"

"Yes. Want some coffee before we start?"

"That'd be grand. Good mornin', Rose, Mick."

"Good morning to yeh as well, Sean," Rose said. "I'll get that coffee."

"I thought we could talk in the back room. It's more private, although lately the front room's been pretty private too. Where did all the tourists go? Or is the county repairing all the roads around here at once?"

"Ah, Maura, these things are like the tides — they come and go. Be patient. And Rose has been tellin' me about what yer doin' with the kitchen — that could make a difference."

"We hope so. Follow me." She led the way to the back room, which was relatively cool and definitely quiet. "Please, sit down."

"What's this about?" Sean asked.

"Before I start, can you promise you'll listen with an open mind, and wait until I'm done?" When Sean nodded, Maura launched into her story. "It's about that dead man in the fairy fort."

"Ah, I thought as much." Sean nodded. "Do yeh know anythin' more?"

343

"That's just it: I do. I could lie to you and say I didn't know anything, but that doesn't seem right. You've been a good friend, and I don't want to get you in trouble over this, but then, I don't want to get me or any of my friends in trouble either. Do you see my problem?"

"I do. Please, tell me what yeh know, and I'll decide what I can or cannot do with it."

"All right, here goes. We've identified the dead man as Cornelius Hegarty. He and his family lived around here, but the rest moved away when he, well, died. Which does not mean they forgot him. Apparently they're into holding grudges."

"And how do yeh happen to know this?"

Maura sighed. "This is where the tricky part starts. First, Darragh Hegarty is his grandson. Second, several people you and I both know also know this, and more, and they've told me. Mainly because this Cornelius killed my own grandfather — my grandmother Nora's husband — in a fight. Cornelius had been drinking, and Mick Sullivan threw him out. And my grandfather had also been drinking, and they ran into each other out toward Knockskagh somewhere. The fight happened nearer Old Mick's place, and he knew what had happened. And he went after Cornelius, who ended up dead — not on purpose, exactly, but because my grandfather was Mick's friend, and he was only defending himself in the fight. Then Old Mick buried Cornelius in the fairy fort, before the sun came up. He figured that no one would go looking for him there, or anywhere else. He was right, since he didn't turn up until last week, forty or more years later."

"And those who know, they'd be Bridget Nolan and Old Billy, and of course yer gran, who kept in touch with Old Mick," Sean said flatly.

"Yes. But neither Bridget nor Old Billy had a hand in the death, although they knew about what had happened. Certainly my gran knew, and I'm thinking that's why she left so fast with my father. I'm not sure if it was the crime that bothered her, but I'm sure she wanted to get away from the memories. I think her friends put together enough money to bury Thomas Donovan and pay for her tickets to Boston."

Maura took a deep breath. "So that's what I've learned over the past few days, since I found Cornelius' remains. On what's now my land. I thought about not telling you, but that didn't seem fair, and if it came out some other way, I didn't want you to get in trouble. Is there anything that can be done now? Or should we be done?"

Rose came in then and deposited the coffee on the table between Maura and Sean. She looked at Maura and raised an eyebrow, but Maura gave a small shake of her head, and Rose retreated silently.

Sean took his time in answering. Finally he said, "Let me tell yeh what I know up till now. Cork sent us a report on the body, and all they could say was that it was a man in early middle age, and he'd died from a couple of blows — it was the one to his head that killed him, but his neck was broken as well. The body was pretty well decayed, and they couldn't say whether it was a blow or he'd just fallen and hit his head. There were no other identifying features, no scars or broken bones or wounds. And there weren't many other tests they could run with what they had. Now yeh're tellin' me that this Darragh Hegarty is his grandson, so could be they could do something with DNA."

"But then what, Sean? Say they do identify him — is there someone they could charge? The person who killed him and hid the body is dead. Yes, other people knew what had happened, but I couldn't tell you *when* they knew. They chose to keep quiet. I don't know a whole lot about Irish laws — maybe you could arrest Bridget Nolan and Billy for hiding evidence. But what would be the point? The killer is dead, so you can't arrest him. And I don't think you'd make any friends if you arrest Bridget or Billy. And I believe them when they say they didn't do it. So, Sean, what are your choices?"

He stared into space while drinking some of his coffee. Finally he said, "So here's what we've got. The postmortem was inconclusive. No one reported the man missing — I've checked our own files on that. There's nothin' to identify him, unless this Darragh wants to make a stink."

"I don't think he wants to — he just wanted an answer to an old family story. Remember, he's in the same boat as I am: a grandfather he never knew was killed in a fight, up in the townlands here. With my own grandfather. What's to be gained?"

Sean emptied his cup and sat up straighter. "Maura, I'm glad you told me. And glad that the story never spread any farther. I'm thinkin' you don't expect to spread it around now, nor would Bridget nor Billy, after so long."

"Mick Nolan and Rose both know the story now, but I trust them not to tell anyone else."

"So, as yeh rightly point out, there's nothin' to be gained by anyone around here.

347

Sure, and there's more bodies buried up in the hills, but no one knows anythin' about them, or admits to knowin'. There's been a lot of fightin' in this part of Cork over the years. So I would say I won't take this any farther. I might run it by Detective Hurley, for he's old enough to remember some of the local history, but I wouldn't want to put him in a difficult position about decidin' who to tell. So fer my part, I'm willing to keep silent."

Maura released breath she hadn't known she'd been holding. "Thank you, Sean. It's so tangled up with local history, and then with my own life. If that fight had never happened, or if both men had walked away, I wouldn't exist, and I wouldn't be here now. But it's not my battle, and I care about the other people involved — they've kind of become my family here. So I would be grateful if this is the end of it. If I see Darragh again, and I'm not sure I will, I'll sound him out, but I don't think he wants to make trouble. Oh, and what happens with the body? I don't know the cemeteries around here, and I don't know what you do with unidentified bodies."

"I'll ask around, but I don't recall any Hegarty graves or stones nearby, and the family left a long while ago. If Darragh decides to take him back to his family, wherever they are, it could stir up old problems. Yeh can ask him what he thinks. He knows the rest?"

"Yes. We included him when we talked it over. But that's all, so far."

Sean stood up. "Well, then, I'll give it some thought, but unless I find out somethin' new, I think we can and should move on."

Maura stood as well. "Thank you, Sean. I don't want to go around breaking laws, but I'd like to wrap my head around all this, and that will take a little time. Will you let me know if anything changes?"

"I will. How's the kitchen comin'?"

"Really well, I think. My mother's contributing some discarded appliances from the hotel — all perfectly legal, since they've been sitting in a basement rusting for a while, but they're probably a lot newer — and will work better — than anything we've got here. And she's even got a guy from the hotel who can install them. Rose wants us to plan a party when we open the kitchen and start serving real food, and I think that's a good idea. At least it will bring in some more people."

"It sounds like a good idea, Maura. Yeh'll invite me?"

"Of course we will. See you out?"

They walked together to the front door, now open, and Maura watched as Sean walked back slowly to his official car. She was glad he'd seen things her way. Unless something unexpected happened, they were free to move forward now.

Epilogue

"Is the oven working right?" Maura asked anxiously, as she watched Rose move around the newly finished kitchen as though she'd been working in it for years. Maura couldn't remember the last time she'd been so nervous, and she couldn't really understand why she was. She'd agreed that serving real food at Sullivan's was a good idea (as long as she wasn't doing the cooking), and she'd approved every change that had been made. They'd all sampled meals produced by Rose, just to be sure the appliances did what they were supposed to. All had passed with flying colors, including Rose.

Susan was watching Rose like a hawk, ready to deliver a finished plate as soon as it was ready. Maura felt both proud and distressed by that. She was glad Susan had thrown herself into this very ordinary task with enthusiasm and was doing it well, but she was pretty sure her mother had bigger plans for her than serving food. Still, they both knew it was temporary: at the end of the summer, Helen and Susan would be going back to Chicago so Susan could go back to school, and that would mean the end of what had become a pleasant relationship. She hoped Susan would come back to Cork sometime — and she knew Helen would, since the Crann Mor hotel seemed to have gained new life once Helen had gotten to know it and also know what local hotelgoers wanted.

"Yeh've asked me before and I've told yeh before, Maura," Rose said, without stopping what she was doing. "Everything's goin' fine. Quit yer worryin' and go enjoy the crowd."

Maura had to admit she was useless just hovering in the doorway of the kitchen and getting in the way. "Yes, ma'am. But give a shout if you need an extra pair of hands. I'm pretty good at washing dishes."

"I'll keep that in mind. Susan, that plate's for the corner table."

Maura retreated quickly. In the main room she allowed herself a moment to enjoy the sight of people, both familiar and new, enjoying food and drink. It had been a slow summer, for no reason she had figured out, but they seemed to have turned a corner.

She'd be happy to give the credit to Rose and her food — even she could recognize the quality. Maybe she ought to make Rose a partner in Sullivan's — she'd earned it.

Maura slid behind the bar, where Mick was setting up pint glasses with practiced skill. "Everything going all right?" she asked.

He flashed her a quick smile. "Do yeh need to ask?"

"I guess not," she admitted. "It's been a while since we've been this busy. I hope it lasts."

"The word's out. Stop worryin'."

"That's what Rose told me. So I should go look like a successful pub owner and mingle with the crowd?"

"Yeh can take this tray of pints over to that table by the window. And one of them's fer Billy."

"Got it."

Glad to have something useful to do, Maura hoisted the tray and made her way to the corner, stopping to chat with the American couple seated there. Their first trip to Ireland, and Maura now knew enough about West Cork to give them some good suggestions about what to see and do. Then she took the tray with its last glass and went over to Billy. For once he was alone, but he seemed to be enjoying just watching the hubbub. She set the full glass in front of him and dropped into the chair beside his.

"I'm afraid to say anything, in case I jinx it," she told him. "Looks like things are going well. Think it will last?"

"Ah, Maura, don't worry yerself. Yeh've got a good cook, and a cheerful place here. Just keep the pints comin'."

"That's the easy part. But it's nice to see the place busy again."

Billy stared across the room, but Maura wasn't sure he was looking at anything in particular. Then he said, "Could be Old Mick's at peace, and he's givin' you his thanks."

"Was he really so upset by . . . what happened?"

"He never said much, but it didn't sit well with him. He was never a violent man. But he spent less and less time out at Knockskagh in his last years. Maybe it didn't feel like home to him anymore."

"It's a shame. But I'm glad we got it all out in the open. Thank you for your part in it."

"Yeh needed to know. And I'd guess Old Mick wanted you to know. Now we can lay it to rest and enjoy what he created here, and what yeh've made better."

"That sounds good to me."

"Will yer sister be leavin' soon?"

"End of the summer, I think. I hope she comes back."

"I'm thinking she will. Not to stay, mebbe, but I think she likes this place, and her mother'll be going back and forth for a while."

"Good. She's a good kid. If I'd been in her shoes, I would have been a real pain, and probably spent most of my time hiding out and sulking. If I'd come at all."

"Yeh might have noticed, Maura Donovan, that these things have a way of working themselves out. Now, go on and take care of yer customers. We haven't seen Seamus and his gang yet, and they're sure to be thirsty when they arrive."

"I'll do that. Thanks, Billy."

She stood and turned toward the bar, but she was intercepted by Susan. "Got a minute?" she asked.

"Sure. How about outside? You look like you could use some fresh air."

"Great. But not for too long because Rose needs me." Susan headed for the side door, and Maura wove her way through the crowd to follow her. Outside there were a few more customers, but they all looked well supplied with pints. Maura directed Susan toward the edge of the property, overlooking the ravine.

"Something wrong?" Maura asked, as soon as they were far enough away not to be heard.

"Oh, no, no, nothing like that. I just wanted a chance to thank you. We've never had time to talk much, and now the place is crazy busy."

"What are you thanking me for?"

"Well, I guess for being nice. I can't imagine what it would be like to be you and to be handed a pissed-off baby sister out of the blue."

Maura smiled. "If that was your pissed off, you'd better work on it. I was surprised you were polite at all. And at least I had some warning, since I knew you existed. Not that I expected you to pop up in front of me one day. Like your mother did."

"Yeah, we started off really well. But you didn't treat me like a stupid kid, and you gave me something to do, and I've had a lot of fun. More than I expected."

"I'm glad. It took me a while to get there. I got here at a difficult time in my life, and then I kept getting surprises. Don't get me wrong — they were all good, like inheriting a house and pub, but they were unexpected and I didn't know how to handle them. It's taken me a while to get used to the way things work around here, and I didn't know anything about Ireland, or anywhere outside of Boston, really. But I like it now. It's beginning to feel like home."

"You look happy," Susan told her. "Most of the time, anyway."

"Good. I'd hate to scare customers away by looking grim all the time. Look, Susan, if you're trying to find a way to say that you'd like to come back again, I'd be happy to have you. Or if your folks insist you have to go off to college right away, or take some super-serious summer class in astrophysics, I won't take it personally. You can still come for vacations. I bet winters here are better than in Chicago."

"Uh, yeah!" Susan said eagerly. "I just wanted to be sure you didn't think I was in the way or something."

"Not at all. It's just that I'm not used to having family, so I'm still trying to understand how it works. I would be happy to see you here anytime, with or without your mother. Our mother. See? That takes getting used to too."

Susan grinned. "I'll be happy to lend her to you whenever you want." She turned to go back inside, but stopped again. "By the way, I think Mick is cool. I think the two of you are cool together."

Maura hoped she wasn't blushing. "Are we that obvious?"

"Yes." Susan turned to hurry back to the kitchen, and Maura followed more slowly.

Inside the noise level had risen another notch. The sun was low in the sky, turning the interior into gold. And wonderful smells were coming from the direction of the kitchen. People looked happy and well fed. Maybe this was all going to work.

She slid behind the bar again and came closer to Mick.

"Problem?" he asked.

"Nope. Susan likes me, and she'd love to come back here when she can. And she approves of you and me. Us, I mean. Smart kid."

"She is that."

"Do you know, I'm almost afraid to be happy?"

"What do yeh mean?"

"Business is going well. We've made some great improvements. Helen and Susan and I seem to be getting along. And then there's you and me."

"So?"

"So I finally feel I have some control over my life. It's not perfect, but it's getting closer. I never expected that when I left

Boston. Now I have a place where I think I might belong. And I have you. At least for now."

"Fer as long as you want."

ACKNOWLEDGMENTS

I've been visiting Ireland, and West Cork in particular, for more than twenty years, and now I own a home there. But even before I put down roots, I was on a friendly basis with many of the local residents, quite a few of whom turned out to be relatives of some sort. What's more, they could explain how we were related, which often went back several generations. It was clear from the beginning that memories are long in rural Ireland.

The people there love to talk, but they are careful about sharing information. It's a small country, and where past events have had unhappy outcomes, they are reluctant to talk about them, especially with people they don't know well. In a way you have to earn their trust, and having the surname Connolly, and knowing which branch of the family I come from, has been a big plus. And by listening carefully, I've learned a lot about the area and its people.

While this story is fictional, many elements are true. There are many fairy forts in the region, and they're still a bit mysterious (and they're not to be confused with stone circles, which are much fewer). Nobody's quite sure what they were intended for — cattle pens? Protection from marauding Vikings? Yet they have survived for centuries, and local farmers still treat them with respect and mostly leave them alone. Most scholars will agree that they were not burial places, but many raths still remain to be explored.

I've joked that in Ireland, family members either left the country because of the Great Famine in the nineteenth century for American or Australia (I can claim some of each), never to return, or they stayed on the same land where their families had lived for centuries, and they're still there. And family stories were passed down by storytelling rather than in writing. I've had an old woman tell me that a Connolly great uncle of mine used to stable his horse behind the pub I write about. Another local woman once handed me a baby picture of my father, born in 1919, which I had never seen. The past is still treasured there.

My protagonist, Maura Donovan, arrived

in Ireland knowing little about her Irish family, and readers may have wondered why I didn't explain her background. Now I can, because Maura has earned the trust of those who remember her family there and have welcomed her as one of their own.

Yes, this is a murder mystery, and more than one man died. But only a few people have known all the facts surrounding those deaths, which have remained hidden for years.

I need to thank all the people who have welcomed me to County Cork, and all the friends and relatives I have met by pure chance. My Irish family has grown substantially since I've been traveling there. Former garda Tony McCarthy (now retired) gets a special thanks, because he has shared a wealth of stories and more than a few hints about some less well-known events, without betraying any confidences. And it has been a joy to watch Sam McNicholl take the old pub, Connolly's of Leap, that his father and mother made successful, and raise it to a new level (details of which I've borrowed shamelessly, but he doesn't mind. And I can't wait to see the new pizza oven!).

ABOUT THE AUTHOR

Sheila Connolly is the Anthony and Agatha Award-nominated author of over thirty titles, including the Museum Mysteries, the Orchard Mysteries, and the County Cork Mysteries, in addition to the Relatively Dead paranormal romance e-series, the standalone books *Once She Knew,* a romantic suspense, and *Reunion with Death,* a traditional mystery set in Tuscany, as well as a number of short stories in various anthologies. She lives in Massachusetts with her husband and three cats and visits Ireland as often as she can. This is her eighth County Cork mystery.

The employees of Thorndike Press hope you have enjoyed this Large Print book. All our Thorndike, Wheeler, and Kennebec Large Print titles are designed for easy reading, and all our books are made to last. Other Thorndike Press Large Print books are available at your library, through selected bookstores, or directly from us.

For information about titles, please call:
(800) 223-1244

or visit our website at:
gale.com/thorndike

To share your comments, please write:
Publisher
Thorndike Press
10 Water St., Suite 310
Waterville, ME 04901

CPSIA information can be obtained
at www.ICGtesting.com
Printed in the USA
BVHW032231051120
592663BV00001B/24